Praise for *What Hell Is Not*

'A beautifully written novel, translated from the Italian, with a heart-warming story...The language soars like a symphony. The notes are in perfect pitch.'

New York Journal of Books

'Rich in figurative language...equally rich in characterization and setting.'

Booklist

'D'Avenia convincingly conveys the extent of the deprivation and of the reach of the Mafia's influence and control...[He] has a lyrical touch amid the violence and the squalor.'

Herald, Scotland

'If, like me, you are a fan of Elena Ferrante's Neapolitan Quartet, I urge you to check out *What Hell Is Not*...a gorgeous, authentic book.'

Literary Hub

'A mature work that looks the theme of evil and violence in the eye.'

Libero

'Each short chapter of this book is a work of poetic beauty, some showing the transformative power of love and some showing the devastation that hate brings into the world.'

Marjorie's World of Books blog

'The dark story of Father Pino's passion and death is a long shriek of grief, but it is not in vain: it is also a hymn to love that becomes beauty.'

Antonia Arslan, author of *Skylark Farm*

Alessandro D'Avenia teaches Ancient Greek, Latin and Italian Literature at a high school in Milan and is a regular contributor to the newspaper *Corriere della Sera*, writing on the subjects of literature and education. His debut novel, *White as Milk, Red as Blood*, was translated into twenty-two languages and turned into a film. Together with his second novel, it spent three years on the Italian fiction top ten bestseller list, selling more than one million copies in Italy alone. *What Hell Is Not* is his third novel.

Jeremy Parzen studied Italian at UCLA. He is a translator, blogger, musician and wine writer. He lives in Houston, Texas.

What Hell
Is Not

ALESSANDRO D'AVENIA

Translated from the Italian by Jeremy Parzen

ONEWORLD

A Oneworld Book

First published in North America, Great Britain and Australia
by Oneworld Publications, 2019

This paperback edition published 2019

Originally published in Italian by Arnoldo Mondadori as *Ciò che inferno non è*, 2014

Copyright © Arnoldo Mondadori Editore S.p.A., Milano, 2014
English translation copyright © Jeremy Parzen, 2019

The moral right of Alessandro D'Avenia to be identified as the Author of this work has been
asserted by him in accordance with the Copyright, Designs and Patents Act 1988

ISBN 978-1-78607-683-0
eISBN 978-1-78607-274-0

Co-funded by the
Creative Europe Programme
of the European Union

The European Commission support for the production of this publication
does not constitute an endorsement of the contents which reflects the views
only of the authors, and the Commission cannot be held responsible for
any use which may be made of the information contained therein.

This book has been translated thanks to a translation grant awarded by the Italian
Ministry of Foreign Affairs and International Cooperation. Questo libro è stato
tradotto grazie ad un contribute alla traduzione assegnato dal Ministero
degli Affari Esteri e della Cooperazione Internazionale italiano.

Typeset by Hewer Text UK Ltd, Edinburgh
Printed and bound in Great Britain by Clays Ltd, Elcograf S.p.A.

Oneworld Publications
10 Bloomsbury Street
London WC1B 3SR
England

Stay up to date with the latest books,
special offers, and exclusive content from
Oneworld with our newsletter

Sign up on our website
oneworld-publications.com

MIX
Paper from
responsible sources
FSC® C018072

To Marco and Fabrizio,
Brothers who taught me to have fun
and to fight, to speak and to swear . . .
All that is needed for boys to be brothers.

What is hell? I think it is the suffering of one who can no longer love.

(Fyodor Dostoevsky, *The Brothers Karamazov*,
Book 6, Chapter 3)

I believe I am in hell, therefore I am.

(Arthur Rimbaud, *A Season in Hell*, 'Night of Hell')

By first light, a boy spies her.

She is enveloped in the salty, windy ambush of the virgin dawn as it rises up from the sea only to dive into the semidarkness that pours over the streets.

The boy lives on the top floor of his building. From there, he can see the sea and he can peer into the houses and streets that belong to the men. Up there, he casts his gaze until it loses its bearings. And where the gaze is lost, the heart remains entangled as well. There's too much sea spread out ahead, especially at night, when the sea vanishes and he can feel the void beneath the stars.

Why is this scene reborn every morning? The boy has no answer. The rose's withered petals sting more than its thorns and when he looks in the mirror each morning, he sees a castaway. He touches his face and with the sea stuck inside, he looks in his eyes for what still lives. What still lives is her light, glowing on the last day of school. He studies it like the mysterious maps he loved to contemplate as a child hoping to recover treasure and see those islands, ships, and waves.

The boy watches her. She's the one who rummages through his heart, in the tangle where dreams grow. Things bathed in too much light cast the same amount of shadow. Every light has its grieving.

Every port its shipwreck. But boys do not see the shadow. They prefer to ignore it.

He covers his gaunt face with his hands, as if he could somehow interpret his expression by touch. He is like a sailor, standing on the pier, waiting to set sail again after his time back on shore. He continues to watch her. Without end. He allows his flesh, his thoughts, to be molded by the light, the wind and salt.

Light, wind, and salt ought to do as they please. Millennia have transformed even the infertile rocks that lie on the edge of the sea. God put a heart in his chest but he forgot to add the armor. He does this with every boy and in this, for every boy, God is cruel.

The boy is seventeen years old and has a life to invent ahead of him. Seventeen holds no promise of good luck. At seventeen, even ugly actors believe they will grow into handsome men. Blood runs hot and when it presses hard against the heart, they are forced to decide what they will make of themselves.

He has all the questions but the answers will arrive only after he has forgotten them. At seventeen, supply and demand are mismatched.

He pinpoints her in the June light and he is scared because this is the last day of school and on that day summer's escape resides alone in the soul. But he has a thousand questions. Life seems like those equations in his maths book. The answers are there, at the bottom of the page, but he can never quite get the workings right. And it doesn't make any sense to him that two minuses make a plus. A minus is always there somewhere.

Like a siren, all of that sea and all of that light enchant him. And without a struggle, he allows himself to be ensnared by that enchantment. He looks down from above, as boys his age love to do when they try to solve a maze without entering it. He has no thread to unspool to avoid becoming lost in the pathways of his fears.

What do boys know about becoming men, anyway? What do they know about using the nighttime or its shadows or its darkness? Boys always expect joy out of life. Little do they know that it is life that expects joy out of them. He would like to have a simple life. But life has never been simple. Even though everyone enjoys life, endures life, speaks of life, and writes of life, very little is known of life. Perhaps he is the simple one and he ought to leave his maze of light and grief to life.

Light on the rooftops and grief in the streets, just like a Caravaggio painting. It is the aesthetic paradox of a city inhabited by men and not suitable for spellbound boys. They do not know the pain that it takes *to become* and how much courage is needed to shake off illusions. The boy knows even less than the others: He has little flesh around his dreams.

For an instant, she stops bewitching and enchaining him. She has eyes to gaze upon him, jealously, with claws to clutch him as voraciously as any siren, as if to reveal the night that he hides jammed in his heart.

His city.

Palermo.

1993.

PART I

A Never-ending Port

Panormus, conca aurea, suos devorat alienos nutrit.
(Palermo, the golden shell that devours her own but feeds
strangers.)

(Inscription under the statue of the
Genie of Palermo in the Palazzo Pretorio)

The sea is the land's edge also, the granite,
Into which it reaches, the beaches where it tosses
Its hints of earlier and other creation:
The starfish, the horseshoe crab, the whale's backbone.

(T. S. Eliot, *Four Quartets*, 'The Dry Salvages,' 1.16–19)

1

The streets are quiet, despite everything.

With each tenaciously slow puff of the sirocco wind, curtains flap sinuously against the heat-besieged windows. A dog wanders about, trampling oases of shade. A rare gust of sea breeze tempers the heat. Even the undercurrent is exhausted by the grind.

Don Pino raises the dust with his big shoes. It turns to gold at the touch of all that light. His gait is fast, not because he's in a hurry but because he's running late in a city that was founded on slowness. He approaches his sunbaked, rusty-red Uno. The child is sitting on the hood, his feet dangling beneath him. He's six years old and has a white t-shirt, soiled shorts, beachcomber sandals, and a mother named Maria at home. She can be tough. End of story.

'Where are you going at this time of day, Father Pino?'

'To school.'

'To do what?'

'The same thing that you do.'

'To give my classmates a beating?'

'No, to learn.'

'But you're a grownup. What do you need to learn?'

'The more you know, the more you need to learn . . . You're not going to school today?'

'School's out for summer.'

'Are you sure? Today's the last day of school. But there is class today. Otherwise, yesterday would have been the last day.'

'School's over when you decide it's over.'

'Since when?'

'Damn, you ask some tough questions!'

'What are you doing here?'

'Waiting.'

'For what?'

'Nothing.'

'What do you mean, "nothing"?'

'Why do I have to be waiting for something?'

'How about this?' he asks as he gives the boy a pat on the cheek.

'Is your school a school for big kids?'

'Yes, it is. Sixteen-, seventeen-, and eighteen-year-olds.'

'And what do they learn them?'

'They are *taught*, not *learned*. They study things that big kids study.'

'I learn myself things like that.'

'In this case you say, "I learn them myself."'

'Damn, what a pain in the neck! *Teach, learn*. It's all the same.'

'Well, you're right about that.'

'So what do they learn?'

'Italian, philosophy, chemistry, math . . .'

'What are you gonna do there?'

'You get to know the secrets behind things and people.'

'We have Rosalia for that.'

'Who's that?'

'The hairdresser.'

'No, no. At school, you learn secrets that even she doesn't know.'

'I don't believe it.'

'Too bad for you.'

'Well, tell me a secret.'

'Do you know what "Francesco" means?'

'I know it's my name. That's it.'

'Yes, that's true. It's a name. But it's an ancient name. It was used for people who descended from the Franks.'

'Who were they?'

'They lived during the time of Charlemagne.'

'And who was he?'

'Francesco, when is this going to end? The Franks were called Franks because they were *free*. Frank means *free*. Francesco means *a man who is free*.'

'And what's that supposed to mean?'

'I'll tell you another time.'

'So what do you learn them?'

'"I teach them" is the proper way to say it. I teach them religion.'

'What does religion have to do with it?'

'Religion teaches you the most important secret of all.'

'How to steal something and never get caught?'

'No.'

'Then what?'

'If I told you, it wouldn't be a secret.'

'I'm no snitch. I won't tell a soul.'

'That has nothing to do with it. It's a secret that's hard to understand.'

'I'm going to be seven soon. I can understand just about anything!'

'Someday I'll tell you the secret.'

'Do you promise?'

'I promise.'

'Do you perform miracles?'

'No, I'm too small for that.'

'But you're, like, 150,000 years old!'

'Fifty-five years old.'

'But isn't that more than 100,000?'

'Watch it, kid. Who do you think you are?'

'But if you're so small, why do you have such big feet?'

'To walk far and get to the people who need me.'

'And what about those ears? They're huge, Don Pino!'

'They let me listen more and talk less.'

'You have really big hands, too . . .'

'I just can't get anything past you, can I?'

Don Pino smiles, puts his hand on the boy's head, and messes up his red, Norman hair. It's just like those blue eyes: Uncut diamonds that the Nordic peoples mounted on the Arabs' dark skin after they had snatched up their cities.

Francesco smiles. And his eyes sparkle like magic. History is layered in those eyes.

'Damn, you know so many things, Don Pino.'

'Come on. I've got to get going. Otherwise, I'm going to be late.'

'But you're always late, Don Pino.'

'Look who's talking!'

'And why the bald head? Why is your head so smooth?'

Don Pino pretends to give him a kick in the butt and starts laughing.

'Do you see how beautiful the sunshine is here in Palermo?'

'But we're not in Palermo! We're in Brancaccio!'

'Fine. It's the same difference. My bald head helps to reflect the sunlight so that people can see better.'

He bends over to show him up close and Francesco places his hand on his head.

'Damn, you have a hard head, Don Pino!'

'It's for breaking through the thickest of walls,' says Don Pino, grinning like a boy as he speaks. A small boy, like a seed in the ground, like flower seed that his mother used to keep on her balcony, like the lumps of yeast that she used to put into the bread dough.

'Would you be my daddy, Don Pino?' says Francesco.

'What on earth are you talking about?'

'Well, I only have my mother. I don't know where my father is. It's a mystery. Maybe you know the answer since you know so many things that are hard to understand.'

'No, Francesco, I don't.'

Don Pino fumbles for his keys in his pocket but they wriggle free like fish caught in a net that's been hoisted aboard a fishing boat.

Francesco looks down at the ground, motionless.

Don Pino finally finds his keys and starts to open the door. But Francesco doesn't budge. Don Pino leans over so that he can look him in the eye.

'What's the matter?' he asks him.

'Everyone calls you "father." But you don't want to be my dad even though I don't have a dad.'

'That's true. But I'm not your father.'

'Then why does everyone call you "Father Pino"? Do you know why?'

'Well . . . because . . . It's a figure of speech.'

'You're a father and you belong to the Church. But aren't there some fathers that don't belong to the Church?'

Don Pino stands there in silence.

'Come on, Francesco. Let's just say there's some truth to what you're saying.'

He takes him by the hand and the child gets down from the hood of the car and smiles.

Don Pino smiles, too. He gets in the car and makes the sign of the horns.

'You've got horns! Pointy ones!' says Don Pino.

'So that I can break the "thickest walls" just like you.'

Francesco closes the door and sticks his tongue out at Don Pino.

Don Pino pretends to be angry and he starts to drive off.

But the child knocks on the window with a worried look on his face.

Don Pino rolls down the window.

'What's the matter?' he asks.

'When you perform a miracle, do you promise you'll tell me?'

'I promise.'

'But it needs to be a big one, like making it snow in Brancaccio.'

'Snow in Brancaccio? You're asking the impossible.'

'I've only ever seen snow in cartoons. What kind of a priest are you, anyway?'

'Okay, sure.'

'Ciao, Father.'

'Ciao, Francesco.'

As he drives away, Don Pino looks in the mirror and sees a somber face.

He can feel those kids kicking in his heart like babies in their mother's womb. One of these days, they'll rip that little heart of his right out of his chest. And who knows how much time he has left? Who will take care of Francesco and all the rest of them? Who will take care of Maria, Riccardo, Lucia, Totò . . .?

He's run out of time. There's no time left yet there are all those kids, just like seeds scattered in a field. The thorns wish to choke them. Hungry crows wish to devour them.

The train crossing's barrier has been lowered. The train crossing that separates Brancaccio from Palermo like a ghetto. A little girl stands beyond the barrier on the other side of the tracks. She looks out toward the arriving train. She leans over as if there were a line that she shouldn't cross. A doll dangles upside down in her hand.

Before Don Pino can get out of his car, the train bolts by him and swallows up the girl. Her hair goes wild in the suction of the train cars. She focuses on them like film unspooling at the movies. Her imagination follows that train as her thoughts are filled with every possible destination. She would like to get on it, with her doll, so that she can take it far away. She doesn't know where the trains go but she knows they go far. Just like the ships that go behind the sea. Who knows where they end up? This is the reason that the only thing she enjoys more in the world than her doll is when her father teaches her how to swim. So that she can go see what's behind the sea.

She disappears with the last train car. Don Pino stands motionless halfway between the barrier and the car door, looking at a mirage. He doesn't know who that girl is. He knows only that he saw her fly away toward a train with her colored dress, out of reach. What if she had been run over?

The barrier rises up again. Don Pino slowly gets back in his car, looking for any signs of her presence. And as if on cue, a car horn starts honking. Where could they be going in such a hurry in a city where parking is a mere aspiration?

'Where are you off to in such a hurry? Your wedding?' says Don Pino to the driver sarcastically.

'Yeah, I'm marrying your sister, Father.'

Don Pino tells him to get lost with a good-natured smile. He leaves again and thinks of the girl. He doesn't know who she is but he understands her. There's a train to catch. It's just beyond the barrier that stands between us and our fear.

Wherever that train takes you, it spits you out of hell. His grandfather worked for the railroad and he used to tell him stories about his trips on the tracks. He was just a boy back then and he couldn't understand how the trains could walk or how the tracks seemed to be endless. If a train were running backward, how did they pick it up so that another train could pass by? And where did all the trains go anyway?

The children's questions stick with him because he is weak like them. He is afraid like them and dreams like them. He trusts like them and forgets things right away like them. And he does not give up, just like them.

There's only one thing that's different about him. He can't ignore death like they do.

2

Wind and light lash the streets of Brancaccio, a neighborhood composed of houses that resemble the scales of a fish that writhes ever more slowly as it dies, gasping all the while for water and life. A dark area of Palermo's endless port with the sea at its back, Brancaccio rises from the debris that every sea discards along the coast. The Hunter walks across those bits and pieces.

He's nearly thirty years old. He has a name, the one his mother gave him when he was born, the one that they repeated in church when they baptized him. But now this is his real name. He got the name 'the Hunter' thanks to his silent determination in doing what must be done because a man is someone who does what a man must do. The way he sees it, the world is divided into two groups: Predators, the group to which he belongs; and prey that has been sniffed out, identified, hunted down, and killed. He walks with his head held high and his gaze is never distracted from the line of sight. Aim without distraction is a sign of strength. Three decades into this life and he already commands respect, like a father commands respect from his sons. And sons he has, three of them. Then there are all the rest of them. They're guaranteed a bright future just as long as they stay in line and obey. The Hunter.

Nuccio is with him. Roughly twenty years old with a long nose that makes him look like a bird, thin lips, the night before stuck between his teeth like his ever-lit cigarette. His eyes are sad. Not because he's sad but because sadness has shaped his features.

They monitor their surroundings as they wander without any apparent destination through the sirocco maze.

As shutters are raised, they reveal a hive of activity behind a sign that they all share: '24-HOUR-ACTIVE CAR-RIAGEWAY. DO NOT BLOCK.' Yes, it's called a 'carriageway' because in another era carriages went in and out of buildings. Sides of beef hang on hooks and shamelessly show off their meat and limp entrails. Motor scooters waiting to be repaired are dirty with grease. Loaves of bread, their crusts covered with sesame seeds. Brooms, detergent, perfume, toys, soccer balls. And everything else you can imagine. Wicker and wooden chairs, still empty, stand ready outside the shops for breaks between clients. Here, winter lasts three or four months if you're not lucky. Otherwise it stays away.

The Hunter glances around him before his eyes are once again motionless and steady. He spits on the ground and his saliva mixes with the dust in the street teeming with double-parked cars and trash cans already fermenting in the violent heat of the early hours of the day. The acrid smell of things rotting mixes with the sea-soaked morning to create a bittersweet odor that pervades the neighborhood and the entire city. Heaven on one street, hell around the corner.

A woman hangs her languid sheets in the still air. She's wearing a robe and curlers. Groups of children roam the streets in search of dogs, cats, and lizards to torture; in search of adventure among things that have been discarded by grownups; in search of asphalt patches for a soccer game, a break from the cement and from their boredom. Their threadbare leather ball is so light that it nearly floats away.

They say hello to the Hunter and he smiles like a father smiles at his children.

'What's your name?' Nuccio asks one of the children.

'Francesco,' he answers, his chest puffed up after being called upon.

'Very good. Very good. You always need to tell me the truth. And when the cops come around?'

'Never tell the truth.'

'Very good. And how old are you?'

'Seven. Well, almost.'

'Only seven years old and you are already this tall? Damn, it won't be long before you can kill a cop.'

'How would I do that?'

'With a gun. How else?'

'But I don't have a gun.'

'When the time comes, you'll have one.'

They all stare at him as he leaves, their eyes magnetized by his swagger. Anyone with a cigarette and a gun is a hero. Francesco wants to be like him, with a white shirt open at the collar, cigarette between his lips, and some serious attitude.

In the meantime, the Hunter has kept walking. Nuccio watches him from behind. He'd like to be that powerful. That's why he's following and learning from him. It's the food chain of respect. The Hunter has closely cropped hair as curly as an Arab's. Few in Brancaccio could dispense justice with a gun like him.

'You gotta do what you gotta do,' he tells him over and over.

It's the right thing to do.

The family doesn't do anything that's not right to do. And it guarantees order in a city where chaos is just another type of order.

If it weren't for them, Nuccio would get bored. He wouldn't even have the money he needed for cigarettes, and he'd have to find a job on his own. His parents have told him a thousand times. But he has no intention of spending his life breaking his back like his mother and father. Why would anyone want to do that?

All you get is a broken back. No, he's twenty years old and he has other plans. He wants to get himself a villa by the sea where he can take his girlfriend. He's already promised her. As sure as his name is Nuccio. He was born, raised, and still hasn't died in Brancaccio.

The Hunter stops in front of a fishmonger's stand and presses his finger against the head of a swordfish which stares back at him from its bed of ice with a crazed white eye. Nature has condemned fish to live without eyelids so they see everything, even when they die. The Hunter doesn't utter a word. Attitude is everything if you have power.

A restless man is wearing an apron soiled with blood and scales. He slices off a piece of swordfish with a knife twice the size of his hands. He wraps it in butcher paper and places the fish in a bag. He slips in an envelope and hands the Hunter the bag without looking up at him.

The Hunter checks the contents of the envelope. Nuccio observes his calculated coolness. He spits the butt of his cigarette and lights another. He snorts in the summer air and the smoke hovers above him in a halo that slowly dissipates. It's going to be a hot day today. When the smoke remains suspended like that, it will always turn out hot.

'So?' Nuccio makes the sign of the cross in the damp air as if to say, 'Are we sending a man to the cemetery?'

'It's fine.'

'What do you mean "fine"?'

This guy needs to learn how not to ask the same question twice.

The swordfish eyeball screaming from its socket reminds the Hunter of his first victim. A bullet is instant destiny. The eyes of prey aren't like fish eyes. They drain immediately. Fish eyes take too long to die. Either way, everyone dies sooner or later. The way they die is just a detail. You gotta do what you gotta do. He has a family to feed, three marvelous children that he loves more than anything in the world. And the 5 million lire that they give him each month mean food and future and even more importantly, they mean health. If you have that, you have everything.

Killing doesn't lead to all the remorse that they talk about in the movies. It's much easier than on film. The wolf has to deliver the meal to its pack. And that's how some people are born to be prey and others to be hunters in this world. Nature is the one who decides. The rest just falls into place. Killing is simple equilibrium. Cops, rivals, traitors. They are human animals. If blood needs to be splattered when you strike, it's nobody's fault. Life is made with blood. Destiny? Fate? Or however the fuck you see it. He needs to protect his children and raise them right. The Hunter became the Hunter for them, from the very first time he robbed someone.

He was fed up with hearing his friends brag about things they had never actually done. And he needed money. It was a day like any other day and he put on a ski mask and robbed a jewelry store. That's it. There was nothing else to add. Little by little, hit after hit, prey after prey, he earned himself his name: The Hunter. Planning and acting and playing it cool like a snake. The secret is that receiving and executing an order are the same thing. Obedience is the only form of loyalty required. It's the devotion due to the neighborhood gods so that their wishes are fulfilled.

No one wants to upset Mother Nature's balance. The cops

don't need to come to the neighborhood looking for fugitives. They don't need to come and check up on things like that priest from San Gaetano who fills up the church with babies and children and cops, and that center he opened next door, the Holy Father Center. Amen. He needs to keep an eye on him. Something really ugly could happen in there. People come all the way from Palermo, from the rich people's neighborhoods. They show up with their designer clothes and they think that they can teach us how to live here in Brancaccio. They speak fancy Italian. Once his kid went to play soccer at the Holy Father Center and he had to give him a good beating to make him forget how much fun he had. He made him slash the tires of the cars that belonged to those smart-aleck kids who speak Italian. He gave the job to his son and to two other boys, a couple of kids that were just standing around waiting for something to do. After fifth grade, that is pretty normal for Brancaccio. Children go to school when they feel like it. And they're the ones who assign the homework.

He stopped going to school after fifth grade. And then the street became his classroom. You should take what you want with your hands. Or with the claws that pop out when you don't get the piece of meat that you wanted. It's just like what happens to wolves. In the fury of grabbing for the meat, they can't stop their claws from popping out.

Nuccio hasn't killed anyone yet. He's still waiting for the right moment. When they call on him to do it, he will and that will be the end of the story. He knows that's the test of obedience that can make your career. At the moment, he's just dealing, collecting, and looking after a few whores. He knows how to do his job but that's not all. He's also capable of skimming a little off the top just for the hell of it. But the Hunter doesn't know that.

The Hunter watches out over the empty street. The street is what makes a man a man. They know the street and its rules. Anyone who doesn't learn will die like a fish who tries to breathe out of water because it thinks the water's dirty. That's the water where you were born and where you have to swim. You have to dominate so as not to be dominated. It's not a question of good or bad. And that priest just doesn't want to understand. It's a question of dignity.

'Take this to Maria,' he says to Nuccio as he hands him the fish.

'Sure thing.'

Nuccio couldn't ask for anything better.

And with the package with the fish arrives the answer to Nuccio's earlier question about the cemetery: 'It's like putting a piece of metal into a piece of flesh. Nothing more, nothing less.'

Nuccio goes into the courtyard of an apartment building with crumbling balconies and blinds colored pink by the sun. The aroma of boiled vegetables descends like a veil over the space. The sky is clear above, and what a beautiful day it is: Bright and warm, a day for the beach. Before he heads up, he looks in his bag and notices there is an envelope. He opens it and there are 200,000 lire for Maria. He puts the envelope in his pocket and walks up. He rings the doorbell and a girl with dark eyes like an Arab princess and blue bags under her eyes like a prostitute barely cracks open the door.

'This is for you.'

'Thanks.'

Maria extends her hand to grab the bag without opening the door any more. But Nuccio pushes her back firmly.

He goes into the kitchen and tosses the swordfish steak on the table. He turns and sets his eyes on Maria. He moves closer and puts his finger on the mascara streak that runs down her cheek. He presses the skin on her face and squeezes her mouth between his thumb and index finger as he takes what he is due.

Maria can feel hell enter her body. Her eyes are like those of a fish dumped out onto the shore. In their desperate bid to return to the water, their violent convulsions threaten to sever the fine thread that still binds the animals to life.

Flesh can wound as much as any weapon.

3

They are children like all children. But they have the uncontrollable sneer that strays have on nights when the sirocco blows. Francesco watches them. They laugh and he laughs, too. But he's just pretending because he doesn't want to feel left out.

The dog has a broken leg, a missing eye, and black liquid smeared on its side. He's whimpering so he must have another hidden gash in his bag of bones. He's as big as a German shepherd but he's a mutt. You can tell from the unusual blend of colors and shapes he wears on his fur.

The apartment building is still under construction but has been forever abandoned to its mattresses and syringes. You can see roofs and uniform swaths of sky. Everything is rusted over and sharp, like the rods that emerge from cement blocks, like iron bushes.

They drag the dog to the edge of what would be the kids' playroom in the best of all possible worlds. That's where he is supposed to lie down and dream of hunting and eating meat. Francesco wishes he were at school but this morning his mother didn't drop him off, nor did she tell him to go on his own.

She didn't even get up. And when she's like this, all he wants to do is hit the streets. Last night, he heard her laughing until late. And then he heard her sobbing after she'd been left alone. He opens his eyes during the night and can hear his mother and the men who laugh with her. Then he closes and reopens them again to see if he's dreaming. But even in the dark, the sounds are still there.

So in the morning, he got dressed by himself and he took to the street. The first street took him to Don Pino's car and then his encounter with Nuccio. And then the street took him where it wanted to, where it decided to take him, where it ends.

Now Francesco wishes he were at school with Ms. Gabriella. She smells nice. There are colored walls in that little classroom where you don't have to listen to the creaking bones of an animal won in a dogfight by a man who bets on its pain. No, it's not night-time there. It's far from the basements of Via Hazon. That dog doesn't have a name. A fighting dog doesn't ever have a name.

There's a big poster on the wall of the classroom with a large letter D. And there's a drawing of a dog that's not bleeding and doesn't have a broken leg. It's a whole dog and it's clean, the way things should be. It's a dog with happy eyes. But everyone knows that at school they teach you things the way they should be, not the way they are. Francesco can see the red drool drop from the muti-lated teeth of the dog with no name.

He closes his eyes and then reopens them. But the drool is still there, dripping. There is no mirage, no nightmare, and no miracle either. Everything is real in Brancaccio, for better or for worse. He'd like to call that dog by a dog name. But he doesn't know any dog names. Pino does, for sure. He repeats this to himself, as if the dog could hear him. The first name that comes to mind: Dog. He'd like to see him get up again and be healed like the dog on the poster at school. But a dog can't hear you if you just call him Dog. He could try Charlemagne, like the King of the Franks. That would be a perfect name for a dog. Everything is perfect, just the way it is supposed to be, on the posters at school: Cherries, gnomes, butterflies, fish, bottles . . . Ms. Gabriella knows some great stories about the drawings on the signs, like the one about the boy who is so good at swimming that he reminds people of a fish. They call him Colapesce, like the legendary Sicilian 'fish man.'

One day, he stays in the water trying to find the bottom of the sea as everyone waits for him to come out. He goes to the beach when he's worried that he will run into Colapesce. He's afraid that he'll see the fish man come out of the water. And that's why he never swims far from shore. Then there is the story of the mermaid who wants to become a girl and she sprouts legs. But they are very sore because she's never used them. Francesco loves these stories that mix men and fish and it's not clear whether it's a fish or a man or both.

His favorite time to go to the beach is when his mother comes with him and she puts on her green bathing suit and lets her beautiful hair down. Swimming underwater and opening his eyes and seeing all the things mixed up together the way they look when you open your eyes underwater. Then his eyes start burning. But he likes the silence underwater and he likes diving into the waves, under the waves, with the waves. The sea and his class at school are the only things that he likes.

Aside from his mother, everything beyond the posters at school is ugly. The houses don't have roofs and white smoke coming out of the chimney tops. The dogs have broken backs and empty eye sockets. Cherries? He's never even seen one, and bottles are used only for breaking with rocks.

And he's scared. Especially when the hot wind outside is so strong that it makes the windows burst open. But he doesn't have the courage to get up and go close them because maybe the wind will snatch him up and he will fly away. And he doesn't have a dad who would go looking for him and bring him back home.

His friends kick the dog in its stomach and it makes a muffled gurgle. Then the dog whimpers and grinds its teeth. They break its ribs. Francesco doesn't know how to repair a broken dog. The only thing to do now is for him to break it, too, so that nothing living and suffering is left. That would be worse than death.

He kicks it on its snout and it creaks. The trembling spreads from the tip of his foot all the way to the inside of his head like a whip cracking. The only way to shake it off is by giving the dog another kick and kicking harder and harder. And hell is when you no longer feel the pain of shattering something, when you no longer feel it in your spine, in your bones, in your head, in your heart. Hell is the anesthesia that makes you no longer feel the life in what is living. But Francesco has something that resists inside of him even as he kicks the limp, loose flesh.

He goes over the subjects in the posters, just as the teacher asked his class to do. Let's repeat together. The letter B is for the bee that once stung him. The letter Z is for the zebra that reminds him of the Juventus soccer club and Roberto Baggio and how he wants to be like Roberto Baggio even though there are still some who prefer Schillaci. The letter F is for the frame that he would like to jump through. The letter E is for the eggs that he likes when his mom makes him zabaione with sugar. He can't remember what the letter I is for. He just can't remember it at all.

And so he just keeps on kicking and he seems like anything but a child. He and his friends quench their thirst with that crushing, wounding, and destruction. The dog's missing eye opens with each blow, emptier each time.

Then they push the carcass over as it still gasps for life. They aim for a cinder block with the rods sticking out. The dog ends up on its side and one of the rusty iron rods punctures it, slicing through like a piece of paper. The dog moans hoarsely and falls back on the ground as his innards, now turned to mush, spill out freely. One last convulsion decrees the end to its instinct for survival.

The children shout. The dog is dead. Losers deserve to die. The children laugh. They cheer like crazy people who know only the game of making sacrifices to the faceless god of apathy.

Francesco opens the eyes that he had closed because of his fear. But it's all still there and he can see blood splattered like fireworks around the dog as the flies and wasps began to flutter around it. He still can't remember what I is for. He cheers as well because he doesn't know what else to do. The mob mentality has swallowed him up and he can feel the buzz of destruction in his slender arms.

H must be for hell. But there is no hell on first-graders' posters. If anything, there is F for fire. But hell and fire have nothing to do with one another. Hell is pure subtraction. Hell is taking away all the life and all the love from within.

4

It's over.

Noontime is the only moment on the last day of school worth remembering. The school bell rings like the Seven Trumpets of the Apocalypse. The summer, which the kids wish were eternal, swallows them up and casts its spell over them. It abducts and scatters them.

The sunlight is so strong that it practically drowns them. It sparkles on the rooftops before falling on and gushing over the streets of men with amazement. It bathes and warms all the salty surfaces of the sea. Only an impossible rain could crack that blue marble sky. Amid a tide of bodies and souls, you can hear a voice if you lend an ear.

I like to find the right words. Words and their sounds are what saves me. I learned this at elementary school when everything is, well, elementary: I use words to anchor all the things that drift on the sea inside my heart; I dock them to the port in my head. This is the only way to stop them from crashing into one another, from running aground and breaking apart.

When I didn't know the name of something new, I would invent it. And that was all it took. When I was a child, the thing that was hiding under my bed in the dark of night was called Nero. And that made me less afraid. I didn't even know of the existence of the Roman emperor Nero. And when I discovered there was an emperor named Nero, I was convinced that I had created the tyrant myself.

I love wordplay. I love rhymes, assonance, and adverbs. But especially adverbs. But when conjunctions connect clauses or sentences (something that I learned at elementary school but later forgot), it has a cathartic effect on my brain.

'Cathartic' is an anchor-word. It's one of those words that can dock a large number of things. I learned it when I studied ancient Greek tragedy and it can help you to relax when you are afflicted by the greatest causes of stress: Fear and anxiety.

I, too, am docked to the four syllables of my name. I pass my time quietly in the port as I watch the world from the shore. My name is regal: It's composed of the imperial eagle, veins of gold that emerge from my hair, and the wholly confident blue (at least, I'd like to think that's the case) of my eyes.

My name is Federico. I was named after Frederick II, the Holy Roman Emperor. This city was the jewel of his empire.

That was also the name of my grandfather, commander of ships, who died seventeen years ago. But I know his tomb well. It's between the cliff and the sea in the shadow of Mount Pellegrino. A tomb with a view of the sea, just like he wanted it. I have no idea what kind of tomb I will have, and it's not exactly the moment to be thinking about it. But I want it by the sea, too.

Federico came from far away and he crossed many lands and seas to get here. That's how he built his empire. Unless I'm a complete loser, my name will force me to do great things in life. I'm not saying I'll become an emperor. But I do want to have a view of the open sea.

There are days when the emptiness nips at my chest and the void frays my insides. I know that I should really get a move on but all that emptiness and that void leave me paralyzed. I want for nothing but am still not happy. I don't even understand how all of this space can fit inside of me. Blood, muscles, and nerves don't leave much room for emptiness and according to the laws of physics, there is no such thing as a void. But inside of me, a few cubic centimeters are lurking. You can't see them. They are hidden. It's as if they had been smuggled in.

In the byzantine golden light, this guy's bicycle shimmers to the point of seeming like it could float away. If you look carefully, you can see that he has his bathing suit hidden under his jeans, a common sight around these parts starting in May.

He turns his back on Vittorio Emanuele Classics High School and a year that was both boring and beautiful. Then he heads down the ancient road that leads from the belly of the city to the port where it dives into the sea.

But here, the port is everything. There are thousands of cities that men and nature have set up along the sea. But there is just one that can claim this name by its very essence, brilliance, and fate.

Palermo, *the never-ending port*.

The Phoenicians called it Ziz, *the flower*, because of the rivers that flow like petals to the city's center. The rivers aren't there anymore. And don't even bother looking for any traces left by the flow of water.

Pan ormus.

The name meant *never-ending port* for the Greeks and Romans.

The original meaning really hasn't changed. It was the name that ancient mariners used to call it when they managed to moor there after surviving storms or being becalmed.

Ships were welcomed by these docile sands like heads resting on silk pillows. And the bay would nurse the tired sailors with a feminine embrace: *never-ending port*. An embrace that was kilometers and kilometers in size. Ever loyal. At least in appearance, just like everything that boasts of being never-ending.

But you mustn't ever forget that an embrace can also be used to strangle you. Ambushes set for those who are taken in by such sweetness and lower their guard: Ports are full of sailors and scoundrels, deals and dangers. Double-minded souls suited for an ambiguous place. Once upon a time and forever more, just like there will always be young dreamers ever ready to set out to sea, with no particular destination, because they are unable to see the horizon without wanting to break it in two.

I believe that someday I will be a poet. I might already be a poet but a poet who leans toward baroque exaggeration. That's what my Italian teacher says but, then again, he doesn't mind a touch of baroque. He also says that I'll heal someday. He was like this, too, when he was seventeen years old. If you ask me, he hasn't changed a bit and he's trying to correct a defect in me that he still has as well. I love the quick-wittedness of the baroque style, the metaphor that dislocates reality and the great plays on words used to raise the ante.

Maybe that's the reason why the boy plays with the city and the city with him. He walks through the alleys that lead to the sea like the Cretan Labyrinth. Sudden darkness hides the sun and offers an unexpected coolness. For every light, there is a shadow: In a city lashed by light, the whipping of the shadows can be just as violent. The never-ending port.

Never-ending cargo, never-ending negotiations, never-ending money, never-ending conmen, never-ending brothels, never-ending wine, never-ending arrivals, never-ending departures.

From the heart of the ancient Arab city, he can slip through the old alleyways all the way to the actual port. He passes by the Arab–Norman cathedral on his way. It looks like a sandcastle built against a shade of blue for which no adjective has yet been invented.

The coral-colored cupolas of San Giovanni light up while the gold in the mosaics of the Palatine Chapel do little to pay homage to the Eden that once existed there. Only a few tiles remain. The rubble left over from the Second World War is real as well. It has long since petrified and now stands motionless in the streets of the city center, like a black-and-white photo that refuses to fade.

He might brush up against the immense ficus as the sun bathes it in light. If he does, he will smell the sea as it impregnates the tophus stones. If it weren't their natural color, you'd think that it were an exaggerated shade of yellow. But it's just the effect of the sky, which acts as a backdrop. It resembles a magic lantern from *One Thousand and One Nights* more than any other city. All you have to do is to rub a few stones together and some genie will appear. Not just any genie: A wheeling-and-dealing genie who will inspire more wishes than he will grant.

An Arab geographer once said that 'to look out on to Palermo is to make your head spin.' It's all knotted up together, so much so that it can dislocate your brain as if it were your shoulder. The never-ending port. The never-ending embrace. The never-ending crush.

The boy's senses are well trained. He lets himself be guided by Ariadne's thread, which, in this case, is a humble aroma of *sfincione*, the classic Sicilian pizza, piled up high on a Piaggio Ape, a three-wheeler, known as the Lapino in Palermo. The fragrance of the pizza is mixed in with the dust and noise emitted by low-horse-power exposed motors as they burn gas that has been mixed unwisely with oil. The boy is heading downhill on his bike and he's nearly as fast as the Lapino. You can have lunch around these parts for just 1,000 lire. Poverty has never been ashamed to show itself here. The simple things are cheap because people have learned to make do with what they have to survive. *Sfincione* is also a good cure for the blues. To tell the truth, there's no room in a port for sadness. Those who are sad know the best place to hide it: In the words of the stories. Never-ending port. Never-ending stories. Never-ending voices.

He stays on the trail of this three-wheeled cart and inhales the smell of onion on a slightly charred bed of tomato. Everything and nothing seem familiar because everything and nothing are constantly being improvised on these streets. Every day and all things are different, even if nothing has changed from day one. The fishmonger knows this. He constantly rearranges his all so as to confuse even the most eagle-eyed of ladies. A raucous voice gurgles through a loudspeaker, promising flavors as comforting as a mother's bosom.

'You won't believe how good this *sfincione* is,' it says in the Sicilian dialect. 'Damn, it's good! Treat yourself today!'

The vendors hawk their wares like Arab merchants in their souk. And with their words so full of *ahhh*, they have been imitating the same voices and vocal chords for centuries. They transform their goods into vowels that promise the heavens. It's all thanks to the repetition and the modulation of their voices. It's something that has penetrated a people's dialect and flesh so deeply that it can no longer be removed. Words are as valuable as the wares around these parts. Actually, they are more valuable. Words that push and force you to do things. The boy calls them siren words. They seduce and bewitch even the coolest of brains. A language that was created to seduce and take charge. A language not intended to serve truth. Never-ending port, always open for business. Never-ending sales. Never-ending words. ('Never-ending words' is what they should call Palermo!)

But how do you tell a boy who's made out of thin air that reality always overflows from a bed of words?

I feel like singing, though I'm tone-deaf. *Though.* How wondrous the world of possibilities hidden behind a *though*! And I'm going to sing at the top of my lungs because school is over and everyone's going to the beach; because girls are a mix of light and flesh and maybe there's one out there for me; because I'm going to England for a month; because I can read whatever I feel like reading into the early hours when books open up like flowers in the morning.

As the street floods with young bodies and hopes, I realize that I'm not going to miss much about school. Italian class, Ping-Pong on the teacher's desk, exams I passed without studying, and chats with Geppo the janitor who keeps a bottle of the worst vodka and the best Marsala in his closet along with his manuals. He uses them to console himself and the students. We even invented a magic potion, a cocktail that we call Orabuca, made with Sambuca and mint, jasmine (borrowed from Geppo's wife's stash, which she uses for cosmetic purposes), and orange peel (Geppo always has at least two kilos of oranges on hand and he wolfs down at least one every hour). Orabuca can help you get over even the most painful disappointment. It makes you remember where you were born and it reminds you that you have no regrets. However badly it's gone so far, life goes on and you still have everything you need.

I've never studied much. Instead, I've practiced the noble art of improvisation as I've used my intuition to master certain subjects about which I couldn't care less. The only thing that interests me is literature and words that can be used to imitate reality or to stab it as I counterattack. That's why I love to say things like 'variety is the price of life.' But I'm the only one who laughs. I'm convinced that every soul is made of at least five words. Everyone should have a list of five words, their five favorite words. Your five words are the ones that reveal the air you breathe. And everything depends on the air

you breathe. My five are: *wind, light, girl, silently,* and *though.*
Everyone should write a poem with those five words. At least that
way their souls can dock in safe harbor.

Here's my poem:

> *Where are you, the only*
> *One who can sew up my*
> *Soul silently?*
> *Girl full of light,*
> *Can you mend a boy*
> *Made of wind?*
> *I search for your name*
> *Though you have none.*

The strangest thing is that I use words as my anchor. And then it's
those same words that push me toward the unknown, like maps that
need to be filled with places. It's because every word that's uttered
precisely opens an empty space around it, like the pier of a port.

I read poetry because my house is full of books and I have
always loved poetry books since I was a child. I couldn't understand a thing with all those line breaks but I loved to doodle in the
empty space. When my mother found out, she wasn't pleased,
especially when she found a copy of Cesare Pavese's *Hard Labor* full
of scribbles.

My brother calls me 'Poet' and he makes fun of me because I
couldn't grow a beard even if I wanted to. My mom thinks that I got
my wide, doe eyes from her. They are too trusting of the beauty in
the world, she says. Dad claims it's better that I didn't get anything
from him. That would be a shame, he says. He pretends to be tough
but he knows full well that my heart is as delicate as his and he can't
stand to see me suffer like he does.

My passion for Dostoyevsky has also earned me the nickname 'the Idiot.' My classmates saddled me with it the day I spoke about that book with a geek's enthusiasm during an oral exam in Italian literature. In that book, it's written that beauty is the thing that will save the world.

My classmates say that the world will actually be saved by beautiful girls. They might be right, but my experience in the field is pretty limited and so I prefer putting my trust in writers. I'm getting my experience through them.

I'm lost in my entirely useless thoughts when I notice a small, black figure among the confetti of t-shirts. It stands out against the festive colors surrounding it.

'Father Pino! I missed you today!'

Here he is, '3P,' someone I will actually miss now that school is out. '3P' is what we call Padre Pino Puglisi, otherwise known as Father Pino, our Bible studies teacher, with his big shoes, his large ears, and his calm gaze.

'Ready for summer vacation?'

'I am. I'm going to study English in a town near Oxford. I've seen photos of it. It's all green and there are tennis courts and grass soccer fields. Real grass, Don Pino! It's paradise! And what are you up to this summer?'

'Who? Me? Who needs to go on vacation when you live in a city like this? We're always on vacation. Just look at what a gorgeous day it is!'

'You work too much, Don Pino!'

'I love what I do. In Brancaccio, there will always be children that remind us that summer is a special time of year.'

'I've never been to Brancaccio.'

'I was born there, and I can tell you that you're not missing much. No grass there. Just cement. There's a lot of work to do . . . all of those children. Sometimes I feel like I'll never make a difference. I need more manpower.'

'Do you need a hand?'

'I could use three hands! Why do you think I asked you to come visit when you have time? I really need to do all I can this year because this summer is different.'

'Maybe I'll stop by before I leave . . . as long as we don't have to talk about God.'

Don Pino smiles. It's a strange, peaceful smile, as if it had emerged from the depths of the sea while there was a storm above on the surface.

I can still remember my first lesson with him. He came to class with a cardboard box. He put it in the center of the classroom and asked us what was inside. No one guessed right. Then he jumped over the box.

'There's actually nothing in it because what's important is what's outside the box. You need to think *outside the box* to get out of the box.'

And he was right. He's someone who can break open the boxes where you hide. The boxes that cage you. The boxes full of empty words. The boxes that separate one man from another. Boxes that act like the thick walls in the Pink Floyd song.

Don Pino's words distract me from this unexpected but indelible memory.

'What's the sense in talking about God? If I explain love to you, will you fall in love? When you fall in love with a girl, do they have to explain what a girl is beforehand?'

'No, they don't. First I see her and then I want to meet her.'

'Very good. You can tell that you're one of my students. We must be given God before they explain Him to us. Either you touch God or there is no theorem that can make you like Him.'

'So how do you do it?'

'What's this? Are you talking to me about God now? Didn't you just say that you didn't want to talk about God?'

'Well, just out of curiosity . . .'

I watch him and I'm actually hoping that he will answer because when it's just us, I have no problem talking about God. I think about God often, especially at night when I'm alone. After a storm, too, when all the things swallowed up by the sea are gently deposited on the beach: Messages, wrecks, dead people, and treasure.

'Come give me a hand with the kids in Brancaccio.'

'I wouldn't know how. They need people who know what they're doing. I don't even know how to get there.'

'Do you know how to play soccer?'

'Sure.'

'Do you have any free time?'

'A little before I have to leave.'

'A little is more than enough. Do you know how many tiles there are in the mosaics in the Duomo in Monreale?'

'No, I don't.'

'Neither do I. No one has ever had the courage to count them. And yet it's the largest mosaic in the world. And every tile, no matter how small, is important. I'll look forward to seeing you there. At the Church of San Gaetano. You'll find me at the Holy Father Center. Write down the number. Call me before you come and I'll tell you how to get there.'

He says goodbye with a hug. I'm not sure how to hug a Bible studies teacher and so I stiffen up as he wraps his arms around me with a warmth I wasn't expecting. I can feel his strong hands on my back like someone who leans on and supports you at the same time.

Don Pino smiles and leaves.

I continue to watch him as he walks away. He's dressed like always. Black pants, a little too wide. A pair of giant shoes that make him look like he's anchored to a base more than to his shoes, like my brother's Subbuteo players. A shirt and a blue jacket. He wears the same thing whether it's cold or hot outside. He's short and between his height and his thin gray hair, he looks like you'd expect a country priest to look.

That's enough now. Time to get out of here. June is for orange blossoms and the beach. I pump the pedals on my bike as I head to the harbor where I'll sit and dream about taking the girl in my poem there.

I'll tell her that I'd like to talk with her for the rest of my life, or we can just sit there and let the sea say it itself. The sea is so sparkly today. It's as if the sun had blown its light into it. I can't resist jumping in. I swim until I run out of breath. The more you push, the better you float, according to some strange principle that we studied at school. It's like that in the sea and maybe in life, too. And then I give myself over to the water and the sky, and I float like a dead man.

5

Don Pino heads up from Piazza dei Quattro Canti di Città toward the hills. That square is also sometimes called the Teatro del Sole or Theater of the Sun because at any given hour of the day, the sun cuts through one of the eight wedges that form the piazza. Nature and power. Sacred and profane. Pagan and Christian. Light and grief. Here, they mix. It's the true center of the city where the Càssaro – the ancient Phoenician road that connects the port, fortress, sea, and necropolis, now called Corso Vittorio Emanuele – runs into the street that was built at the end of the sixteenth century by the Spanish Viceroy Maqueda. Where they come together, they form a perfect cross, a cross that no one wants to bear. A cross and a mixed blessing.

He's returning from the umpteenth pointless battle fought in the corridors of bureaucracy, where every challenge is lost to fatigue and disenchantment. They will never build this middle school in Brancaccio, nor will they ever let them use the basement in the building on Via Hazon to make a school hypothetically possible in the meantime. These are all properties owned by the township and they have been taken over by squatters and their criminal activity. They are like Dante's circles of hell, except they have addresses and zip codes. A multifunctional hell: A warehouse for weapons and drugs, a pit for dogfighting, an alcove for a prostitute's young flesh. But the permits never come. The permits for normality never arrive, either. But Don Pino won't give up. He won't ever stop trying, even if it means working his knuckles to the bone from knocking on the doors to the permit office.

That's Palermo. The well-lit, sparkling neighborhoods of the rich and newly rich lie just a stone's throw from a constantly growing hell. It's a hell where men's misery is needed for the Mafia to show that the State means nothing. Don Pino knows why they say no. He knows who says no. But he continues to prod, just like a drop of water on a stone. One day he goes to present a request. One day someone from the housing cooperative board goes. One day a friend goes, another day . . . Drop after drop, the stone will finally break in two.

' "Give me time," said the water drop to the stone, "and I'll make you budge." '

His mother used to repeat this to him over and over again to teach him the patience that he didn't have.

The Holy Father Center is simply not enough for all the neighborhood's children. It's a place where they can play, study, and be together but it's nothing close to the work that is done in a school. The kids need to go to school in the morning and the center in the afternoon. That's the only way to keep them off the streets and away from the rules of the street. They have to be able to touch beauty in order to want it. Hell is the place where space for desires is already taken. That's where you take your orders head-down.

Sometimes people think that the Mafia is about extortion, murder, and bombings. But Don Pino knows that the real violence comes in the form of a neighborhood where 10,000 souls live but there is no middle school.

As the congested traffic swarms, he remembers the story of the greatest pianist of the twentieth century. She became great possibly because she also worked as a schoolmistress. In a Russian school, where there's a naughty child, despised by everyone and impossible to educate, he is regarded as a motherless and fatherless boy. He steals from his classmates, he insults the teachers, and he hits the little girls. One day the child almost kills another with his blows. They decide to expel him. The teachers line up like a firing squad. The principal stands behind him in silence and escorts him like a prison guard. The schoolmistress watches him leave. He is alone among teachers who fire upon him with their eyes and don't hide their satisfaction between their tightly drawn lips. And she begins to cry. The little one, with his gray eyes full of apathy and hate, hears her sobs and turns around. These eyes have a glow of goodness that no one has ever seen before. He stares at the schoolmistress while the principal pushes him forward.

He manages to break free and runs to her. She hugs him and shouts out that he will change, he will change, he will change. From that day onward, he remains attached to her skirt, like a dog. No one can explain this transformation. But he confides his secret in her.

'No one has ever cried for me.'

All this child wanted was to make someone love him but he didn't know how to do it. That's why he wanted so much attention and that's why he broke the only rule that life had taught him. Those who don't know how to build something know only how to break something. And maybe they break things that others build so they can learn how to build themselves, so that they can at least exist a little.

We need a school like that. And just like the Holy Father Center, it needs to be an alternative for these kids. No one cries for them, no one cries for the lives of these children.

The Holy Father Center was opened last January so that there would be at least one place in the neighborhood where young people could gaze into the eyes of someone who saw the value of their lives. When they found out that it was Father Puglisi who was opening the center, the landlords, who happen to frequent certain circles, doubled the rent. The money had been collected lira by lira and in less than two years, the dream had become a reality. He's not an 'anti-Mafia' priest, as some say. He's never been *anti-* anything.

He parks and gets out of his car. His knees are aching and it's not always easy to smile in the face of men's evil. He walks up the same street he did in the morning. It's always the same one, with its apparently muted beauty and its silence pregnant with possibilities, like an expectant mother in the first month.

Children are playing soccer in a little lopsided piazza.

'Why don't you come see me? You can play ball at the center and relax instead of playing here like stray dogs,' he says, smiling but with a firm tone. He knows that he needs to prod their pride first and then their souls. The one that seems to be the biggest among them stops the ball. He has goalie gloves on and he's standing in front of shutters that haven't been opened for as long as anyone can remember. They've been battered by soccer balls the kids have kicked up against them. There's a sign on them that reads '24-HOUR-ACTIVE CARRIAGEWAY. DO NOT BLOCK.' It's their goal and it rattles every time someone scores.

'We like it fine right here. What do you expect, priest?'

Don Pino moves toward them and then kneels on one knee. He looks up at the boy and their eyes lock. He can see all the reckless toughness you find in people who are afraid of being weak. The boy clenches his jaw. He doesn't know how to defend himself from someone who bows before him and no longer commands him.

43

'You're right. This is a great place to play. At the center, we have goal posts with nets and the lines are drawn on the field. So you can do corner kicks, throw-ins, and even penalty kicks. But I get it. It's better here with the cars coming through and without the lines. But you could at least use a referee . . .'

The boy stares at him in silence. He just can't give him the satisfaction of hearing him say yes.

But Don Pino knows that silence means yes around these parts. He takes a whistle out of his pocket. He's won more battles than Frederick II with that little whistle. He draws it to his lips and blows as hard as he can.

'I'm dressed in black like a referee. Put the ball in the center of the halfway line. Where are the captains? We need to do the coin toss!'

'This is the final match in the Champions Cup as Brancaccio faces off with Milan. Who's playing for Brancaccio?'

The boy from earlier gives him the ball and smiles. He raises his hand. His team gathers behind him.

'Is the Brancaccio captain the famous goalie?'

'Gaetano Passalacqua.'

'It's really him!'

'Passalacqua's men certainly won't be intimidated by Milan. And now here's the other captain.'

A child, six or seven years old, with dark hair and black eyes as deep as wells. He approaches without saying a word.

'What's the name of the Milan captain?'

'There's no Milan here. We're from Brancaccio, too. Get it?'

'Of course! Milan was eliminated by the other Brancaccio in the semi-finals!'

'The other Brancaccio? What are you talking about? We play for Brancaccio, too!'

'Yes, you're right. Of course. Brancaccio has *two* teams. Just like Milan has two teams: Milan and Inter. And Rome has Roma and Lazio. Let's just say that it's Brancaccio vs Also Brancaccio. Okay?'

The little boy softens up and begins to smile. This man is barely taller than they are and he has very little hair left. He's nice.

'What's the name of Also Brancaccio's captain?'

'Salvo. My name is Salvo Imparato.'

'Okay, perfect. Imparato and Passalacqua. Come over here and shake hands. Heads or tails?'

The two boys do as he says and their eyes sparkle. And this little corner of hell is transformed into a real man's game.

'Also Brancaccio wins the coin toss. Brancaccio gets to choose ends.'

Gaetano points to his shutters. The end is more important than anything else.

Don Pino puts the ball in the center and blows his whistle.

The hot sun is cooking the asphalt. Don Pino runs and sweats as much as the kids and it's hard to tell them apart. Watching them have so much fun, it would be easy to think that heaven is a soccer game with a referee who's not a jerk.

Salvo shoots and scores on the volley and Gaetano only manages to partially block the shot.

The referee blows his whistle.

'One-nil. Brancaccio kicks off!'

It's a ring around the rosie made up of children with ripped, faded t-shirts, some of them in their undershirts, others shirtless. And it seems to make time stand still.

As the game starts up again, Don Pino notices one boy standing to the side apart from the rest. He's watching with his arms crossed.

'You're not going to play?'

'No.'

'Don't you want to play?'

'No.'

'Are you sure?'

'Yes,' he answers, with his eyes betraying him and revealing the truth.

'Weren't you playing earlier?'

'I was. But then you got here.'

'You're not playing because of me?'

'My father doesn't want me to.'

'What?'

Silence.

'What's your father's name?'

'You ask too many questions.'

'You tell your father to come see me. I'll explain to him that it's okay for you to play. I'm harmless.'

The child steps away from the dirty, crumbling wall. He moves toward the halfway line.

'What's your name?'

'Giovanni. What team should I play on?'

'The one that's losing.'

Giovanni runs to take his place on the field and smiles, even though he's a little confused.

He doesn't know which father he should obey.

Don Pino watches them play. For a second, their hearts seem to be made of flesh, not asphalt. Their yells ring through the streets like waves crashing on the rocks on days when the wind lashes at the land and at the hopes of men.

6

The day after school lets out, everyone goes to the beach in Mondello, our own personal Caribbean. It's a collective and mandatory ritual and it's the real last day of school, when the sea, sand, and sky are our teachers. I go to Mondello on my bike, even though I'm sopping wet by the time I get there. But there's nothing like tossing your bike down on the ground just one meter from the shore and diving into the water like a seagull making a nosedive in search of prey. Then I head up to Notarbartolo where I live. It's a neighborhood with shop windows so shiny they look like mirrors, and freshly cleaned stuccoed buildings. The morning here is prodigious, squandering away its light on streets and gardens that look like jade, emerald, and malachite, depending on the hour of the day. Oversized trees explode from sidewalks. Too big for their stony soil, they taunt the highest balconies, like the enormous ficus in front of the house where Giovanni Falcone lived.

Everything slopes toward the sea and the wind rises along the street unimpeded. My street is named after Emanuele Notarbartolo. He was a mayor of Palermo and the president of the Bank of Sicily in the late 1800s. His battle to wipe out corruption in the customs houses of the time earned him twenty-seven stab wounds on a train that was traveling to Termini Imerese. As the steam soiled his white nobleman's collar, he was probably looking out peacefully at the sea when the assassins killed him. They had been sent to kill the determined politician by his colleague, Deputy Palazzolo, who was close to the Mafiosi who ran contraband. Naturally, no one was ever convicted of the crime, except for the killers themselves.

Then there's Falcone's house, its tree laden with drawings and letters. It was a Saturday afternoon, May 23 of last year. I will never forget it. We were all at Gianni's house. He's one of my classmates and he has a villa on the sea with a pool. We were taking turns between acrobatic dives and watermelon slices, relaxing on the white beach chairs with lemon ices. Water polo and water volleyball and contests to see who could hold their breath underwater the longest. The competition was so fierce that you felt sorry for the losers, whose faces would turn white when they couldn't take it anymore. And when they came up for air, we burst out laughing and razzed them. We watched the girls whose bathing suits stuck to their smooth skin, taut as the drums of an imminent war. It was as if we were suspended in time, oppressed by the wait for something that seemed never to happen in the distracted succession of our games. Maybe it was just the beginning of summer with the wait for its promises over. The crystal-clear water lapped up against the dark blue tiles. The reflections were hypnotic.

Then Gianni's mother called us and our playing was silenced by images from another world, the world of doomsday movies.

'What movie is this?' asked Enrico, who joined us after a cool shower, with a Coke in his hand.

Nobody answered. Our swimsuits were still dripping wet and we felt naked and inadequate. We were attending a funeral in bathing suits. And what's more is that this was our own funeral, our city's funeral.

An entire stretch of highway had exploded. We would have taken that same route to get home.

It had blown Giovanni Falcone and everyone who was with him to bits. The images were inconceivable when viewed from so close. They belonged to another dimension. But when we realized that it was our own dimension, we got dressed and waited in silence to go home.

In that moment, I realized for the first time that safe borders in life are an illusion. At seventeen, you dream of nothing more than a swimming pool, maybe because life is beginning to seem so vast that it's best to put up a fence around it. From then on, the pool became my surrogate for the open sea where sailors drown. We were swimming-pool swimmers, gold fish in a fishbowl. We knew nothing of the sea and its cruelty. And I still feel safe in that perfectly illuminated water, in that parallelepiped where everything is controlled and controllable. No waves, no whirlpools, no undercurrents. A sterile perception of tranquility.

I cross the city and cut through Favorita Park without engaging with my thoughts. They are too heavy for a day like this. It's incredible to think that hardly a year has passed. The trees freshen up the air as I pass by. They are like oxygen odalisques. The last stretch of road extends before me in a straight line like an asphalt rug over an oasis.

Everyone is there: Gianni, Agnese, Marco, Eleonora, Margherita, Leo, Giulia, Teresa, Daniele, Manuela, Alessio, Luigi . . . I can feel a burden lifted from my shoulders as I am thrown in the water with my clothes still on. That's the price you pay when you arrive late to an obligatory ritual like the first swim after the last day of school. Then there are water games, human towers pitted against other human towers, dodgeball, volleyball, contests to see who can stay underwater the longest and who can swim the farthest. Grazing the bodies of the girls from my class reminds me that I am made of blood and flesh. But the girl from my poem is not among them.

'What are you doing for the summer?'

'I'm going to England at the end of the month.'

'I'm going to America.'

'I'm going to our family's house on Pantelleria.'

'First I'm going with my parents to the Aeolians and then to Elba with my friends.'

'I'm going InterRailing around Europe.'

'What cities will you visit?'

'Palermo, Rome, Florence, Milan, Venice, Vienna, Munich, Berlin, and Paris and then I come back.'

'How long does that take?'

'However long it takes. You get on the train and then get there when you get there.'

'Sounds great!'

'What are you going to be doing in England?'

'I'm going to the college where my brother went. I'll be away for a month and a half and I'm going to learn English.'

'How's your hot brother doing?'

'He's taking it easy. He has the most beautiful girlfriend in the world and he works in the most beautiful place in the world. What more could you want?'

'He sure has done well.'

'He has. And I want to learn to speak English perfectly, just like him.'

'How come?'

'So I can impress at least half of the girls in the world.'

'And what about the other half?'

'I'm planning on studying Spanish on my own. And if need be, I'll do French, too. That way, I'll have at least three-quarters of the world covered. Of course, you have to keep in mind that I don't care for Asian women. So that should be enough to keep me satisfied.'

'You're so full of it, Federico.'

'You'll see. You'll see.'

'What are you going to major in in college?'

'I'm not sure yet, but definitely something in the humanities.'

'All those books have turned your brain to mush. What's so interesting about the humanities?'

'The essence of life. Leopardi said that art concentrates what is scattered in nature before our very eyes.'

'You are such a pain! You're always complicating your life with these theories. Take a look around: Sea, sand, sun, girls. And you're talking about Leopardi? What's wrong with you? What else do you need?'

'Obviously, you've never had a Spleen,' I respond with an intellectual air.

'What's that? Some type of drug?'

'No, it's a cocktail.'

'What's in it?'

'When the sky weighs upon your soul like a lid. When it rains inside of you. When all this or this *all* that you say is never enough.'

'Do you hear what you're saying?'

'I'm just playing.'

'See what happens when you read all those poems?'

'What do you mean?'

'You end up full of doubt, uncertainty, and questions.'

'Well, what's literature for? If not for asking questions?'

'I dunno. It's "required reading." What good is that?'

'To free you from clichés. To never take anything for granted. To test the status quo.'

'Like what, for example?'

'Like "the clear knowledge / that anything pleasing in the world is just a brief dream." '

'What's that from?'

'The last line from the first poem of Petrarch's *Songbook*.'

'Please! Anything but Petrarch! Dante's okay. But Petrarch? No way! He's the lamest poet in the top ten of lame poets.'

'Don't you understand?'

'What?'

'Nothing.'

We stand there in silence. It's one of those moments when I'm joking but I realize that I can see everything from afar. I love words that put distance between me and other people. I give names to things that others don't seem to see. And so I retreat to the folds of silence and hope that someone will someday find me there.

Another swim washes away all melancholy. We have a pastry for lunch. It's a prodigious balancing act between ice cream and butter cream, not dissimilar to the great artistic masterpieces. And so we let the sun, sand, and salt smooth out our green lives.

All of a sudden, I remember that I made a plan with Don Pino. There's something sharp in that thought, like something annoying sticking out from your soul.

Wherever you turn, it pricks you. And this leads to the umpteenth unanswered question. I have a box full of them tucked away somewhere. I dig up my 'poet in the grass' notebook and on the first blank page I find, this is what I write, using my odd handwriting:

'What is all this life disconnected inside of me? Why can't I give it a name?'

7

When the game is over, they all swarm off as the alleyways swallow them up. Dripping with sweat, Don Pino stands there alone. He looks at his watch. He realizes that he's running late and that he'll have to skip lunch. Just like always.

A girl, five or six years old, is sitting in the corner. Black ribbons run down her arms and legs. The writing on her t-shirt is no longer legible. It's written in a language that could have descended from the Tower of Babel. Her hair is messy and knotty like a baby Medusa. She's tormenting an unclothed doll, ripping out and replacing her arms and legs. The doll's face is blemished like the girl's and its blond hair is clumped. She looks at every-thing around her with the blue and ever-open eyes that dolls always have.

As Don Pino approaches her, he can smell the acrid odor of urine in her clothes. He recognizes her. He saw her this morning at the train crossing. It was as if she hoped the train would scoop her up in its gust of air.

'Aren't you going home for lunch?'

The little girl continues to torment the doll.

'What's your name?'

She raises her head to reveal eyes that are as black as tar. For an instant, it is as if another child is dancing in those eyes. But then rage and diffidence prevail and the black becomes even more dense and threatening like the sea by night.

She doesn't answer and she crosses her legs together with her arms. Her legs are so thin that they look like dried-out branches. She looks the doll in the eyes. She buries her head between her legs. And the doll stares at Don Pino. She bends over and the odor caked on her skin and clothes becomes even more acrid.

'Where's your mother?' Don Pino asks the doll, as she offers the eyes that the child denies him.

The girl shakes the doll.

Then Don Pino sits and leans against the wall. They sit there in silence for a minute, two minutes, three, four . . . He reaches out to stroke her hair.

She recoils like a wounded animal. She jumps to her feet and shrieks before running away. She's holding the doll by its foot. She stops once she reaches a safe distance and shoots him a dark look. Then she runs away without turning back. She practically stumbles because her slippers are too big for her.

Let the children come to me.

For the Kingdom of God belongs to them.

In hell, even that seems like a lie to him.

'Forsake her not,' Don Pino asks his silent God.

When he gets home, Mimmo, the policeman who lives upstairs, is looking out his window with his ever-lit cigarette in his mouth and his theories about criminal goings-on in the neighborhood. They'll do him no good at work but they are invaluable when it comes to getting to the truth.

They nod at one another and then Don Pino mimes a puff on a cigarette and shakes his head.

'It's the last one,' announces Mimmo with an air of innocence.

'Really?' asks Don Pino, pretending to be surprised.

'Yeah, the last one in the pack.'

8

My bedroom is a port. Petrarch also said his room was a port. There's nothing sentimental about it. Not because my stuff is so well organized. Actually, sometimes you need a map to get around in my room. It's because I know where to find everything.

My poster of Bono from U2 reminds me of who I wish I were and never will be. A row of school books, a hodge-podge of novels and poetry books. They remind me of who I am and who I would never want to be: A jumble of words still not articulated in the syntax of the future.

A syntax mastered by my brother Manfredi, my partner in laughing at nothing; in epic fights that culminate with someone biting someone else on the calf; in soccer and tennis matches; in voracious consumption of television shows, especially *MacGyver* and *The A-Team*, and cult animated movies and shows like *They Call Me Jeeg* or *Captain Tsubasa* or *The Rose of Versailles* or *Lupin III*. He totally looks like Jigen. He's confident, someone whose deeds speak more loudly than his words. But he doesn't smoke cigarettes. When he sets out to do something, nothing can stop him. He's seven years older than me and he just began his specialization in neurology. He knows everything about the brain and how it works. And one day he will be the best neurosurgeon on the block. He can be detached. He always gives scientific answers and he improvises the rest. But there's not much he can't answer with science. I wish I had his confidence instead of this heap of disconnected words. This is the reason I go to him when the precarious balance between words and reality is off. There's never been a time that my brother got it wrong. There has never been a time when he couldn't solve my math equations on the first try. I am convinced that we are the perfect couple of brothers from the 1990s.

This summer I'm going to the college where he went while I was in high school. My parents are obsessed with us learning English. If my brother agrees with them, it means they are right. My parents are only right when my brother says they are. He's my trick shot, the bank on the pool table that guarantees that my Oedipus complex will be less bloody than expected.

When I ask him too many questions, he reminds me that, given my age, I produce testosterone every two hours. An adult, on the other hand, only needs to replenish it every twenty-four hours, he explains.

'You're overdosing on wasted energy, Federico. If you would find a girlfriend instead of reading all the time, you wouldn't be on the verge of collapsing and drowning in your production surplus. And then, to make matters worse, you keep asking all these questions . . .'

He's stupid when he says stuff like that, but I know he's right. After all, his girlfriend is the most beautiful girl in all of Palermo. Sometimes my friends come to my house just because they are hoping they will run into her. Her name is Costanza. She's the daughter of an important Palermo businessman, a real big-shot. I've never been able to understand why God lavishes certain gifts on certain people in a disproportionate manner when there are other people whose lives would be tolerable if they just had a little bit of that same good luck. Beauty, intelligence, and money. Some people have a rigged horoscope.

Of all the gifts in life that one can have, I was saddled with the least useful: A love for words. Of all the things I've studied up until now, there's nothing I love more than Petrarch, which makes me an *ipso facto* strange guy. But his ability to return obsessively to the same terms, honed down to the point where they become transparent, really hits home for me. Petrarch is someone who concentrated all the things in the world into a few select words. He was someone who knew how to stow and dock the chaos of life. I got the idea for the five words from him. Our teacher spoke endlessly about Petrarch's 'monolingualism' and his ability to let the soul breathe with just a few essential words that had been cleaned like polished diamonds.

Dante, on the other hand, assimilates everything, the coal along with the diamond. Compared to Petrarch, he's dirty, even to the point of stinking. I could use some polishing myself because there's more than enough chaos out there to go around. Especially when it comes to love. And Petrarch can simplify love to the point of it becoming a diamond.

The other day my brother and I took a swim together far from the shore. It's the place where I'm never afraid to ask him questions that I'm embarrassed about. Maybe because my body is hidden underwater and the motion of the sea mixes up the embarrassment.

'How did you manage to win Costanza's heart?'

She's the one that first called me 'Poet.' And my brother always gets a laugh out of calling me that.

'Federico, when it comes to women, it all depends on strength. When they see a man worthy of this name, they allow their hearts to be won. It's not that you win them over. It's not a hunt. Don't act like a drooling adolescent. The point is to be a man. Women are women because there are men, and vice versa.'

His argument is flawless but the problem is *what does it mean to be a man?*

'Knowing how to make decisions and taking responsibility for your mistakes. Never being afraid to be alone because you are determined. The opposite of a man is a chameleon, someone who resigns himself to whatever situation and just blends in, someone who doesn't make a choice.'

'That's it?'

'No. You also need to be a gentleman. Not as an affectation but in the sense that you know you have something extremely valuable in your hands. Federico, men are not just males. Males want one part of a woman. Men want the whole woman. Men are willing to give up a little bit of love to have sex. Men want love, and sex is part of that love. A woman falls in love with your hands because that's how she can tell that you know how to protect her, caress her, take care of her, entertain and possess her.'

Treading water slowly so that I could keep myself afloat, I looked at my hands and decided they were too small for such tasks. I don't even really know what I want, let alone whether or not I am able to make decisions and take responsibility for my mistakes. The fewer mistakes I make the better it is. I'm like a warrior from the era of knights in shining armor, except someone stole my armor. Without protection, how can I go out and search for monsters, beasts, and my enemies? What good will all these words do me when I'm out in the woods so full of danger? Sometimes all I have is words, and I'm not immune from acting like a chameleon. But to be a man you have to have vertical motion. Manfredi is vertical. I am like all the poets that we studied in school. I zigzag.

This is another thing I blame God for. He exaggerated with my brother. I might as well have been made out of what was left over after he made Manfredi. I'm just an incomplete vagabond, like Michelangelo's statues with the bottom half still stuck in the stone. I can spend hours drawing new paths in my self-imposed maze without finding an exit. Sometimes I think that you generally have more courage as a child. Then you have to become like a rock to tolerate the waves of life.

Sleep hits me like a lead pipe and I am freed from my thoughts. I wake up and I'm still wearing my clothes and it's already nighttime. I dreamed of Don Pino's smile. I don't usually remember my dreams but I can remember this detail, and Flaubert used to say that God is in the details. Who knows if that's true or not. When the abyss devours the walls of my room, I hope I will be able to fall asleep on command. It's the only way to escape from yourself.

9

Hell does not exist. If it does exist, it is empty. They say.
They probably live in neighborhoods with gardens and schools.
    They are unaware.
Hell is the enormous cement buildings, decrepit hives abandoned
    by beauty. They turn to cement the souls of those who inhabit
    them.
Hell makes its nest in the basements of these buildings crammed
    with white dust, cut as best as it can be cut, and a balance of
    human flesh.
Hell is an insatiable hunger for bread and words.
Hell is a child who has been scarred from the outside in, from its
    skin all the way to its heart.
Hell is the lament of lambs surrounded by wolves.
Hell is the silence of the lambs who have survived.
Hell is Maria, a mother at age sixteen, a prostitute at twenty-two.
Hell is Salvatore, who has scarcely enough bread for his children
    and who drinks his shame away.
Hell is streets without trees and schools and benches where you
    can sit and chat.
Hell is streets from which you can't see the stars because no one
    has given you permission to lift your eyes.

Hell is a family that decides who and what you will be.
Hell is the cold feeling of knowing someone else's desperation.
Hell is making someone else pay the price so that they will taste the bitterness that we chew.
Hell is when things don't get done. Hell is every seed that doesn't become a rose. Hell is when the rose becomes convinced that it doesn't smell nice. Hell is a train crossing that opens up on to a wall.
Hell is every form of beauty that's been voluntarily interrupted.
Hell is Caterina who jumped from a tenth-floor window holding an umbrella because she no longer wanted to live in hell and she hoped that an angel would grab her before she hit the pavement.
Hell is potential love never acted upon.
Hell is hating the truth because loving it would cost you your life.
Hell is Michele with foam at the mouth and a blank stare from the umpteenth overdose.
Hell is a nameless old man who dies in his house and goes undiscovered for days.
Hell is no longer seeing hell. In this neighborhood of the city, men rule over two demons. They don't have esoteric names. Astaroth? Malebranche? Gog and Magog? No. Misery. Ignorance. Those are their names. Just like the horsemen of the Apocalypse. Will mercy and the Word of God be enough to stop them?
Hell exists. And it's here. In these ferocious streets where wolves make their dens. And the bloodied lambs remain silent because their lives are dearer than any other thing. And blood is the mark of life because when words cannot save them, blood will have to do.

What Hell Is Not

Hell is a father who takes his children's lives.
Hell exists and it's full to the brim.
Not over there but over here, with maps and addresses. It's all in
     the 1993 A to Z.

10

A naked girl rubs a dry bar of soap on her thighs in an empty bath-tub as if she were trying to wash away something invisible. The water isn't running.

'What's for dinner, Mommy?' Francesco shouts, standing outside the bathroom with his ear stuck to the door.

Maria keeps on rubbing the bar of soap on her legs. She's on her own, with a six-year-old boy and no wedding dress in the closet. She's gorgeous, with dark eyes hidden by her long hair. Her beauty would fit right in in a fairytale. But it's all wrong for reality.

'Mommy? I'm hungry,' the boy insists, just hoping for an answer at this point.

'I'm coming. I'm coming, Francesco. I'm taking a bath right now. Go watch cartoons.'

'Okay, but what are you making? I'm hungry.'

'Swordfish.'

'But I don't like fish!'

'Well then, I'll give you the sword and I'll keep the fish.'

'Come on, Mommy! I don't like it!'

'That's what's for dinner.'

'Well then, I'm not eating. And you're mean.'

Maria is silent. As she rubs the soap against her legs, she wonders if she's more of a bad mother or a mean mother.

Francesco kicks the door and starts sobbing.

'I didn't mean to kill the dog, Mommy. I didn't mean to.'

'What dog?'

The boy sobs against the door.

Maria opens the door and picks him up.

'I don't want to break everything. I want to fix things, not break them.'

'I'll help you, sweetheart, my darling boy.'

She sits in the tub with him, turns on the water, and lets the water run over him just like that, still dressed. Francesco tries to get loose but his mother holds him tight and tickles him to the point where he can't resist. He laughs and hugs her. He feels her warmth as he hugs her. That hug can fix anything. It's the type of hug that only a mother can give. Even when she's a mother despite herself.

There are places hell can't reach, even in hell.

11

Alone and deep in thought, just like Petrarch, I walk along. He would steal away in order to conceal the signs of burning love so evident on his face. I don't have anything to burn, nor do I have anything to hide. It's myself that I hide for the very reason that I don't have anyone to love. The thing that keeps me in a state of awe is words. As I write a few of them down on white pieces of paper, they sprout up in sequences that are anything but mathematical.

I attempt to connect words that have a similar sound.

I'm playing with the word 'rise,' which sounds like 'rose.' And I'm trying to capture their hidden kinship.

> *Regardless of its thorns*
> *I prefer the rose*
> *Rather than the rise.*

But that's not to mention that a small change can take you to a completely different place:

> *Regardless the hour*
> *I prefer to rouse*
> *Rather than to raise.*

As I am trying to find another variation that involves a Russian who is rushing, my exercise is interrupted by my mother.

'So should we go shopping for all the things you'll need on your trip? If you're going to be in England for a month and half, you're going to need a lot more than paper and pens.'

Shopping with my mother is always one of the most bittersweet experiences in my life. It's sweet because it allows me to become a little boy again for a while. And however much I protest like a seventeen-year-old male, I actually enjoy it.

It's bitter because my mother always likes to haggle, even though she has plenty of money. And it embarrasses me, as if I were a thief. It must be something that she learned at home when she was little. It's a conditioned reflex common among the generation that lived through World War II with rationing and substitute products. She was born in the 1940s and I was born in the 1970s. The discount is the abyss that divides our generations.

'You're going to need a windbreaker. You know how much it rains there.'

'I know.'

'You're going to need a pair of comfortable rain boots.'

'I'm sorry?'

'That's right. So that you'll be comfortable when it rains.'

'Mom, I'm not going to India during monsoon season. I wear tennis shoes no matter what the climate, and that's what I'm taking with me. Come to think of it: Look! I'm already wearing them! Problem solved.'

'Federico, London is not Palermo! Let's see if we can't find a pair like the ones I had in mind.'

'That's not how it is. Let's forget the rain boots.'

'And you're also going to need some long johns.'

'What are those?'

Sicilian mothers are convinced that to leave Sicily is to dive into unexplored lands, like you were a new Cortés or Shackleton. They predict every possible natural calamity and outfit you with all the equipment you need for the highly probable grasshopper invasion.

It's really just their way of showing you how much they love you.

12

Don Pino looks at his misshapen shoes and they remind him of the ones his father used to wear back when new shoes were a luxury. The afternoon light hugs the streets less ferociously than usual and lots of people are out enjoying the milder weather. They chat outside their houses, sitting in armchairs that aren't really suited for the outdoors, but they are comfortable nonetheless.

Dust. Basil and mint. Laundry hanging. The kids begin their ritual: They stroll back and forth along the piazza and the main streets to see and be seen. You could say they shuffle up and down the street but it's more like rubbing up against each other with their eyes than with their bodies. They move the way farmers used to plow the land in another era, up and down, down and up, planting words and every type of gossip, news and commands and stares that reinforce the status quo.

Everything can be done and undone in this city with words and stares. The rest is silence.

Don Pino treads across that same piazza and those same streets as he tries to make eye contact with the boys and girls. Some look away, others make fun of him, and yet others smile at him. A boy sidles up beside him and pulls on his pant leg, asking when they will go out for pizza and French fries again.

He looks into the eyes of the grownups and then back at his misshapen shoes. What kind of shoes are best for walking in hell? No one really knows. Maybe he knows since his father was a cobbler and he passed down his trade with his hands and his sweat. He repaired more pairs of shoes than he could count. And Don Pino carefully stores his father's work tools the way rich people lock away their silverware and jewelry.

Maybe there are no good shoes for walking in hell. All he knows is that you need to do as God does: He wears their shoes and dust as he walks up and down the streets of men. 'Before you judge a man,' goes the proverb, 'you need to walk a mile in his shoes.' And this is what God did for thirty-three years, thirty of which he spent crafting tables with the hands and sweat of a man. And this is what Don Pino has been doing in Brancaccio since October 6, 1990, the day on which he returned to the neighborhood where he grew up. He was born on September 15, 1937 and he cried just like all babies cry when they are born, as if they know that they will have to atone for nine months of warm darkness with years of painful light. He wanted to see, to touch, and to sweat on the streets of the men in his neighborhood. And they needed to see him on those streets, a familiar presence with his shoes encrusted with that same dust.

He knows that in this city, there is one of the five senses that you need more than the others: Your sight. In any port city, everyone watches everyone else. In a vast port city, they do it vastly. And there are not enough adjectives in the world to describe the various ways in which people watch other people.

Someone once said that Sicilians could impregnate even a balcony with their penetrating stare. And whoever said that was right. If a stranger watches you closely, you say, 'What are you looking at?' You need to define the nature of the hierarchy between two interlocutors. An ingenuous stranger doesn't watch. He stares.

People who are born in Sicily know how to watch. They all watch and they see everything. But the art of living is that of seeing and pretending not to have seen. And knowing how to remain silent when you have seen too much. Seeing too much can often be fatal.

He knows that he has to do the exact opposite: Watch, see, be watched, be seen. Openly, with his head held high. And he mustn't pretend when he sees something that needs to be changed. The beginning of hell is when you lower your head and close your eyes, when you turn away and reinforce the only spontaneous form of faith that Sicily knows. The easy-to-come-by, fatalist faith that says 'no matter what you do, nothing will change.' His peace is fed by this war on things that never change, on the status quo. And he keeps his eyes wide open. How many times has he told his children the same thing? Heads held high. Walk with your head held high. When someone walks by on those streets, people lower their heads. Visual submission is one of life's cardinal rules. If you look up at people, you are provoking them. And he looks everyone in the face and in the eye.

He left the neighborhood during the war. The walls and rooftops still show the signs of wounds that were never sutured properly. But ever since he came back, he has walked down every last alley hoping to rekindle the memory of strolls with his parents, when they would swing him between them as they pretended to launch him into the air.

And he knows the men of these streets the same way Mafiosi know their territory. In the end, he's a 'don' like them.

The Hunter is among those men. Don Pino watches him like he watches everyone else. And the Hunter returns the favor with his steely looks. Don Pino is attracted to those eyes. He searches them out. He stares at him and he smiles. The Hunter turns the other way. He has nothing to say to that smile and his air is indifferent, as if he hadn't realized that the stare was intended for him.

When people watch the Hunter, they need to make a slight bow or keep their heads down.

Don Pino is a don without power, a don without strength. His strength is unarmed. It's not greater than violence because violence transforms the flesh. But it goes *beyond* violence because his strength transforms the heart.

It trumps violence, not in space but in time. Only time can vanquish space. There are men who master space and there are men who are masters of time. It all depends on which god they believe in.

13

One of the other events you can't miss before summer vacation is the posting of our grades. It's a way for us all to see each other after school is out. We all go in together and we look up our names among the hundreds of rows and boxes posted on the wall. This jumble of numbers quantifies not only your grades but also your relationship with your pride, with your sofa, and with your television . . . and with every other form of mass distraction you can think of. That's all grades are: The margin of pride among the prideful kids or the confirmation of laziness among the lazy kids.

We meet up with Gianni, Marcello, Marco, Margherita, Giulia, and Agnese. I've mentioned Agnese last not because she's the least important. In fact, I mentioned her last because, at different times in my life, she becomes the most important. I share my sweet nothings with her and she manages to keep them to herself. I share my enthusiasm and my rage with Gianni because he's a boy and boys can't share feelings of deficiency. They can only share feelings of overabundance.

The first box that we probe is the very last one. It's the one that lets you know whether you'll have to retake your exams in September. Smooth. Everyone is smooth, just like drug traffickers who cross the border without being noticed. There's nothing like school to make you feel like a juvenile delinquent. We all yell in unison to let the world know that our summer is safe. I had no doubt that I would pass. My parents would never send me to England if I had to redo my exams in September. School comes first at our house. Everything else revolves around this cause. And by no means can it be neglected.

I've never had problems at school. I've always been intelligent enough to do well in the subjects that I like and to arm myself with well-honed strategies in the subjects that I don't feel as comfortable with. It's all thanks to Latin, which taught me to distinguish between strategies and tactics when we had to translate passages from *The Gallic Wars* by Julius Caesar.

I had the good old Castiglioni–Mariotti Latin–Italian dictionary by my side, the only true veteran of a greater war and a uniter of generations. It was my mother's and she gave it to Manfredi and he gave it to me. The cover had been reduced to a sieve and its pages were densely filled with declensions and cryptographed exceptions that had been masterfully dislodged, especially in the Italian-to-Latin part, which we would have never used. Julius Caesar served me well when he taught me how to get an A–.

According to my Italian dictionary, strategy is defined as follows:

> *In the military arts, a technique used to identify the general and final objectives of a war or to project and direct the larger military movements and operations of a campaign by readying the means necessary to achieve victory (or desired results) with as little sacrifice as possible.*

It's the perfect definition for my strategy at succeeding in school. The final objective is the grade board. Based on my yearly plan, it's always best to ready everything I need to achieve the desired numeric result with as little afternoon, weekend, long weekend, and vacation-sacrifice as possible.

And that brings us to my tactics:

Techniques, principles, and methods for deploying military or naval forces in order of battle or combat with the enemy.

Here's where the whole difference lies: The object of strategy is the general execution of the war or the deployment of large units that cover ample ground; but when you come into contact with the enemy, tactics come into play.

I love Julius Caesar as much as I love Petrarch. It takes a great general like him to balance the bigger picture and the details.

High school is *divided into three parts* just like Gaul. But contact with the enemy has names and last names, subjects, class schedules, fellow soldiers, and fortified hills. It's one thing to have to deal with math. It's another thing to have to deal with your math teacher. Your ability with the latter doesn't necessarily make your ability with the former necessary.

We were victorious. Our yells of joy wiped away any doubt of that. Then everyone rushed to see each box to find out the actual scores in the art of succeeding at school. Mine were beyond what I had expected.

I had a bunch of A–s (even in physics, though I don't know how that happened), three As (Italian, Greek, and philosophy), and a B+ in math. It was a report card worthy of a double backward somersault. And it was all thanks to Julius Caesar. And to my brother Manfredi who helped me with math.

'You're a nerd,' says Gianni. 'And a bit of a brownnoser. You and your Petrarch and your Ariosto, your Tasso and your Machiavelli . . .'

75

'What are you trying to say?'

'Is it really possible for someone to get three As without kissing someone's ass?'

'My good grades have nothing to do with that. And you know that, too. I just happen to like those subjects. They're fun.'

'You're just making things worse, you idiot.'

'You should be thanking me for all the translations I gave you. Dumbass!'

'The world's champion of dead languages! It's no wonder you have so many girls swooning at your feet. Maybe you should study hieroglyphics and date a mummy!'

'To the crows with you!'

We both burst out laughing and remember all of our cursing as we searched through the pages of the Rocci *Greek Dictionary*, a tome that has left generations of Italian adolescents shortsighted. In Greek, when you tell someone off, you send them to the crows who will devour your cadaver.

Giulia kisses Gianni. Or Gianni kisses Giulia. I don't know which. I can forget about cruising around next year with my best friend on his moped now he's dating Giulia.

If I had to define what love is in this moment, I would describe it as nothing more than something that comes between you and your best friend. From Gianni's point of view, love is just like friendship except for the fact that it comes with kisses, caresses, and hugs . . . A qualitative difference, but I would also contend that it's quantitative as well, just like the quantity of kilometers that I will be forced to cover on foot or at the mercy of public transportation.

Especially the 102 bus. It's a bus that resembles providence because of how it mixes up the destinies of poorly assorted individuals: Palermitan matrons with monstrous shopping bags; pickpockets who are the same age as me; students spread out over the seats like butter; a glance from a girl who quickly turns her head as soon as she notices a book in my hands; and sleeping senior citizens who have been on the route who knows how many times. And this is why I had to get a bicycle. It's much more responsive when it comes to the needs of my anarchic inner self.

Nearly everyone in my grade is dating someone. Over the course of my seventeen long years, I've only ever had one kiss. And it was probably by mistake. I'm holding out for Petrarchan love and I still haven't found it. What are the ingredients for such love? I've written them out in one of my lists. Schematically.

- *A woman: No need for explanations here. The right woman.*
- *A name: The right name that has multiple metaphorical and metaphysical meanings. For example: Laura.*
- *A good heart: Something that has to do with what my brother says.*
- *Eyes: Love is always made with the eyes; its roots are in the heart.*
- *Fire: Blood is highly flammable.*
- *War and peace: The oxymoron is the most common literary figure in love, even though I don't really know what this entails except for the self-evident contradictions. I'm not sure how they can be reconciled.*
- *Pain: Nourishment for any true love. It manifests itself in the form of crying. If I could, I would do without it. But from Sappho onward, it seems that the two things can't be separated. Bittersweet.*
- *Luck: That's what I'm going to need to meet the woman in the number-one spot on this list.*
- *Words: All the words needed to talk about it. Including books, stories, and poems.*

And, I'm not sure why, but a declaration of love for Petrarch has also tumbled out of me. Poets are the guests of honor in life.

And this confirms my suspicion that I am in need of a specialist.

When I come back into contact with reality, I realize that not everyone around us shares our triumph. There's a girl sobbing, head in hand, with her boyfriend comforting her. Her summer has been ruined, probably by math or Greek.

Now all that's left to do is head to the beach. After finding out our grades, we always go to Addaura beach and dive from the rocks, five meters high, into the sea. As we hit the water, we shout out insults intended for our teachers and we encourage them to head to the most ancient place in the world.

'When are you leaving?' asks Agnese.

'In ten days.'

'Are you excited?'

'I can't wait. Off to conquer the Brits, just like Julius Caesar. Better yet, off to conquer some pretty British girls.'

Agnese's mouth twists as she smirks.

'Can you give me a ride?'

'I'm on my bike.'

'That's why I'm asking. Otherwise I have to take the bus.'

'From here to Addaura with two of us on my bike?'

'Come on! School's finally over. If you don't do it now, when will you ever?'

This has got to be one of the most titanic undertakings of my life. As soon as she gets up on the handlebars, she leans back onto my shoulder.

Luckily, she's on the smaller side. Her hair smells good. As her skin comes up against mine, I know it's trying to deceive me. But I know that Agnese doesn't live deep inside of me. She lives – case in point – on my skin.

By the end of the trip, I'm exhausted and sweaty. She gives me a kiss on the corner of my mouth.

'You're my hero.'

I think I'm blushing. It's a luxury I allow myself despite my better judgment. I take refuge in the sea.

The slender body. The bare feet. The vertigo brought on by a dive into the water from up high. Certain things require courage. The sea above and below and the world could fit in my pocket.

14

The children are expecting a question because that's his style.

'What does *love* mean to you?'

They watch him in silence. Not because the question is too much for them but because the answer is too big to fit into a single sentence.

'Give me an example.'

Francesco decides to answer.

'When someone loves you, they say your name in a different way. It's like your name is safe in their mouth.'

'Who are you talking about?'

'My mother.'

'What about your father? Where's he?' asks another child as he starts laughing meanly.

Francesco wishes he could punch him. But luckily a little girl says something to distract him.

'Love is when your mom gives your dad the best piece of chicken.'

'I think love is when your dad comes home from work and he's all stinky and your mom tells him that he's more handsome than Tom Cruise.'

'Who's Tomkroos?' asks another little girl.

'An actor.'

'I think love is when your grandpa puts nail polish on your grandma's fingernails because her arthritis is so bad that she can't bend them anymore. But then grandpa got arthritis, too.'

'What's arthritis, Don Pino?'

'When you get older, your muscles aren't as flexible as they once were. Your bones get stuck together and it gets harder to bend them.'

'Do you have arthritis?'

'Am I so old?'

'Yeah, because you have gray hair.'

'But I don't have any hair!'

'That's even worse.'

'Well, either way, I don't have arthritis.'

'Thank goodness!'

'I think love is when my dad buys me a new ball and we play with it together. And it's also when he tickles me.'

'Wow, you know a lot about love! You certainly know more than I do. Think about how God is the sum of all this love put together,' says Don Pino with a smile.

'That's a super love,' concludes Francesco.

A little girl stands in the corner as she squeezes her doll and rocks from one foot to the other. She's wearing a red dress and it's surprisingly clean and ironed.

'What does it mean to you?' Don Pino asks her.

She remains silent. Everyone is watching her. Francesco moves toward her and takes her hand. He sits her down with the group. She keeps biting her nails. Without lifting her head, she starts to form her words.

'When my dad teaches me to swim where the water is deep.'

'Can I come, too? I don't know how to swim,' asks another little girl with glasses resting on cheeks that are as big as tomatoes.

'Damn, you don't know how to swim? Just like a girl,' says Francesco, but without being mean.

'I'm not a very good swimmer either,' mumbles Don Pino as if he were talking to himself. He remembers that time he took a swim during high tide and he was so scared that he sank like a *balatone*, the Sicilian word for rock.

'What does love mean to you?' asks Francesco.

'You.'

15

The train crossing goes up. The bicycle bounces over the tracks and slices through Brancaccio's thick air. It knows the road well. There are certain places where you mustn't ever reveal hesitation. His saliva no longer moistens his lips and it won't be long before the dryness reaches his mouth as well.

The heat weakens his knees and burns his lungs. Fear of the unknown takes care of the rest. But he has the innocent, wild courage of a boy who believes that places actually reflect their depiction on the map. Just like people who go to Iceland and then discover that you can't tell from the map that it's dark there for half of the year. The uniform light of atlases and maps is something you shouldn't trust all the way. This boy is about to find out for himself.

I find the church. I lock my bicycle to a pole and take a look around. As the sun kneads the asphalt, it sinks under the soles of my shoes. The air is still. You need to move slowly so as not to succumb. Occasional passers-by, overwhelmed by the summer heat, stare at me. I feel like a tourist and yet I'm in my own city. My house is just a few kilometers away and my school is even closer.

I can feel eyes piercing my back as curious blinds are raised. What was I thinking when I decided to come here? And on my bike, to boot! I should have come in an armored car. I keep my head down and look straight ahead in an attempt to hide the clandestine nature of my presence. It's like when you're at school and you look for something in your backpack during an oral exam as if looking away would make you invisible somehow. I go into the church and the yellowed walls seem as if they are about to burst into flame. It's like an oven in here as well. There is no escaping these sweltering days. Every once in a while, a gust of wind from the sea offers hope that the blazing heat will come to an end. White tuff. Lime plaster. Red lamps.

The church is empty. Scaffolding supports the roof and the area below is cordoned off. There's just one man with a black shirt sitting in the first pew. His head is bowed. I'm worried that I will disrupt this heated silence and I proceed on tiptoe.

Don Pino's eyes are closed. His heavy breathing betrays the fact that he's sleeping. I sit down near him and the creaking of the bench wakes him. He looks up at me and smiles as if in the dream from a few hours ago.

'What are you doing? Are you sleeping?'

'Umm . . . who's there? You came! I'm so glad.'

'I hope I'm not disturbing you.'

'I was trying to pray but I must have fallen asleep.'

He moves toward me and hugs me.

'Thank you for coming. When do you leave for England?'

'Next Sunday. That's why I came today.'

'Great! You'll get to enjoy some cooler weather. It never stops raining there.'

'The heat will kill you here.'

'Other things kill here, unfortunately.'

'What can I do to help you?'

'Let's just sit here in silence for another moment if you don't mind. Then I'll show you around.'

'Okay.'

All around me, there are statues of saints and they don't have wrinkles. There's a cross that's not properly hung and looks out of proportion. Underneath it says: 'There is no greater way to love than to give your life for your friends.'

I'm staring at Don Pino: His eyes are closed and he sits there motionless and smiling. His hands are resting on his legs and his back is slightly bent. Who's he smiling at? He opens his eyes and looks at me as if he could see right through me.

'I am so happy that you are here. I was feeling really lonely today. I needed some help.'

'That's why I'm here,' I answer.

I feel embarrassed. He needs me.

'I'm going to pay a visit to a family. Will you join me?'

'You asked me to come lend a helping hand. Well, here it is.'

I show him the palm of my hand. Don Pino puts his hand in mine for a moment.

Then we walk slowly down the neighborhood's sunburned streets. We stick close to the walls, wishing for cover that isn't there. The homes are low to the ground. Small houses with one or two floors. It's all very different from Via Notarbartolo and its apartment buildings and its patches of green. Bunches of basil, parsley, and mint, indispensable for cooking succulent sauces, dot the windowsills. But that's all the color there is.

We enter an alley where the trash bins overflow with garbage bags. The humidity-soaked air makes the edges of things tremble and liquefies their shapes. There are small buildings that look like garages.

Don Pino heads toward some half-opened blinds. I'm at his side and I'm hoping his diminutive body will be my shield.

'Anybody home?'

'Don Pino!'

'Sorry I'm late.'

'When have you ever come on time? You know that our door is always open.'

A woman is putting something away in a corner that appears to be a kitchen. The air is compressed but fragrant. Sauce. Oregano. Wicker furniture. Dignity trumps frugality and is transformed into grace.

I have my own room where I keep my records, my cassettes, my CDs, my posters, and my books. Here, instead, everyone keeps everything in this one room. In the opposite corner, there is a couch where three children are sitting and watching television. There's an old man sitting on a chair who's doing the same thing but he appears to be in a daze while the children seem to be hypnotized.

This room is everything. Or nearly everything. There's a scattering of beds, a rickety chair or two, and a cupboard. There's a table near the kitchen covered by a plastic tablecloth with orange flowers and dewdrops.

'May I get you something?'

'A glass of water. It's so hot outside!'

'Children, say hello to Don Pino.'

'Ciao, Don Pino,' they answer in unison without looking up from the screen.

I'm still standing in the doorway. I don't know what to do or how to do it. When you go to your friends' houses, you act a certain way depending on the room in the house. Here, I don't know what position I should take. There are too many places all in the same space. I don't even know where to put my hands and what I should be looking at. My pockets turn out to be useful for hiding my hands.

'Come over here and let me introduce you to Gemma. And

those juvenile delinquents watching TV who don't even say hello. What are their names?'

The children present themselves one by one, shouting out their names.

'Domenico.'

'Caterina.'

'Massimo.'

Don Pino moves closer to them and knocks on each of their heads. They try to defend themselves as they laugh.

'And this is Signor Mario,' says Don Pino, speaking more loudly than usual and enunciating every syllable so the gentleman will hear him. 'One of my parents' dearest friends. Isn't that so, Signor Mario?'

Signor Mario nods and reveals his toothless gums. He smiles a crooked but genuine smile and his dewy old man's eyes light up. He drools a little from one side of his mouth as he kisses Don Pino's hand. His visitor retracts it delicately as he gives him a caress on his cheek.

I decide to come inside and I shake Signora Gemma's hand. Then I wave to the children and Signor Mario. I can feel my skin bristle the way it does during an oral exam while you're waiting for your name to be called.

'What can I get for you?'

'I'll have a glass of water as well, thanks.'

'Is tap water okay? We only have tap water.'

'Of course, that's fine.'

Gemma fills a carafe with water from the faucet but she lets it run for a little bit first.

'The water's not very cold. It's too hot outside. I'm sorry.'

We sit down at the table with her.

'How's it going?'

'What can I tell you, Don Pino? We're getting by. Giuseppe's working construction. And now Giovanni is giving him a hand, too.'

'What about Lucia?'

'Lucia helps out when she comes home from school. And she's looking for babysitting jobs. She loves reading. I don't know how she manages to read so many books. I don't know how to read, but I have a daughter that can read all the books I should have read.'

'I'll ask around to see if I can find a family that needs someone to help out with their kids. And I have plenty of books to lend her. I have too many! Lucia needs to go to college, Gemma.'

'You're right. She's a special girl. The guy who marries her will be one lucky fellow.'

I listen to their conversation like someone watching a documentary about an exotic country. You can see the goodness in her eyes and in her tired face the sacrifice of someone who has never kept anything for herself.

I drink the water to keep my mouth busy. I have no idea what to say. Words fail me, when I'm usually the one who can't keep his mouth shut. Not even Petrarch comes to my aid.

The children laugh and banter over Tom and Jerry's misadventures.

'And what about you? What do you do?'

'I . . . I'm a student. I'm in Don Pino's class at Vittorio Emanuele High School. Near the cathedral.'

'Damn, you're in the right place! Don Pino knows everything. And he has a heart as big as a house.'

Don Pino smiles.

'He's younger than your boy, you know? No mother in Brancaccio can even touch Gemma! And her sauce! No one can make it like her. How's your father doing?'

'Just look at him. He's like a baby. Sometimes he drives me crazy.'

'Just like your babies.'

'Yeah, it's like having another child to take care of. Except he's eighty years old!'

Gemma gets up from the table and wipes the drool from Mario's mouth.

At that moment, a girl walks in. She's maybe sixteen years old. Her skirt has flowers on it and she's wearing a thin white blouse. She has wavy, shoulder-length hair. Her skin is dark and her green eyes sparkle against her oval, tanned face. She is a melting pot of Norman and Arab ancestries. Grape. Topaz. Dates. Centuries of Mediterranean history live within her. I always let words get the better of me when I see a girl I like. Maybe it's just to make her less inaccessible.

'Don Pino! How are you?'

She moves delicately. Her presence doesn't belong to this place. She seems to be above it all.

'I'm fine. What about you, Lucia? Did you finish that book?'

'Yes, you need to give me a new one.'

'I have it here with me.'

Don Pino opens the bag he always carries with him and he hands her a novel. She takes it hesitantly. Then she rushes to the corner of the room and grabs a book that she gives back to Don Pino. Her hair leaves behind a silken whirlwind in her wake.

'You keep it.'

'Really? Can I?'

'Yes, it's a gift.'

'I really loved Dickens. It was like I was walking through the streets of London.'

Her eyes shine like sunshine on the morning sea.

I'll be in that city in just a few days and I'm wondering, considering how big the book is, whether he lent her *Oliver Twist* or *David Copperfield*.

'This is Federico. He's a student of mine.'

'Hi.'

'Nice to meet you.'

My face is already warm because of how hot it is outside and I can feel the temperature and my embarrassment rising another degree. I'm just hoping that she won't notice if I stay out of the light. Her hand is slender but her handshake is firm.

'What do you study?'

'Classics. I just finished my fourth year.'

'Everyone who goes to Classics High is super-nerdy. They think they are better than everyone else.'

'What high school do you go to?'

'Teachers' High.'

'Do you want to be a teacher?'

'Among other things. What do you want to be?'

'I don't know yet. I like words.'

There are certain things that you don't really understand even when you say them yourself. My answer makes her smile in a fleeting instant of light.

'What's it about? Which city does it take you to visit?' she asks Don Pino as she points to the book.

'It's the story of a boy who lives by himself in a city where the sun is always setting. St Petersburg. It's the city where Dostoevsky was born. He loved that city more than any other place in the world. One evening, that boy meets a woman on a bridge. She is crying. They talk late into the night. But it's not night because there is a constant light there. So they decide to meet every night on the same bridge to talk. He falls hopelessly in love with her. Or, at least, that's what he thinks. And then . . .'

It wasn't Don Pino who answered her, for the record. I was the one who answered her. I've fallen prey to a terrible disease that one of the girls at school calls the 'Petrarch syndrome.' Our teacher has ruined Petrarch with hours and hours of lectures on the poet and his love of books. He was one of the first to have his own private library. He took it with him everywhere he went, and some of his books were true one-of-a-kind works at the time. I never go out without a book in my hands and my room is a disorderly library. If I'm going to spend money, it's going to be on a new book, even if I'll never read it. In owning books I find a joy that I call 'libridinous': Arousal created by the presence of a book and by its accessibility combined with distance, since I still haven't read it.

'And . . .?' Lucia asks me with a look of amazement on her face.

'Read it!'

'This one is worse than you, Lucia,' Don Pino interjects.

'Where is this city?'

'In Russia,' I answer.

'And how do you pronounce the name of the author?'

'Dostoevsky.'

'Have you read his books?'

'He's one of my favorites.'

'Why's that?'

I start thinking again about the summer between middle school and high school. I was beside myself with boredom and I was sick of hearing how high school would be more interesting and more challenging. I opened a copy of *Crime and Punishment* that we had at home. And everything became more interesting. Not because of high school. But thanks to that book. That novel confined me to my room for many afternoons in a way totally different than the other books I had devoured up to that time, like *The Lord of the Rings* and *The Neverending Story*. *Crime and Punishment* didn't seduce me. It repulsed me. It scared me.

I enjoyed reading it because of how harsh it was, a transgression not sweet but rather dangerous. At every turn of the page, I was expecting to discover the umpteenth hallway in the labyrinth of the human heart. I couldn't believe that there could be so many things in someone's soul. So many dark and light things at the same time. Then I read 'White Nights' because it was short and because I thought that the character was my literary alter ego, holed up in his attic as he dreamed of a love as perfect as it was unattainable.

'I don't know.'

'You don't know a lot of things for someone who studies Classics. But you like words and books. I love books that describe faraway places and distant cities.'

Lucia says this with a smile. She seems accustomed to saying what she thinks, without hesitation.

'How are the *Little Orlando* rehearsals going?' asks Don Pino.

'Great, but we still need a Charlemagne.'

'We'll find someone. You'll see.'

'How can I play the part of the queen if there is no king? I'm also having problems with the lyrics. Sometimes I can't seem to find the right words.'

'Can I come and play soccer with you, Don Pino?' asks one of the children out of the blue.

'I wanna come too!' exclaims the other automatically, even though he hasn't understood what they are talking about.

'Of course. Come with Lucia. That way your mother can have a little bit of time to herself.'

'Only if they are good.'

'We're always good!'

'Are you sure about that?'

'We're not always good. But mostly we're good! We're good more minutes than we're bad!'

'Well, okay then!'

We laugh. I watch Lucia laugh. Her profile in that small, cluttered room seems like a port. I don't know why but I want to read her 'White Nights' even though I don't know her and we have nothing in common except for a book.

As we head back, Don Pino is stopped by a woman.

'Father, would you be so kind as to bless my son? Maybe that way, he'll find a job.'

'Is he looking for a job?'

'No.'

'Well, then I'm going to give him a kick in the pants! Not a blessing!'

We walk along in the spongy June air and the street swallows up our feet. I can't stop thinking about that crucifix I saw in the church.

'What does it mean "to give your life for your friends"?'

'It means that you protect them and make their lives better with your own.'

'How?'

'With your time.'

I look around me without focusing on anything. I feel like I'm stuck in my inner traffic. Too many thoughts haphazardly parked.

'And with ice cream,' adds Don Pino with a smile.

'I don't think I've ever turned down an ice cream in my life, which has admittedly been short. Ice cream's almost up there with books, if you ask me.'

As I answer, I linger on the pauses and emphasize the most important words with a very serious look on my face.

'Here in Brancaccio there's a guy who makes ice cream so good that it could raise the dead.'

'That's impressive, coming from a priest!'

'Do you remember the time we took that trip to Monreale?'

It's one of the things that made the school year not a total waste. You always learn the best things outside of school. 3P came with us and so did our art teacher, a skinny waif of a man who could make a painting come to life like in Kurosawa's *Dreams*. He was the one who showed that movie to our class and the fallout was devastating.

'After St Sophia in Istanbul, it's the largest mosaic in the world. And the largest in the West. Six thousand four hundred square meters of tiles subdivided into 130 enormous scenes and single figures, all immersed in a sea of gold that peels away the texture of the stone and transports the viewer into the paradisiacal light of God. The Duomo was built like a great theological study of light. It was conceived so as to follow the light of the seasons. The light reaches its greatest intensity on December 21, with the winter solstice. And it reaches its lowest intensity on June 21, with the summer solstice. It's illuminated all year long by physical and meta-physical light so that the light shines on the Byzantine-era gold of the tiles on the right day of the liturgical calendar,' our teacher explained.

'What's the liturgical calendar?' Gianni asked me.

'What do I know? It must be something to do with the Church.'

'The world is safe where the light shines. It frees the world from darkness. Nothing is left to chance in this building. Unfortunately, the windows are covered up and so you don't get to enjoy the scientific precision in play here. Whenever you hear people talk about the Middle Ages in disparaging terms, you can answer that nobody today would be capable of such scientific, technical, and theological mastery. The first tile in this allegory of light was set in 1174.'

'Allegory of light? What does that mean?' asked Gianni again.

He holds me (rightly, I might add) to be the greatest expert on the useless encyclopedia of rhetorical figures that you find in literary anthologies.

'It means that the light represents something other than the light itself.'

'And what does that mean?'

'Maybe, if you shut up and listen . . .'

Gianni raised his middle finger and it wasn't intended as an allegory.

'The Duomo of Monreale, the cathedral, and San Giovanni degli Eremiti share the astronomic alignment with the winter and summer solstices. The temple was meant to be the physical representation of the teachings in the images: God is the creator and the architect of the world and man has been called upon to be the same. To distinguish between dark and light and create order out of chaos.'

The mathematical laws used in their construction were based on the language that God had used for creation. Anyone who entered had to walk along a path of purification through light, and the stories on the wall marked each stage of this progression. It culminated in the eyes of Christ Pantocrator from which everything flows and returns, just like the lines from Dante's *Paradiso*, as Don Pino pointed out:

> *The glory of He who moves all things*
> *Seeps through the universe and shines*
> *In one part more and in another less.*

'I really can't stand Dante,' Gianni started up again. '*Inferno* is okay. Just okay, though. But *Purgatory* is like boredom via suppository. And *Paradiso*? Let's not even go there!'

'Petrarch is much better, I know.'

'Petrarch is like taking a laxative.'

Don Pino snaps me out of my freewheeling, anarchic flow of memories. They are capable of absenting me from the present, causing me to lose my way.

'Just think of the tiles that make up those mosaics. First they are millions of tiles separated from one another, each with their own color, shape, and imperfections. Then they come together to compose an image. The image of God. We are like those tiles, each one of them arranged next to another, and together they make up God's mosaic in the world.'

'But I don't really care so much about being part of a mosaic. I'd like to understand something about the little tile itself.'

'And how can you, if you don't consider them as a whole?'

I had thought I'd fulfilled my duty by going to Brancaccio. But now here I am, lying on my bed and thinking that I need to go back, because Don Pino has asked me to. I should be thinking about my summer vacation and going to the beach. I should be thinking about England and not about that priest. And I shouldn't be thinking of Lucia, either. But there are certain thoughts that we don't think. Those thoughts think about us, just like words from songs that pop into your mind for no apparent reason. Those are the thoughts that I fear the most, boats that arrive in the port without warning. You can only imagine what cargo they carry and where they come from.

Manfredi comes into my room, without knocking, as usual.

'Hey Poet, what's all this melancholy going on in your room? It's like the attic of one of those young bohemians who died young from sadness and TB.'

'Since when did you start working in the "other people's business" department?'

'Poets either die from TB or from love. Which one is it?'

'Sometimes they just die from the overwhelming desire to smack someone in the mouth.'

'You're all talk,' says Manfredi. He smirks like De Niro in *The Untouchables* and pretends that someone is holding him back and keeping him from jumping me. He's obsessed with that film and he especially loves the scene where they are having lunch and someone's brains get splattered all over the table with a baseball bat.

'Would you please leave me alone?'

'What's the matter with you, brother?'

'There's nothing the matter with me. Nothing.'

'There's more something in your nothing than you're letting on. And you know it.'

He's right. But this time, my 'nothing' is just a way of alluding to something that I can't wait to tell him so that I can get his advice. It's just that I need to figure out what is happening to me before I let someone explain it to me. For once, I want to be the first one to arrive at the appointment with myself and I don't want anyone else to get there first, even Manfredi.

'Are you coming to the concert with us?'

'Of course I'm coming.'

'Well, you better get a move on.'

I had forgotten about the concert tonight. It's only the biggest event of the summer, and I forgot all about it. What's wrong with me?

16

'The priest is hiding the cops. Believe me. With all these people coming and going.'

So decrees the captain of the Brancaccio crew.

'Are you sure?' asks Mother Nature.

'He even went on television. And if the journalists get started, we're finished. They will make us look like assholes.'

Mother Nature remains silent and keeps thinking about the words uttered by the man from Corleone: 'We need to break that priest's balls. The kids like him too much.'

In Brancaccio, it's Mother Nature who gives the orders.

Mother Nature and his brothers are part of a Trinity and they control the neighborhood like Father, Son, and Holy Ghost: One of them gives the orders; one looks after their finances; and one pulls the trigger. The only difference with this earthly trinity is that you need to substitute the word 'love' with 'respect,' the perfect synthesis of loyalty and fear – something even God can't afford.

'I eat and I make it so others can eat.' That's their motto. And it's something that not even a Holy Father, with his Daily Bread, can guarantee.

The Corleone family has given them its blessing to rule over Brancaccio, and they have been grateful for the opportunity to do so after Michele 'the Pope' Greco's hold on power began to slip in 1984. They are known as 'the Boys.' And they are the definition of the term. They know everything. They see everything. And they do everything. With the help of others: The Brancaccio crew, including the Hunter.

They are young and determined. They are the family's new muscle. The Mafia capo is the god who knows and decides. He is the eyes, the mind, and the word. He exercises pure power.

The three of them bear down on those streets like a low sky. They guarantee protection even when the price that you pay is sometimes asphyxiation.

Power is control. There is no such thing as good power that loves its subjects. Power is necessary. It ensures balance and survival. And when no one is going hungry, there's little reason to complain.

'Are you ready?'

'Whatever you say, Father.'

Mother Nature pretends to be counting money.

'He didn't even want the spare change we offered to fix the roof at the school. You know how stubborn he is. He even found the money to build his center, though we had doubled the price. He's one hard-headed priest. After they marched for Falcone, we blew up the van from the construction company that was working at the church. But he just keeps on going . . .'

'Is the rest of him as hard as his head? Let's soften him up a little bit. Just like they do with octopus. But we need to make sure that we get him by his tentacles. And let's give his friends a little massage, too.'

17

It must be the fifteenth time that I've reread the same page. Sometimes I feel like my brain has been jailed for so long that not even books can succeed in unlocking my imagination. There's always a word stuck edgewise between the words on the page that continues to make me lose my train of thought. Or could it be that it puts me on a train of thought that leads me back to my own self? Lucia. I need to keep reading this truly interesting book while the music in the background deadens the noise coming from the street. I need to dream about my trip to England and concentrate on what I need to pack. Lucia. I need to stop losing control of the words that I am thinking. I need to find the way to do it. Lucia. I must. Lucia. I must. Lucia. I've had enough!

Even though I am a series of *though*s, my head is filled with thoughts of love. Maybe it's because love is what unifies the threads, the pieces, and the fragments and molds them into gold. And love always waits to ambush you, just as day turns to night. Love with a capital L, as Petrarch wrote, like a hidden god that you suddenly discover in your room waiting to mess everything up and give you that sinking feeling in your gut. When that happens, all you can do is lie on your bed and stare at the ceiling, listening to some melancholy song on the radio, about how even raging war can't take away from the love felt inside.

How is it that writers think our thoughts? Is it because we think their thoughts? Lucia puts down the book after having read only the first few lines . . .

The sky was so starry and so bright that, when looking at it, one could not help but ask oneself whether ill-humored and capricious people would be able to live under such a sky.

She moves toward an open window that reveals just a sliver of the sky and she rests her arms on the windowsill. She thinks about her siblings. About her parents. About the kids at Don Pino's center and the show she is working on.

She thinks about all the good and all the bad that exist under that sky. It's under that very sky that there are men who do bad things – despite that sky. For an instant, she wishes she could leave sixteen behind and be twice as old. Who can guess where she will be by then? Under an equally beautiful sky but with gentler men. She thinks of the boy she met by chance. He seemed so ingenuous considering the neighborhood he comes from and the world he lives in.

Her father peers into the room and sees her there. He caresses her head softly to remind her that it's late. She lays her cheek in his rough construction worker's hand and gives into its motion as if her father could cradle her face.

'Why are you still up?'

'I was reading but then I started thinking.'

'What were you thinking about?'

'Nothing. Just thoughts.'

'It's okay. Everything will be alright. Now get to bed.'

'How do you know?'

'Know what?'

'That everything will be alright?'

'When you do right, everything will be alright. And you are a good girl. Everything else will work itself out on its own.'

Lucia smiles with melancholy-speckled eyes. She wishes she believed him. But she knows, all too well, the limits of the world into which fate has placed her. Being good isn't enough in this city.

Dreams are a luxury afforded only by the books she reads.

I'd like to read a million books, visit a thousand cities, learn hundreds of languages, and grasp the essence of the world around me. If there is truth, there is only one truth. I want to be strong and courageous, like Falcone and Borsellino, or at least like Manfredi. But where will I find courage? Maybe I should talk with Don Pino. But I'm worried that he will talk to me about God and I don't care about God because I want to be a free man who lives without the Ten Commandments, the Seven Sacraments, and however many Beatitudes there are.

All I need is a little bit of truth. A woman to love and something good that I can do for my friends. You don't need God to do these things. I'll worry about God posthumously. *Posthumously* is a word that fascinates me: Being published after death, just like my beloved countryman Giuseppe Tomasi di Lampedusa. My grandmother used to see him every morning eating a pastry and a granita for breakfast while he was already writing new pages of his book. What in the world were they thinking when they turned down the greatest novel of the twentieth century? Posthumous.

If people could hear what I'm thinking, I'd probably end up being committed to a psychiatric ward. Manfredi explained the following to me but I'm not consoled by it: Recurring thoughts are our most frequently used circuits. They are well-worn pathways and well-oiled synapses. I must have oiled the wrong gears. Science explains how it all works. But I need something more.

The only science subject I like is chemistry, especially the periodic table. It looks like the letters for the alphabet. That's probably why I like it. Words help me to relax and so does the periodic table. Despite its apparent multiplicity, it's a finite list of elements all positioned in the correct order. Our chemistry teacher explained the most important ones and the strangest ones. The one I identify with the most is francium.

It's the most unstable element of the entire periodic table. Twenty-two minutes. It has a half-life of twenty-two minutes. And that's if everything goes well. At this very moment, there are only twenty-eight grams of francium on the face of the planet. And then it decays.

I'm like francium. The certainties of my life are constantly decaying. They don't ever last more than twenty-two minutes. And they have a rough density of twenty-eight grams. I've rechristened francium as 'federicium' because I am the bearer of those twenty-eight grams.

I wish I were more stable, like the carbon in diamonds. But it was my destiny to be more like francium, I mean, federicium.

There are some kids who think silent thoughts at night. And unlike the sea, it always takes a long time for those kids to understand the changes that are happening inside of them.

18

There's a table and there's Mother Nature. There are others seated around the table. A knife and a pistol have been placed in the middle of the table. And there's a card with a drawing of St Mary of the Annunciation next to the pistol.

'Will you be loyal?'

'Like a shadow.'

'Are you ready for anything?'

'Anything.'

'Even killing?'

'I've already shown that I'm ready to kill.'

'And remember: We never touch women who belong to made men. If you change territory, you have to let your capo know. Don't ever do anything that you haven't been told to do. And always be available. If you end up inside, we'll take care of you and your family. The important thing is that you are loyal.'

As the list continues, every command is accompanied by an eloquent glance at the pistol and the knife. Then Mother Nature takes his hand, pricks his finger with a needle, and lets the blood drip on the card with the sacred image of St Mary. He takes out a lighter and he lights the card. It curls as it burns on the table. He takes the man's hands and presses them against the flame, holding them like a vise. The flame burns his skin and it begins to peel away. Standing still, he grits his teeth.

'Like the card, I burn you. Like the saint, I adore you. And just like the card burns, my flesh must burn if I ever betray Cosa Nostra.'

He recites the formula that evokes hell. Actually, he creates it for the first time.

'If you fail, your skin will burn by my hands.'

He squeezes his fingers to let him know that what he is saying is the law. They stare each other in the eyes. Now he belongs to Cosa Nostra and Cosa Nostra will guarantee his livelihood and protection.

In the banquet that follows, an hour passes between each course. Everyone compliments him and shakes his hand, reminding him each time why it burns. And they give him two kisses. Finally, after a long period of observation, he has been presented to and accepted by the family. It's not something that happens to everyone. Only to those who are ready for anything, those who are obedient and devoted. And those who are, above all, silent.

He heads back home. A breeze rises from the sea as he races through the streets like a wild animal that's been mortally wounded. The humidity rises in waves from the asphalt, making the world around him feel like a mirage in the desert. When he was a child he would try to touch the water in those images on the pavement. When he was a child. But the water would disappear as soon as he drew near. He's no child anymore. Even though he would love to run after those mirages for a moment or two and watch the water cool the heat. He remembers how his mother used to take him to the beach. 'Curly' is what she used to call him. He was really happy then. But happiness belongs only to children. Life is something entirely different. You can be happy enough. But no more. He could even be happier if it weren't for that ball-breaking priest that makes his bile rise. His blood boils at the thought of those five minutes. Priests should stay in church. They should lead processions, not revolutions. Live and let live is what they should do. This priest just can't stop himself from going out, talking to people, and making waves. But he'll teach him how to take it easy. And he'll get over his love of making waves, talking to people, and not staying put. It's not for nothing that they call him the Hunter.

19

I've been staring at my book collection for a half-hour and I'm still looking for something for Lucia. I want to lend her one of my books but I'm not sure which one. It will be the book that chooses her. I close my eyes and spin around, three times toward the right, twice to the left, another four times to the right, and one more turn to the left. With eyes still closed, I raise my right arm and I point it toward my bookshelves. My index finger lands on the spine of a book. I open my eyes. It's my Petrarch. The *Canzoniere*. Who better than him? I slip it into my bag and head out toward Brancaccio. Petrarch's never been to Brancaccio. That's for certain. At least I hold one record in the history of literature. I was the first to bring him there.

The afternoon passes slowly, like a goodbye. Minutes roll into one other, running over each other like an undertow. Don Pino asked me to referee a soccer game so that he can take care of some unfinished business at the church. He should be here in no time. Nothing galvanizes these kids like being refereed.

'No one ever looks after them,' Don Pino said to me. 'And a child not looked after is a child lost,' he added.

The only thing I need to do is get the game started.

The lopsided, sunbaked soccer field is teeming with restless boys. I have a referee's whistle, an object that wields catalytic power.

'Dark shirts versus light shirts!' I declare, confident in my experience from playing soccer at school.

'Who the hell are you?'

'I'm one of Don Pino's students. I'm reffing the game today.'

I must have screwed something up. I can tell by the sullen looks on their faces.

I still haven't told them my name.

'We want Don Pino. What the fuck are you doing here?'

I try to hide my annoyance at their warm reception. But the tone of my voice betrays me.

'He asked me to sub for him. Come on! Don't be like that!'

'Take a look at this guy. He's a nobody who thinks he can come in here and boss us around,' one of them says in Sicilian. 'And listen to the way he talks. Seems like Italian.'

My instincts tell me that I should find a way out of this tight spot. I start messing around with the ball, juggling it on my feet, head, chest, and knees. They seem to be impressed.

'Did I forget to mention that I'm a star player?'

'Wow! You're good! Who learned you how to play like that?'

I keep going.

'No one did. That makes fifty. Let's see who can top that!'

One of the younger kids steps forward and grabs the ball from me. He starts juggling. His hair is as straight as a rake. His legs and arms are so slender it doesn't seem possible that he can perform such extraordinarily smooth moves.

He gets to fifty and does one more. Then he stops and gives me the ball back.

'Take that.'

'You've got me beat. Good for you! What's your name?'

'Riccardo.'

'Okay, great. Riccardo's a captain. Who wants to be the other one?'

Another boy steps forward. He's wearing goalie gloves. No one dares get in his way.

'And what's your name?'

'Gaetano. And we will choose teams. None of this "dark shirts versus light shirts" business. That's for girls.'

They end up picking teams by taking turns at choosing players. They're so serious they might as well be World Cup coaches. The only thing missing is the Italian national anthem.

'Heads or tails?'

'Tails.'

'Tails. Kick-off or pick sides?'

'Kick-off. Picking sides sucks.'

I blow the whistle and the air plunges into chaos under a bitter sky yellowed by sand and sirocco. Their t-shirts are immediately impregnated by sweat and dust. The children follow the ball mirage in the seaside light of a June afternoon. The racket of their cursing and blasphemies deafens the piazza.

I watch them and I see their smiles, scabs, and frenetic legs; arms, tackles, and steals.

The boy still doesn't know the stories of these kids with their names as short as biography titles. Those biographies already contain hundreds of pages of pain and a few lines of joy. The boy sees them play soccer, just as he has done thousands of times. He still can't see everything. It's too early.

There's Dario, with eyes lined by sadness. He doesn't say a word. His father is in jail and his mother has to work to feed him and his brothers. And his mother doesn't know what happens to Dario when he doesn't go to school, nor does she want to know. Nobody knows. Nobody wants to know. Dario turns out to be the one who scores a goal. They all hug him and he hugs them back. And he laughs in a sincere embrace.

Then there's Riccardo. The smartest kid in Brancaccio. He's the one with sculpted black hair sticking straight up like a rake. He's quick-witted and light on his feet. He always has a zinger ready to go. Always on the lookout, he knows everything that's happening in the neighborhood. Just ask him who deals drugs and who takes them, who goes to school and who doesn't, and who does it with whom. The other kids always do what he tells them to because he is a sharp-tongued merchant of information. He's destined to be somebody in this life. But he's going to be the one to decide who that will be. His family is well known to be involved in the Mafia.

He once saw a boy who had overdosed. He was lying in his own feces in a lonely alleyway, with his eyes rolled back in his head and a blood-soiled syringe by his side. He saw hell for at least ten minutes before he started trembling as he sat there alone. Don Pino had found him that way, curled up and shaking. And he had told him everything.

He had asked where the dead boy would end up. Don Pino spoke to him about heaven and hell and he admitted that he didn't really know. Riccardo insisted that he wanted to go to heaven and Don Pino suggested that they go together.

'Do you know how to get there, Don Pino?'

'Yes, I do.'

That's why Riccardo goes to the Holy Father Center to play soccer. Because Don Pino knows the way to get to heaven. He even knows which bus you need to take. That's what he said.

Then there's the shy kid. His name is Totò. No one knows if his name is short for Antonio or Salvatore. But his name is Totò, just like his grandfather. His father works in a factory and his mother is a hairdresser. They're one of those couples who quietly work and try to educate their children the best they can. Totò has good table manners, unlike the better part of his friends. And he goes to school every day.

He gets teased a lot for the schoolboy smock that he wears. And the other kids have it in for him because he wants to be an orchestra conductor. He decided that's what he wanted to become after he saw a man dressed in black on TV who was waving a baton and all the musicians did what he told them to do. That man had wind-swept hair and his eyes were closed as if he were lost in something truly beautiful. The musicians obeyed this beautiful thing. Music is a beautiful thing for Totò. He's hopeless when it comes to soccer. But he's the best at music. They make fun of him because of his girly dreams.

'When I grow up, I'm going to buy a gun and kill all the cops in Palermo,' said one of his classmates one day. Baton and music just don't really cut it.

He watches them play, and oblivious to their stories, he sees what's missing in Brancaccio compared to the neighborhood where he lives: It's the space for imagination. The space for wishes that burst open during those August nights when the stars fall but the sea seems to return them to the sky as each moment passes. That fragment of pavement, sized to fit a lopsided soccer field, just isn't big enough for storing their wishes.

The team that's behind scores and ties. But the opposing team protests, claiming that the attacker got control of the ball thanks to a foul. The boy confirms the goal and the kids start attacking him with curse words.

'You're a sell-out, ref!'

'Cuckold!'

'Your mother is a whore!'

It doesn't take long for there to be a shift from joy to panic.

I can feel my blood churning under my skin. Who do they think they are? I eject the kid who insulted me. He walks away in silence but as soon as I turn my back on him, he surprises me by suddenly appearing in front of me and punching me in the face, just below my nose. This kid is barely ten years old.

My chin is not even eye-level for him. So when the punch lands from below with the strength of his jumping up at me, it busts my lip open. I run my hand over my mouth and it gets covered in blood. Something like this has only ever happened to me once. It was a basketball that was hurled accidentally at my nose. And from that day onward, my nose has been slightly crooked.

I always thought that punches in the face were something you only saw in the movies. I wouldn't even know how to punch someone in the face. And getting punched in the face? I never thought it would happen to me. The other kids push in around me. The pain stings my soul and my lips. But my rage has the upper hand. Something inside of me is deciding to do something without asking me first. More kids come onto the field, the ones who were waiting for their turn to play. They want to see how this ends up.

'Who the hell do you think you are? You come here, from your nice house in Palermo, with your fancy shoes . . . and you kick me off the field in the neighborhood where I was born? Why don't you go back to that whore of a mother of yours?'

Something inside of me starts to act. I grab the kid's t-shirt and begin to shake him as I push him to the ground. I put my knee on his chest and I threaten him with my fist. I watch myself as I do this. The boy flails under my knee and tries to kick me. He spits on me.

'Now get out of here. Or I'll give you the rest of what you have coming!' I yell at him.

'Just try it and I will kill you. You aren't the one who gives orders around here. Get it? You're the one who has to get the hell out of here. Otherwise I'm going to call my father and we'll see how that works out for you.'

I sit still without saying a word. Something inside of me is breathing more slowly now. There are many eyes on me, eyes like those of stray dogs who are ready to defend themselves against a stranger. My arms fall to my sides in desperation. I lower my gaze. I throw the whistle to the ground in disgust and start to walk away.

'Go fuck yourselves and your neighborhood of savages!'

Just at that moment, Don Pino shows up.

'What's happening?'

'What's happening? This is happening!' I yell as I show him my lip.

'Who did that to you?'

'I don't belong here. I don't belong to this place. It was a mistake for me to come here. If you had been here, this never would have happened, damn it!'

Don Pino pulls out a handkerchief from his pocket and hands it to me. Then he turns toward the kids.

'What is this all about? Who did this?'

'I did. This asshole shows up and thinks he's in charge.'

'Is this any way to do things around here?'

'We don't want him here.'

Many of them start nodding and they add their own nasty comments. That's it. I'm going to get out of here before something inside me transforms into tears. But Totò gets in my way and hands me a glass of water to clean my bloody lip. He always brings a water bottle with him when he comes out to play soccer. The water is warm. It does more for the soul than for the lip.

'You need to be careful. He might actually call his father . . .'

'Who the fuck cares? His father should have taught him better . . .'

'His father taught him just as his own father taught him,' interjects a female voice.

Lucia.

I hadn't noticed she was there. She looks at me without pity.

'He busted my lip. And now it's my fault?'

'They are taught to defend themselves, and that's it. If you don't want to become a victim, then you have to learn how to attack. You can't let yourself be humiliated in front of everyone else. That's how they were brought up. It's not because they are bad kids. It's because this is their life.'

'Normal people don't act like that.'

'This is how normal people are brought up here. Nothing that you consider normal is normal here.'

After Don Pino gets the game started again, he comes over. The kids are quick to forget what happened.

'What are you doing here, Lucia?'

'I brought you your sandwich like I always do. Otherwise you'll forget to eat.'

'It's because of the heat. When it's hot like this, I lose my appetite.'

'During the winter, you lose your appetite because it's too cold. During the summer because it's too hot. You always have some excuse for skipping a meal or eating something that's not good for you.'

She hands him a plastic bag. Inside there's a sandwich wrapped in tinfoil and some fruit.

Don Pino smiles as he takes the bag.

'Thank you.'

As I watch the scene, I feel like an astronaut who's landed on an alien planet, or an explorer who discovers a new land that isn't virgin land as expected.

'Let's go. I'll come with you to get your bike.'

Before we head out, I turn to Lucia. She's got her back to me. But then she turns around and our eyes meet for a moment. She has a bitter, wounded look on her face.

'Don't judge what you don't know. What do you expect to learn at Classics High School if you haven't even learned that?'

As I zip up my backpack, I see the book that I brought for her.

It takes more than reading books to be a man.

It takes more than thinking good thoughts to be a good man.

20

The chain is lying on the ground. The pole seems depressed standing there alone without my bike. Don Pino seems even more depressed.

'I'm sorry. Unfortunately, that's the way it goes around here. If you're not from the neighborhood, you have to pay a price to be allowed in. I was wrong to think that you'd be protected by being here with me. Instead . . .'

The street seems inert and unaware. At this time of day, the heat starts to loosen its bite and the sea breeze begins to caress you with unexpected grace. But in my case, it only makes my lip burn even more.

'I'll come with you.'

'I'll catch a bus.'

'I'll take you to the bus stop. I know the way.'

'But you're busy, I'm sure.'

'I'll go with you.'

I'd rather be alone with my pain but he is insisting on being part of it.

'Are all the kids here like that little brat?'

'He's not a brat. He's a child just like any other. How they turn out all depends on how you treat them. Did Lucia's family seem like that to you? Mario used to be one of the farm workers that lived in this part of the city. This used to be green, fertile land. Then they covered it up with cement and tar. The old landowners all got rich and the farmhands now can barely get by. They live in two- or three-room apartments that have been built out of the old farmhouses. Their daily struggle isn't *what* but *if* they will eat. But they live their lives with dignity, despite their poverty. Here, there's dignity around every corner. You just need to know where to find it. There are plenty of people here who know how to keep their heads held high even in the face of the whipping that life has given them.'

We move slowly through a sort of maze that feels as suffocated as it is suffocating. The asphalt has been bleached by the sun and there's no escaping. I can't wait to get the hell out of here.

'There are also a few new families who have come from other parts of Palermo because of how affordable it is. Day laborers, most of them with steady jobs. They keep to themselves. They use the neighborhood more than anything else as a place to sleep. But some of them actually set down roots here. You saw Totò, right? The one who gave you water from his water bottle? He comes from one of those families. A lot of them help me out and they have even started a homeowners' association that lobbies for services they still don't have, like sewage, schools, and public spaces.'

'Are we heading out?'

'We are. But I need to show you something.'

He just can't let it go.

'What's that?'

We end up on a wide boulevard. Via Hazon. Cement giants not only suffocate any hope of seeing the Mediterranean but they also guarantee that you can't feel the sea breeze. The street is dotted with potholes and trash bags. Garbage bins are arranged like barricades used in urban combat. Weeds grow in bushes along the sidewalks.

Little kids play on the pavement with a Super Santos ball and they move like a swarm chasing after the ball, which appears intermittently between their legs.

'Have a look at this building.'

A monolith that stretches up toward the sky like a Tower of Babel.

'Hell is not below the ground. It's in these cement housing projects. Scores and scores of families live here, people who have moved from the historical center of the city. And now they are camped out in these dilapidated buildings. The city has stuck them here, in apartment buildings that have been transformed into evacuation shelters.'

'How do they get by?'

'However they can. Some of them work under the table, if they're lucky. Otherwise they sell contraband cigarettes or drugs, or they work as prostitutes. Many of them are under house arrest. Others are in jail. Nearly all of them are illiterate. The children don't go to school and they learn their parents' trade, whatever that may be. The rest of them live on the street.'

'Why don't they look for something better?'

'If you had been born here, you'd be just like them.'

I don't know what to say. It feels like someone just gave me a slap in the face.

'For months, I've been trying to get access to the basement in this building. It belongs to the city. But it's being used for things you can't even imagine.'

'Don Pino, I don't know what to say. I have nothing to do with this place.'

'You do have something to do with this place. You came here and now you are leaving with less than what you had before you got here.'

'In the end, the balance from my visit is a busted lip and a stolen bike. Not so bad, all things considered.'

'Actually, it's worse than you think.'

We arrive at the bus stop. The street is lined with bands of stray dogs and kids. On the street where I live, elegant women walk their Newfoundlands, greyhounds, and German shepherds. Here there are nothing but mutts and strays. In the unforgiving afternoon light you can see all their misery on display.

The bus stops as its brakes squeal.

'Good luck, Don Pino. I'm leaving on Sunday.'

I don't know what to add. Before the doors of the bus close, he hugs me tightly.

'Forgive me. Have a great trip! Bring me back some tea, some of the good stuff!'

His smile is his farewell.

There are a few empty seats on the bus. I tumble onto one of the benches. My lip still hurts and fills my mouth with the taste of evil and its depths. The clotted blood gives me physical reassurance that I am made of flesh and bone and not of air and dreams.

The sun sinks and stops slapping everything in its view. Sand. Dust. Stone. Then, little by little, other colors begin to prevail. Paint, glass, wind. From darkness we slip into light, passing through every gradation of shadow in between.

The borders of the city I knew are as wide as the space between my eyes, no more. This is all I have been able to see in my seventeen years. I thought I had seen the entire world and not just one tile in a mosaic. Instead, its belly is shadow and grief.

The bus comes to a stop in the glow of Via Libertà's indefatigable light. I get off and I want to smell the clean air. The green plants in the Giardino Inglese seem as if they have been shellacked by ancient potters and decorated leaf by leaf. The trails are now golden in color and even the breeze seems cooler here. Hope is in the air you breathe, the sky, and the things that descend from the sky, the sea and the things that rise from the sea. Everything seems unchanged.

But now I know that not everything is here, just like when I used to point my finger at the blue of the map and it was the sea. And when I pointed to the brown, it was the mountains. And when I pointed to the green, it was the grasslands. Maps hide too many things, and it's best to keep them at arm's length.

The price you pay for reality is too high for me.

21

Don Pino trudges down the same train tracks that I wanted to follow when I was a kid. But I would always get scared and turn back. I never had the courage to make my way to the end.

His grandfather used to tell him that the tracks could take you anywhere. The train, he would say, could even be taken onto a ship so it could cross the sea. He used to listen to him in amazement and he would imagine the tracks as they dove into the sea.

When he was a kid, his father meant everything to him. A cobbler, a day laborer, a man of action, and a man of few words. His mother meant everything to him. A seamstress, she was affectionate with her children and she believed they needed to study to make a life for themselves. He held their hands as he tried to give them the courage you need to die. The mother had passed six years prior. The father, just a year prior.

The voice of a woman who calls someone to a simply set dinner table brings him back to a time when his memories become hazy. The road rolls back up like a spool of film and the show is the same as always: Low-lying apartment buildings, with their frosted windows and yellow windowpanes, enclosed balconies that have been transformed into the spaces needed for living. Everything is poor and ugly.

Their immobile façades are lined with ruffled clothes hanging in the wind. Mimmo, the policeman, smokes his cigarette wearing only his undershirt and underpants. Mimmo has a sharp mind, and he's a special detective down at police headquarters. But there's not much else special about his life. Don Pino feels safe having him in his building, right above him. It's like having a police escort but without having to tell anyone about it and without the inconvenience of having it follow him around everywhere he goes.

Actually, it's like having an underwear-clad guardian angel. Mimmo shares his insights about the neighborhood, about unexpected changes and the painfully slow metamorphoses. Connections are dissolved and created, almost as if there were a chemist busy with chemical reactions unseen by the inexpert eye.

When he gets home, after a day at work, Mimmo gathers all the data from his attentive observations and builds maps of the geography of power and criminality. He basks in the contemplation of the web of intrigue but doesn't do anything about it other than take pleasure in its perfection, as only a Palermitan mind can do. A mind like that can keep cool even when the subject at hand is burning hot.

He's lost in ruminations worthy of an Arabic alchemist or a tangled murder mystery. He stares off into the void. But the arrival of his friend shakes him out of it.

He says hello to Don Pino with a nod and he awaits the good-natured perfunctory admonition that comes every summer evening. It's a scene written in a script that has been repeated over and over again for years.

'You smoke too much, Mimmo.'

'You gotta die from something, Father.'

22

'I'm not hungry. I'm going to sleep.'

'But where have you been all day?'

'At the beach, Mom. I told you yesterday that I was going to Mondello.'

I avoid eye contact and try to hide my face with my hand by pretending that I'm scratching my nose.

But my mother understands something's wrong without me having to explain it to her.

All it takes is the tone of my voice.

'What happened?'

'Nothing.'

'What do you mean, "nothing"?'

'Nothing, Mother, nothing.'

'Federico.'

'It's stupid. A ball hit me in the face when I was playing soccer.'

'A ball? Come over here. Let me put some ice on it.'

I give in to the alarmed tone of my mother's voice.

'Just look at what you did to yourself. What on earth for? You and your soccer. You're both obsessed. You and your brother. No, "obsessed" isn't the right word. You're both sick with it!'

The ice eases the pain and I start to notice the state my body is in. I stink and I can feel my foul mood all over me.

'Poet, what happened to you?'

Manfredi comes into the kitchen. I'm sitting at the table with my mother and she's holding the bag of ice to my face.

I start to mumble a 'nothing' but my mother pulls my hand away from my face for a minute and shows my brother the work of art that I'm wearing.

'Unstill life with a perpendicular slant,' comments Manfredi. 'How did you manage that? Did you fall out of your stroller? Or did you get in a fight with someone because they were better at reciting Petrarchan sonnets?'

'GO OOO ELL,' I tell him, emphasizing each syllable as much as I can with ice pressed up against my lip.

'Aaa you shuh?' says Manfredi, mocking me.

'Yeah, go on and go right ahead.'

He moves toward me and slaps me on the back of my neck.

'Be respectful of your brother.'

'Take it easy, both of you.'

'So what happened to you?'

'I got in a fight.'

'Didn't you tell me it was a ball in the face?' my mother asks.

'It was over a girl, right? That would be understandable. But first there would have to be a girl worthy of our family name. And she would have to be capable of seeing beyond the fact that you are a toad. And then she'd have to be able to stomach being with you after your first kiss. Or maybe it was a girl that did this to you after you tried to kiss her?'

'It was this one kid . . .'

'Better one than two . . . Who was it?'

'This one kid.'

'You never forget your first busted lip. Poet, you are becoming a man.'

'And you're the same asshole as always.'

'Federico, stop talking like a juvenile delinquent.'

'Why should I? Do you have a problem with juvenile delinquents?'

'Fede, if you don't cool it, I'm going to bust your other lip,' says Manfredi, laying it on thick.

I jump out of my chair, lunge at my brother, and I start punching him willy-nilly. He's not quick enough to stop me and I manage to punch him in the stomach. He bends over in pain.

My mother tries to grab me but I manage to wriggle free.

'Leave me alone. I said, leave me alone!'

I hole up in my room and let the anger seethe into every cell in my body. I've become violent with some of the people I love most, and it only took a few hours to get this way. Hell has latched onto me and now I've brought it back to our house like an unknown virus.

I feel like a stranger in my own home, in my own city. I feel like a stranger to myself.

23

Hell has a minimal and indivisible unit, an identifiable molecular state: The interruption of accomplishment, the compression (not the comprehension) of life. Hell is everything that sullies, wounds, closes off, interrupts, and destroys, and every possible variation on the theme of interruption. To oppose hell you must repair, resume, reconcile . . .

Don Pino knows that hell works more efficiently on tender flesh: Children. Their souls must be protected before they are evicted from their bodies. Their most sacred possession must be looked after.

He knows that only children go to heaven. Children, or those who become children once again. But not because they are good. He wasn't a good child either. He never wanted to go to Mass. He preferred playing and beating up other boys. And he loved to pull girls' braids. He tortured lizards and swiped apples from the fruit stand just like other kids. Children only know how to receive. And the ones who inhabit heaven are those who know how to receive love from their parents like a child. They always have a place inside themselves where they can escape. A place where that love goes to live and cannot be chased away.

Don Pino knows that he must protect that place within every child, that piece of goodness that explodes like a seed. If that piece of soul remains intact, it can save that child. It's small at first, very small. Then it becomes roots, branches, trunks, leaves, flowers, and fruit.

In Brancaccio too many children are seeds in the darkness.

Seeds that grow in reverse. There is no space for dreams, beauty, or imagination. Too many of them are destined to die before living out their lives. Too many of them will die before they can begin to reach out toward happiness.

One of these is Giuseppe.

Don Pino remembers everything about that thirteen- or fourteen-year-old boy, who he had surprised as he was trying to break into a car parked not far from his own.

'What's going on?'

'What the fuck is it to you?'

'That car belongs to a friend of mine.'

'Too bad for him.'

'Leave that stereo alone.'

'And if I don't? What are you going to do? Call the cops? A priest who's friends with the cops? You're probably a cop, too!'

'Leave it alone. What do you get out of stealing a stereo, anyway?'

'I don't get anything out of it. But if I sell it, I get to eat.'

'Leave it alone.'

'Are you planning to tell my father? Are you planning to come over to give me the belt?'

'I'll give you money to eat. How long does it take you to break into a car and get the stereo?'

'Five minutes.'

'You'd be great on the job with hands like that. My father was a cobbler and I used to help him repair shoes. You'd be great at it.'

'I don't want to be a cock-sucking cobbler.'

'He was just a cobbler.'

'I'm not interested in getting a job.'

'Well, what do you want to do then?'

'Whatever my father tells me to do.'

'And what if I were to visit your father?'

'He'd kill me. I'm never supposed to talk to cops. Ever.'

'Why don't you come give me a hand with the nativity scene? I could use someone with hands like yours.'

'I don't go to church.'

'You don't have to come to church. You just need to come give me a hand with the nativity. A hand with the wood houses, the Styrofoam, the soldering iron . . .'

'What do you mean?'

'Would you just come and see?'

'How much does it pay?'

'The same that you get for the car stereo.'

'It's not worth the time. I'm better off doing this.'

'But you wouldn't be hurting anyone either.'

'That's his problem. If he has a car, it means he has enough money to scrounge himself up another stereo.'

The owner of the car showed up and the boy ran away, without the stereo. As he fled, he blurted out a blasphemy against God and an insult for Don Pino who in turn yelled back with a challenge: 'The nativity will be waiting for you! We'll see if you can handle it.'

Giuseppe showed up at the church but was very careful not to let anyone see him who might tell his father.

'What are you doing here?'

'I came to see if this was for real.'

'But didn't you tell me to bugger off?'

'It was a joke.'

'There are certain things that you shouldn't joke about. What's your name?'

'Giuseppe.'

'Okay. But before we build the nativity scene, an apology is in order.'

'Apologize to who? To you?'

'No. To God.'

'Why? Are you God?'

'No, I'm not. But you said something awful to him. And you need to tell him you're sorry.'

'Why should I? Do you think that God can hear us? How could he? It's not like he has ears.'

'How do you know he doesn't have ears? Just look here,' said Don Pino as he pointed to his own ears.

'But those are your ears.'

'That's exactly right. But my ears serve God and that's why they are so big. That's what God does. He asks people to lend him their ears, eyes, hands . . .'

'You're still a cop, even if you're God's cop.'

'For example, if you use your hands to build the nativity, your hands will become God's hands.'

'That is *if I build it*. Okay?'

'You have to try. And you'll see what you're capable of. When God uses part of us, we do divine work. We are like brushes in the hands of a great painter.'

'Like a painter who paints walls? I'm not going to be a loser like that.'

'Look at your hands. You could make God come down from the heavens with those hands.'

Giuseppe looked at his hands but they were the same as ever. Nonetheless, he decided to give it a try.

And the 1992 nativity scene was the most beautiful one that had ever been built in San Gaetano. The boy even revealed that he wanted to become a woodworker when he grew up: A carpenter.

'Jesus was a carpenter. And it was his father who taught him. His father was called Giuseppe, just like you.'

'Jesus who?'

'Jesus, the one in the nativity that you built. The son of God.'

'Wow! If he was Jesus, he wouldn't have to work!'

'He did it for you.'

'For me?'

'To help you understand that God likes carpenters.'

Giuseppe's eyes seemed to light up.

He was like one of those blades of grass, thought Don Pino, that appear in the cracks in the cement. That's the way all the children are in Brancaccio. They are initiated into hell by organizing duels to the death between stray dogs, strangling cats or merely torturing them and offering them up to those same attack dogs for their dinner. Then, of course, there's drugs, violence, prostitution . . .

The light turns to darkness and is then substituted by the rage of those who crave destruction yet know not why, the rage of those who learn to dominate before they learn to love, the rage of those who don't realize that love adds something to life and that hate takes something from it. But hate is much easier and immediate. It's a sort of anesthesia that shuts out life and light. Many of them are sexually abused by older kids and they quickly learn how to submit. And the dominated no longer know how to love because they no longer know how to be loved. When Falcone was killed, the children yelled: 'Hurray for the Mafia! The Mafia has won!'

Don Pino had begun to prepare Giuseppe for his First Communion. But when he started to teach him the Ten Commandments, Giuseppe told him he couldn't do it. He could never follow the seventh: Thou shalt not steal.

'Why?'

'Because if I come home empty-handed, my father gives me the belt.'

Giuseppe ended up in Palermo's youth detention center: Malaspina.

He is going to visit Giuseppe today. The Malaspina detention center is a fortress full of renegade kids located in a nice neighborhood at the end of Notarbartolo Street. He's planning to bring him a present, too. But first he wants to call Federico to see how he's doing.

'I'm doing okay. My lip is better. How are you?'

'I can't complain. Listen, I'm planning to be in your neighborhood later today.'

'What for?'

'I'm going to Malaspina to see Giuseppe.'

'Who's that?'

'He's a kid that ended up there because he stole something. I know him well.'

'How is it that you remember everyone so well?'

'Come on. Don't you remember all the people who you love? It doesn't take much.'

'I guess so. I really made a mess at home, Don Pino.'

'We can talk about it if you want. Come with me to visit Giuseppe and you can tell me about it on the way. And that way we can have a proper goodbye. It was all a bit confusing the other day.'

'Okay, sure. But will they let me into the prison?'

'Bring your identity card but don't bring anything else with you. As long as you are with me, it shouldn't be a problem.'

'I hope so.'

24

The rhetorical device that best describes me is the oxymoron. It's the device that belongs to the crazies, the people who say one thing and then do another. Peace eludes me, yet I don't have the means to wage war. But I would like to go to war.

The Malaspina detention center is a stone's throw from my house. You can even see a bit of it from the top floors of our building. Let's just call it the architectural incarnation of desolation. I've passed by it literally hundreds of times and I have seen mothers waiting to get in, fathers with a sense of guilt sculpted into their faces, and children laughing as they wait to visit their brothers behind bars as if it were some sort of game.

We go inside and I don't say a word. I'm afraid that I will be locked up in prison. Don Pino smiles at me and gives me a pat on the shoulder. A series of iron doors opens before me, slowly, one after another. And as each one opens, the feeling of oppression grows. The cells fan out from the atrium. It makes me think of the *Rota Fortunae*, the ancient wheel of fortune, and the blindfolded Fortuna who spins it. The color of the humidity-streaked walls is anonymous. There is a vestibule on one side with a statue of the Virgin Mary. It has so many black spots on it that you'd think it had been struck by the plague from St Rosalia's time, when she saved

Palermo from the disease. The light enters the space aslant, as if it had fallen there by chance.

We are accompanied by a prison guard who shows us the way. The cells overflow with forgotten, tired bodies and they remind me of gaps in the links of a fence. We don't realize how much we have until we lose it or until we meet someone who has lost it. This happened to me once when I met my friend's sister. She had Down's syndrome. On that day, I realized that I couldn't take anything for granted: My racing mind, my responsive body, my hands that can underline a line in a poem. Now I feel that same sense of estrangement, as if I could see myself from outside my body: Pain dislocated.

And so for the first time in my life, after seventeen years, I realize that I am free. This morning, I got out of bed but I could have chosen not to. I took a shower but I could have chosen not to. I decided to go out but I could have chosen not to. I had the freedom to do whatever I wanted. I had everything. And it was all inside of me.

We are led into a small room just a few meters wide. There's a table with two chairs. A boy is seated in one of the chairs. When I see boys like him, I switch to the other side of the street, especially since that time they stole the Swatch I'd saved up for. It took me forever to save enough money for it. The boy jumps to his feet like a spring and he rushes to hug Don Pino.

'Don Pino! Wow! You came all this way to see me?'

'Of course, Giuseppe. Did you think that I would just leave you here?'

I stand next to the cracked wall.

'This is Federico, my student.'

I move toward him and offer him my hand. He shakes it with a smile that immediately melts my prejudice. Giuseppe has big brown eyes. Beyond the color, they don't look much different from mine. I could be Giuseppe. The only difference is that he was born in Brancaccio and I was born in Notarbartolo. If the roll of destiny's dice had been different, maybe I would be here in the Malaspina detention center.

'I brought you a book.'

Don Pino takes a dog-eared copy of *Pinocchio* out of his bag.

'It's the story of a carpenter and his son. I think you're going to like it.'

'But I barely know how to read.'

'Well, this is how you will learn, silly!'

Giuseppe takes the book and slowly leafs through its pages.

'Wow! It's got so many words!'

'I know.'

'Too many words!'

'First read it. And then you can decide if it has too many words. Besides, what else do you have to do?'

Giuseppe continues to leaf through the book and every once in a while he reads a word out loud.

'Puppet . . . fairy . . . log. Wow! It's full of hard words. Who's going to explain it all to me?'

'Make a list of the words you don't understand and the next time I come visit you, I'll explain them to you.'

'Do you promise?'

'I promise.'

'You're the first person who's visited me here. Not even my mother has come to visit me.'

'When you get out, will you come help me again?'

'Sure.'

He squints his eyes as he says this, so as not to let the tears fall.

Then all of sudden he explodes like a coiled spring that's been suddenly released: He starts yelling as he latches onto the priest like an octopus onto a rock.

'Get me out of here, Father, I'm begging you. Get me out of here. Otherwise they'll do it to me again.'

'Do what?'

Two guards rush in and grab him. Paralyzed by fear, I can't even move my hands. It takes both of the guards to peel him away from Don Pino.

'I'll be back again soon, Giuseppe. Don't worry. I'll be back soon.'

Giuseppe gives up and swallows his desperation.

We step out into the dense morning light. I've never felt the air like this since the day I began to breathe. You never really notice the air. You just take it to be one of life's certainties. But when air is in short supply, you start to get a sense of what it feels like. It's solid and tactile.

Don Pino doesn't say a word. His arms are scratched from Giuseppe's fingernails. And in his eyes you can see other signs of pain, other wounds.

'Are you okay, Don Pino?'

'My friend Hamil is from the Middle East. And he always tells me stories about the land where he comes from. There's one in particular that I really like.'

Two men are walking on a beach and a storm has washed up a carpet of starfish onto the sand. It's like an inverted starry sky. The sun is mercilessly burning them up and the starfish slowly become more and more contorted before becoming entirely crystalized.

Every so often, one of them bends over to pick them up and throw them back into the sea. There are thousands and thousands of them.

The other one is in a rush to get back home and he says to the other: 'What are you doing? Are you going to throw all of them back into the sea? You'll never be able to throw them all back. It would take you a week. Are you crazy?'

The other one shows him the starfish that he has in his hand and before he tosses it back into the water, he responds: 'Do you think this starfish would say I'm crazy?'

'That man's definitely crazy.'

'When you fall in love, you'll sing at the top of your lungs and laugh as you walk down the street. And people will say that you should be committed.'

'What's that supposed to mean?'

'That crazy people are those who know how to love. You can always love. This is heaven. As long as you still have your capacity to love, Federico, you will always be able to do something for someone else. Hell is losing your freedom to love.'

We say goodbye with a hug. He thanks me for tagging along and he apologizes for a visit that wasn't exactly pleasant.

'Have a good trip.'

'Thanks, and good luck picking up all those starfish!'

He smiles as he gets back into his car.

This time, it's not just my lip that is busted. My soul is broken as well. It hurts a lot worse than my lip because your soul hurts all over when it's broken.

25

'You're short a lot of money.'

'I don't have it. You have to wait. Things haven't been going so well.'

'I've already been waiting for two months. The time for patience is over.'

Nuccio stares at the small emaciated man, who keeps his eyes low and twists his fingers to keep them occupied.

'Well, that means that you just have to give me a little gift. Your daughter. What's her name? Serena! What a beautiful name! Serena. It reminds me of being out on the water in a boat.'

The man is silent and clenches his jaw. And then he blurts out: 'If you touch her, I'll kill you!'

'You'll do what?'

Nuccio yells in his face, spraying him with a barrage of 'you'll do what?' and pressing his pistol deeper and deeper into his cheek. It leaves a purple circle on his face as beads of sweat slowly drip down the side of his head at the sight of the gun's barrel. The weapon has a piece of lead set aside especially for a piece of his flesh.

'You'll do fucking what?'

'Nothing, nothing . . . just wait and I'll give you everything you want. Just give me a week.'

'See? You're not so dumb after all. But if you don't have the money in a week, first I'm going to fuck your daughter and then I'll make a bonfire out of your furniture and then this gun is going to go bang bang right in the middle of your thick skull!'

When Nuccio leaves, the man tumbles into a chair and dangles there.

He looks about his little furniture shop, 'Home Sweet Home.' There's the photo of Elvira, who's no longer around, and there's the photo of his daughter who's in her first year studying at the university to be an architect. He would do anything for her. She's the only dream he has left. But now he wishes he had never brought her into this cruel world.

Nuccio tucks his pistol in his jeans and walks away as if nothing has happened. He's a quick learner and he knows how to get creative when it comes to following orders. He'll go far and it won't take him long to get there. The thing about the girl was his own idea. He knows which methods to use with people like this. He's had his eye on her for a while anyway. He wouldn't mind taking her out for a ride. Just like a wolf, he devoured his prey too quickly to savor it. But the blood has lit a greater hunger within him and a greater instinct for a new hunt. He can smell his victims' scent in the air and he begins to track them. And so it's done: Take to the hunt, chase down your prey, and then rip its guts out.

26

'What's going on in that sieve of a brain of yours, Poet?'

When I go back to my room, Manfredi is lying on my bed, leafing through one of my books. I don't answer him.

'Just be thankful that I have abs like Tiger-Man's. Otherwise I would have had to kick your ass. I should have made you into a posthumous poet.'

'I'm sorry.'

'So, what's going on with you? Did you decide to become a cursed poet? Did you go from Petrarch to Rimbaud without telling me?'

'No, that's not it.'

'It's time to start talking. Otherwise I'm going to give you a dead leg and set your books on fire.'

'Have you ever been to Brancaccio?'

'I'm actually fond of my skin and would like to keep it.'

'Yeah, well, I'm fond of my balls.'

'You've definitely become a cursed poet.'

Silence. My brother knows that my silence is a sign that says 'ask me a question.' I'll never start talking out of the blue but if you ask, if you ask questions that require only the briefest of answers, I'll respond.

'Did they give you that fat lip?'

'Yes.'

'What were you doing there?'

'My religion professor asked me to give him a hand.'

'Which professor? Father Puglisi? I remember him from school. During break, he would walk up and down the halls and answer the kids' questions. He didn't like the teachers' lounge. He said it had too many teachers. Is he still at Vittorio Emanuele?'

'Yes.'

'The idealist poet stood his ground and took one to the face like a man.'

I pick up a book and start leafing through it aimlessly, as if the words I read could suggest something to say.

'Who did that to you?'

'A child.'

'A child?'

'Yes. They even stole my bike.'

'How did a child manage to bust your lip?'

'Are you done yet?'

'You poets always manage to surprise me.'

'I'm not joking.'

'I'm not joking either. Thank goodness you're going away to England. Hopefully that'll make you get your head on straight again. Do something useful and stop getting into trouble. The next time they'll bust your head, not your lip. You don't know a fucking thing about that world and you think you can be their savior? Stay where you belong. This city wouldn't even know what to do with a hero. Heroes come here to get blown up.'

'I have no intention of being a hero. I'm not sure about anything anymore. I feel like I'm following a script that has already been written. Everything's just like you: The trip, learning English, university, career ... The talented second son who follows in the footsteps of the first son and achieves the same success. But I'm not like you!'

'Well you're right about one thing: Perfection can only be achieved once in any given family. You're the leftovers. All that was left for you were air and dreams.'

'You're the one who is dreaming. You, with your perfect little world, your perfect girlfriend, your perfect future. You think you know about the real world, but our lives are a million miles away from most other people's. You want to know what reality is?'

'Well? Go on then, what is it?'

'It's like some sheltered greenhouse. We grow like plants in a greenhouse and when we stick our heads outside, the best thing that can happen is that we get a busted lip.'

'So now you want me to feel guilty for people who choose to be delinquents?'

'Do they really choose to be delinquents? Are you so sure?'

'Yes, I'm sure.'

'Well, then, take your fancy motorcycle and go with your hot girlfriend to get a drink there!'

'Why are you getting so worked up? One of these days, they need to do some scientific research on poets' brains. I'd like to understand what part of that cranial box is full of dreams and what percentage of reality has remained intact in there.'

'No, my brain is calm. It's my heart that's so worked up.'

'Well, when things calm down, we can talk about it again if you want. Go tell Mom you're sorry. I'm just trying to get you to use your brain. The reality you think you're changing isn't what you think it is. Next time, it won't end so well.'

'Just worry about Costanza. I'll take care of myself.'

'Man up, then. You deserve to get your lip busted by a bunch of kids. You're the same mental age.'

He slams the door as he leaves.

My rage lasts for exactly twenty-two minutes. Then my self-imposed feeling of solitude fills me with bitterness. I'm not cut out for life as an idealist.

27

'What is it?' asks Mother Nature.

'This kid has something to tell us,' answers the Turk.

'And who are you?'

'My name is Riccardo.'

'And do you know who I am?'

'Of course I know. Otherwise why would I have come here?'

'So what do you want?'

'I wanted to tell you that there is a priest who is saying things he shouldn't be saying. Dishonorable things.'

'And how do you know this?'

'Because I go to his center. I play soccer with them. I listen and I see.'

'What did you hear?'

'The other day he made us read "The Young Mafioso's Our Father."'

'And what is that?'

'It's a sort of prayer that's supposed to make you laugh. First he made us learn the real Our Father, the one that you read in church. And then he gave us a piece of paper that said "The Young Mafioso's Our Father," and he said that it was the opposite of the real Our Father.'

'And what does it say?'

Riccardo takes a crumpled sheet of paper out of his pocket and offers it to Mother Nature.

'You read it.'

The terrified child uncrumples the sheet and begins reading.

> *My Godfather and Godfather of my family,*
> *You are a man of honor and valor,*
> *Your name must be respected*
> *And all of us must obey you.*
> *All must do what you say unless*
> *They want to die because it's the law.*
> *You are our father and you provide us with food,*
> *Food and work, and you'll never stop*
> *Taking from those who have,*
> *Because you know that the young must eat.*
> *Those who err must pay.*
> *Forgive them not. Otherwise you'd be wicked*
> *And wicked are those who spy and betray.*
> *This is the law of our people!*
> *Please take me, my Godfather,*
> *Free me from the police and their jail,*
> *Free me and all your friends.*
> *It has always been like this and always will.*

Riccardo stops reading and then adds: 'But I don't think these things.'

'What do you mean? This is exactly what you need to think. Don't you want to become a good soldier?'

'Of course I do! That's why I'm here.'

'You did the right thing. And you are doing the right thing

by telling me what that priest is up to. Come to think of it, let's make a deal. Come to me again and tell me what that priest is doing, okay?'

'Okay.'

'Word of honor?'

'Word of honor.'

'Good boy. You're a good soldier. You'll go a long way with me.'

Mother Nature hands him a 10,000-lire bill.

'Go get yourself a pizza. If you play your cards right, there'll be a lot more of those.'

Riccardo squeezes the money in his hand and he seems a bit taller as his chest puffs out.

Mother Nature messes up his hair and gives him a little slap on the cheek. As he leaves, the boy rolls the prize between his fingers. He's a smart one and he's already become Mother Nature's eyes and ears. He's a natural when it comes to playing this game.

'This priest better say a few Our Fathers,' says Mother Nature sarcastically, 'the real one. Then we'll see which one works better.'

28

'What's college like?' asks Lucia.

'It's hard. It makes high school seem like a walk in the park. But it's great to study only the things you want to study.'

Serena puffs up her cheeks and then lets out the air as she purses her lips. Then, suddenly, her face lights up in a mischievous smile.

'And you, with all the furniture you've seen at your family's store, you must be a fantastic interior designer.'

'It's true. And my mom was so proud when I started studying at the university. She didn't have the opportunity to go to college and so she got caught up in those interior design magazines that she loved so much.'

'Do you miss her?'

'All the time. Sometimes more than others. Whenever I start working on something new, I wish she were with me. I feel so alone. You are so lucky with that big family of yours!'

'Sometimes I wish I could kick them out of the house. It's so crowded there!'

'Have you decided what you're going to do? Are you going to sign up for university?'

'I'm going to go to teacher's college even though what I really dream of is becoming a director. But it's better not to get carried away with dreams . . .'

They stroll silently back home from the sea. Their smooth tan skin is even more beautiful in the bright summer light. The two friends smile and say goodbye. Lucia heads out over the streets where the asphalt is bumpy, where the sidewalks are full of cracks, where the exposed bricks give the houses the definitively temporary feel that defines them. The great sea that lies just a few steps from the heartache of a small crowded house makes her journey all the more painful. The sea is bad for you. Not for your skin but for your heart. Too much future comes from there, from the horizon, and it breathes down your neck as you seek to limit it to those streets and to the relative possibilities. How can you love the sea when it puts so much desire into your heart? How can you love the light when you must abandon it once you've turned the corner?

'Just look at how beautiful this one grew up to be,' exclaims Nuccio when he sees Lucia's face. She looks at the ground and tries to move past him. It takes just a second for fear to sweep away the stupid dreams of a sixteen-year-old girl and remind her of the reality of her flesh. Her legs stiffen.

He doesn't give up. He follows the trail of her scent.

'One of these days, you and I will go for a nice walk. What do you say, Lucia?'

She speeds up.

'What? You don't like me? You should give me a spin. You have the mouth of a girl who likes . . .'

Nuccio is on top of her. His words sting her shoulders like the tentacles of a jellyfish.

'We'd make a handsome couple, you and me. We'd really be something to see. I would protect you. Nobody would ever bother you.'

Lucia stops in her tracks. She musters the courage that she lacks and looks him in the eye as her lips tremble.

'Leave me alone. Understand? Leave me alone.'

'And if I don't? Then what will you do?' answers Nuccio as he grabs her by the arm with his sweaty hand.

The girl breaks free and runs away.

Nuccio bursts out laughing. The fear he strikes in women almost arouses him more than fucking them.

'You'd better take it easy. You'll see. I take what I want when I want it.'

She can't hear him anymore. Her ears have been deafened by fear and her eyes burn from the tears. Hell is not made of promises not kept. It's made of promises denied.

She is terrified by her womanly body. Her beauty condemns her to violence. She needs to take all those hopes and place them in the palm of her hand and blow them away.

When she gets home, she hugs her mother and cries on her chest.

'Why is Lucia crying?' her little sister asks.

Gemma strokes her hair to soothe her but doesn't ask what's wrong. Not now. Not when she can feel the pain of her daughter's flesh.

Tonight, even the roses in the vase are bitter in the sweet light of their home. The escape routes are blocked, even though this city is a never-ending port.

29

'I'll give you the money.'

Maria looks at him with her tired eyes while Don Pino places an envelope with 50,000 lire on the table.

'What do you want me to do with this? Don Pino, they would kill me.'

'You need to look for a job, and in the meantime you need to stop selling your body.'

'A job? I don't know how to do anything.'

'We'll find you something.'

'There's no way, Father. They'll take my house away if I don't do what I'm supposed to.'

'Do you really want to force Francesco to live like this?'

Maria opens her mouth and the sound that comes out is transformed into a blood-curdling wail. Her eyes brim with mascara and her hair covers her face as she sobs.

'Help me. I'm begging you, help me. I can't take it anymore! The only reason I don't jump out of the window is little Francesco.'

Don Pino hugs her and fixes her hair behind her ears the way you do with a child. Tears continue to stream down her cheeks as she wipes them away with her hair.

'Everything will be okay, you'll see, Maria. Don't be afraid.'

'Forgive me, but I don't have the courage.'

'Think about it a little. Take Francesco to the beach. And think it over.'

Don Pino's black shirt is spotted with her tears.

'Would you consider cleaning an older lady's house? Maybe doing her shopping?'

'But everyone knows who I am . . .'

'We'll look for something somewhere else.'

'Why are you doing this, Father?'

'What do you mean?'

'Why are you helping me?'

'Your smile.'

For just a second, Maria lets him have a look at that smile. That's the first-ever smile that Francesco saw. That's the smile that a boy she liked saw for the first time. And that's the smile that she wishes she could wake up to someday after a night of giving away her love.

As the door closes behind him, Don Pino runs into Nuccio, who's on his way to collect from Maria.

'You, too, Father? Good for you. You have good taste!' Nuccio looks Don Pino up and down with those cigarette-yellowed teeth of his.

'Leave this girl be.'

'What are you saying, Father? You can and I can't? What kind of justice is that?'

'What in heaven's name are you saying?'

'Father, there's nothing wrong with you getting laid. We're all men here.'

'No, you are an animal. I am a man.'

'Let's take it easy with the talk. You're already way out of line here.'

'You're the one who talks too much. Maria is a mother and she needs a job. And you need to leave her be!'

'Father, get out of the way or you are really going to piss me off and then things will get ugly.'

'I'm not getting out of the way. Get out of here and don't come back!'

Don Pino stands in front of the door, immovable, with eyes that flicker with determination and fear at the same time.

'Move or I'll kill you.'

Don Pino moves toward him slowly, with his hand outstretched and his palm facing upward, like someone begging for alms. He puts his hand on Nuccio's arm.

'Please, go away.'

He says this with a smile and his meekness reminds Nuccio of his mother's eyes. Something inside of him (he doesn't know what) or someone inside of him (he doesn't know who) compels him to stop.

'Father, this is not the end of this. You need to start minding your own business. Do you understand me?'

Don Pino watches him leave. Suddenly, he notices that his shirt is dripping wet with sweat.

The door opens and Maria comes out.

'What happened?'

'Nothing. Nothing happened. I just felt a little dizzy. That's all. I just need to sit down for a moment.'

'Would you like a glass of water?'

'No, no. I'm already better.'

'You work yourself too hard, Father. And with this heat!'

'You need to get out of here, Maria.'

'You're so hard-headed, Father.'

30

An open suitcase. Only the dragon from *The Hobbit* is worse. It has wide jaws and devours all in its path. If only I knew what to put into it . . . I stand there paralyzed for twenty-two minutes. There, I said it. How am I supposed to know what I'm going to need when I'm in England forty-five days from now?

I start to toss things into it on a purely poetic basis: Books that I want to read in the original language; sunglasses that belong to Manfredi, who's already got himself a new pair, even though I don't really know if there will be enough sun in England to merit wearing them; one or two pairs of jeans and thirty or so t-shirts; a Swiss Army knife that they gave me when I was nine and that I take on every trip, although I've never used it; a few comics in case I get sick. This is my magic suitcase.

My mother is going to check anyway and repack my bags from scratch.

I need to catch my breath. Too much future can be tiring. I begin to leaf through my atlas with its nearly worn-through cover. It's a map of just islands. When I was in elementary school, I would spend all my time drawing maps that led to islands with buried treasure. And so my parents decided to give me a map of all the islands in the world.

I dug for treasure among its pages. I was captured by chimerical creatures. I learned the thoughts of men very different from me. Some of them had four ears. Others had heads where their chests should be or arms so long they touched the ground. That atlas taught me that the map is more important than the treasure itself.

I used to love searching and searching and searching. And sometimes, when I found a treasure chest, it merely contained another map that sent me to another island a few pages ahead. And my journey would begin again. I had a ship that could sail any sea. On maps, the seas are all the same. The only thing that changes is the blue of their depth. But there are always calm waters and my ship, which I called the *Magellan*, slid along on that blue only to dock in semicircular bays shaped like an arm, in fjords as sharp as sea urchins, on endless deserted beaches. Sometimes I think that my natural inclination toward being a dreamer began then.

I would rechristen the islands with names I had invented myself. This is Paradise Island, my favorite. I called it that because I wanted to create my very own paradise. The islands' treasures were the embodiment of what I loved and a promise of what I lacked. In the former category, for example, there were infinite reserves of kids' games and toy soldiers. In the latter category, there were things like a pool, a wolf, a hat that makes you invisible. The treasure was the island itself and it was capable of generating all the elements of my desire in every adventure. I hadn't looked at it for a while but there it was, fixed in time and surrounded by the blue-colored paper.

What would I put there today?

Of the things I love, I would like to have a mountain of books.

Of things I don't have, I would like to have love, courage, and all the stars that have fallen into the sea.

England will be the island where I will find it all.

Tomorrow I leave.

The time for imaginary islands is over.

31

We are at dinner. Costanza, Manfredi's girlfriend, is there, too. Mom cooked for fifteen even though there are just five of us. But everyone knows that here, love is multiplied by three and it manifests itself in the excess calories.

My brother and I have made peace. I don't think we've ever been mad at each other for more than twenty-four hours in a row. After a while, we both feel ridiculous, no matter whose fault it is.

'All ready to go?' asks Costanza. You'd think her body were inhabited by the most elegant animals on the planet. She has a swan in her neck, a greyhound in her torso, a Persian cat in her eyes, and a thousand species of butterfly in her hair.

'Yes.'

'You're going to have a great time. You absolutely have to go to Harrods and to Fortnum & Mason. They have every type of tea, biscuits, essence, spice, perfume . . . It's a paradise.'

'Costanza is right,' says Mom, 'and bring back some of that Royal Blend tea you can only get there. It's on the expensive side but it's worth every penny,' she adds, clearly excited about my trip.

'I want a nice vinyl record by the Beatles, but it has to be an original,' says Manfredi. 'And I also want a photo of Abbey Road, on the crosswalk.'

My brother is obsessed with the Beatles. There was a time when he looked so much like Lennon that I used to call him John.

Dad contemplates his family and remembers his disappointment at not having had a girl. But it was probably better this way. At least for her. I don't know how she would have survived with me and Manfredi.

'Dad, what would you like me to bring you from England?'

'Whatever you want, Federico. Surprise me. I just want you to have a good time and to learn English like a pro.'

'Is there a professional way to learn English? What if I learn a little slang as well? You're all so obsessed with English!' I say, poking a little fun.

'You know how much this trip is costing us, Federico. You need to rise to the occasion.'

'I will, Dad. In fact, I'm planning to save you some money.'

Everyone looks at me intently.

'I've decided not to go.'

'Are you scared, Poet? I knew it. The same thing happened to me. The night before I was supposed to leave, I didn't want to go either,' says Manfredi, smiling.

'I'm not afraid. I have other things I need to do. I'm not afraid, and that's why I'm staying here.'

'What on earth are you saying?' my mother asks.

'I'm going to stay so that I can give a hand to Don Pino Puglisi in Brancaccio. What point is there in going to England if I don't even know half of the city where I live? How can I learn a new language if I don't even know how to speak my own? What good would that do me?'

'Federico, it's not up for discussion. The money has already been spent. When you get back, you can help your teacher as much as you want. It doesn't seem to me that the two things are incompatible.'

'But they are incompatible. You just can't understand. It's not a question of organization. I'll earn the money and will pay you back.'

'This conversation ends right here. You're leaving tomorrow. Period.'

My father never raises his voice but when he does, it's a sign that the conversation really is over. There's no longer any room to negotiate. And so I need to meet like with like.

I get up from the table. I lock myself in my room and I won't come out until after it's time to go catch the plane.

Between being right and being courageous, I have chosen the latter. And whatever the price, I'll pay it.

32

At night, the sea longs for the refuge of a port. It flows towards the shore in an amorous dance.

The smell of the jasmine bushes mixes with the darkness. The hotter the newly extinguished day, the more intense the aroma will be. Two silhouettes rise above a lonely street.

Dario is speaking with a girl whose lips promise the reward of flesh. He is barely ten years old and his face is that of a child who will become a handsome boy. His arms and legs are slender but proportionate to his prepubescent body. The sweetness of his gaze is thanks to a bitter melancholy. His curly hair droops down his forehead like sea foam over the rocks.

'What are you doing here with these wise guys?'

'I buy a lot of clothes thanks to these wise guys. A lot of things that I like. And I feed my family. And you?'

'I'm going to buy a gun.'

'What for?'

'To kill the person who put me here. So that I can leave.'

'Where will you go?'

'Where the wind takes me. On wings that I will build myself.'

For a moment the silence makes space for the faraway din of the city. A television sputters out voices and bits of light from open windows here and there.

At this point, the sea should rise and cover the entire port and wash away all human detritus. But the sea is too ignorant of what happens along the coast that it rubs up against.

A car comes down the street and crushes shards of glass sprinkled across the asphalt. It approaches slowly. A man of about fifty with an unkempt beard and sweaty hair looks Dario over and motions to him to get in the car.

Dario smiles at the girl and mimics a pistol with his thumb and forefinger. He gets into the car and disappears into the dark among the shrubs and abandoned objects: Refrigerators, old cars, sofas.

Dario puts the money in his pocket and walks away. He wanders aimlessly, as if half-asleep.

It won't be long before he buys his gun and before his wings are ready.

In the dark, he lies down along the shore and falls asleep as he thinks about the story that Lucia told him. It's the story of that boy who flees a monster by using his father's wings made of feathers and wax to fly away. He will fly away like that boy but he won't get too close to the sun. That last effort to dream trumps even the hope that keeps him awake and he falls into a deep sleep. He dreams of a woman who emerges from the sea and holds him between her arms as she carries him into the water. The sea approaches with the nighttime undertow, and it's almost as if the water wanted to make him happy and hide him within its waters and by doing so, save him from the bitter light of another day.

33

'If you don't come out of your room right away, I promise you, you won't ever come out again.'

That's what my father said this morning. I kept the door locked until long after my flight took off. And I only opened the door again after I had triumphed. I realized that I had won the battle but not the war when my father came into the room without saying a word, took the key, and locked me in.

I never would have dreamed that I would one day be a prisoner in my own house, in my own room, no less. My little bedroom-port has now become a bedroom-jail. My father feels that I need this time to macerate in my sense of guilt. But the real senses that are being compromised are more mundane, since I am now forced to stay in here without being able to eat or go to the bathroom. I hope that, at least, they will give me some bread and water in a pail. Even political prisoners are entitled to that.

Thank goodness for Manfredi. When my parents go out, he opens the door and lets me gather the basic necessities.

'Poet, you're becoming epic! Sit down for a minute so we can talk. I want to understand better. Did you suddenly grow balls?'

'If I'm not mistaken, I was quite clear.'

'Listen, I'm your only ally and you're not going to do yourself any favors by pissing me off. They've decided that you're not allowed to set foot in Brancaccio anymore. What did you expect?'

'What do you think they'll do to me? You think they'll keep me locked up at home? I'm seventeen years old. I'll call the police!'

'Yeah, go for it. And I'll call the nuthouse. You've got to cool off. Remember: I'm the rational one. Now, you need to tell me what really happened.'

'When you see certain things, you can't ignore them. I can't just turn away and pretend that they don't exist.'

'Don't you think you're going a little too far with this? Just because you see a documentary about children in Africa doesn't mean you need to go to Africa to solve the problem.'

'That's exactly what I mean. We have become so numb that we see things without feeling them. I know that I have to do the little I can do. I can't ignore what I saw.'

'What did you see?'

'A man who needs help. A man who risks his skin every day and boys and girls whose lives depend on that man. And that's not an exaggeration. I wasn't born just to think of my own future.'

'And what else should you be thinking about? Other people's futures? I think you're being a little self-righteous.'

'I'm not. I want to give what I have to give. And then I saw . . .'

'What?'

'I saw Lucia.'

'Who's that?'

'A girl.'

'That much I can gather. Just like every other poet: You think all you need to do is see a girl once and that's all it takes to fall in love with her. When will you stop being seventeen years old?'

'I don't need your approval. I'm the one who's lived these seventeen years. Not you.'

Manfredi doesn't say anything.

'What's this all about?'

'My seventeen years of life?'

'No, I mean her.'

'She's beautiful. Strong. Real.'

'Real?'

'Yes, real. She's one year younger than me but she lives in the real world, unlike me. She was born and raised in the real world.'

'And you weren't?'

'Yes, but in a totally different reality. A reality made of lights and shadows.'

'Are you sure that this is the right thing to do?'

'I am sure that this is what I want to become. If I don't just dive in now, it will never happen. It's like a day for a seaside stroll when there is no beach to walk on.'

'Who wrote that line?'

'I did. You're either on land or at sea. There is space only for coming and going, there is no threshold between the two, sea and land.'

'Sometimes you actually get to me with your poetry. I'll try talking to Mom and Dad.'

'In the meantime, I need you to do me a favor.'

'What's that?'

'I need you to cover for me. I want to go to Brancaccio today.'

'No, wait until I talk to them. You don't want to sabotage your negotiations before they even start.'

'Cortés burned his ships on the beach when he landed in the New World so that he had no choice but to move forward with his plans. There was no room for remorse. Better regret than remorse.'

'Fede, you are no Cortés.'

'Cortés wasn't Cortés until he burned those ships.'

Manfredi smiles.

'There's something that I need to do. I'll go and come back. You pretend that I'm in my room and that I want to be alone. I'll leave the music on.'

'Hurry. And by the way, there's something that I need to give back to you.'

I look at him quizzically. He punches me in the stomach. I bend over to defend myself but it's too late.

'Now we're even, Don Quixote. Be careful. I'm not kidding. Watch out for kids who know how to do Jeeg Robot's hell-slap. Which reminds me. It's been a while since we watched *Tiger-Man*. You might want to brush up on some of his techniques so that you don't end up laid out on the floor . . . by those kids.'

Reeling in pain and unable to catch my breath, I try to articulate a syllable or two but nothing comes out.

'You thought you were going to get away with it? Remember: Order must be respected.'

Little by little, I manage to breathe again.

'Go back to the cave where you came from. I never gave you permission to leave.'

'You're still my favorite poet even though you're a cursed poet.'

'Damn you! Get the hell out of here!'

'Come on. Get going.'

This is how males resolve their disputes. It's something that women will never understand. Without my brother, I'd only be half of a man.

34

Shoes. Yes, shoes. With books, you can go wherever you want without ever leaving your room. But shoes will take you and your body and everything in it to faraway places. Now it's clear to me how important my shoes are. Thanks to my shoes, I'm going to be able to navigate the maze of life. You can't avoid the maze of life but you have to be careful to follow the thread.

And I know that the person holding the thread is Lucia. I want to see her, even if just for a moment. Apologize to her. Tell her that I am still here. I want to read the manual for using the night. In the end, you can never really escape life. It might be stuck to the soles of your shoes. It might lie in the words you use.

I manage to find the house. I knock and she opens the door. She has 'White Nights' in her hand and she's using her finger to mark her place about halfway through. There is a mix of dreams and words in her eyes. She struggles to figure out which world I belong to.

'I'm back. Do you like the book?' I ask her.

'Yes, I do. You're as discombobulated as the main character.'

'I was supposed to leave for England but I ended up not going. I wanted to see you again.'

'Why?'

'Because I'm a pain.'

'How old are you?

'Seventeen.'

'You don't look it.'

I look down at my shoes as I try to muster what few resources I have left. My shoes traveled all this way thinking this was going to be easy. They have many roads to travel before they will show the age of the person who wears them.

'What I meant was that you have a child's face.' Lucia smiles.

All is not lost. I smile as well.

'I'll be back soon. I have to run.'

Lucia looks at me and continues to smile, without saying anything. I don't know where to look. I focus on my shoes and I watch them as they turn back in the direction from which they came. Gauging from how warm I feel, my face must be bright red.

As I make my way down the street, I see the boy who beat me at juggling the soccer ball.

I juggle an invisible ball and say hi to him.

'Remind me, what's your name?'

'What's it to you?'

'I'd like to remember the name of the kid who beat me at juggling.'

'Riccardo.'

'Okay, see you next time.'

'What's your name?'

'Federico.'

'How old are you?'

'Seventeen.'

'And you?'

'Eleven.'

'Wow! You're already really good at soccer. You could be a pro.'

'My father said that he's going to have me try out for Palermo.'

'That's how it's done.'

'Why are you here?'

'No reason in particular. I have friends here.'

'Who?'

'I'm a friend of Don Pino's.'

'Don Pino's a good man. He knows everyone.'

'That's right. Are you a friend of his?'

'Of course. He promised me that he would teach me the way to heaven.'

'He even knows the way to heaven!'

'Yeah.'

'I need him to teach me, too.'

'I'm first.'

'Sounds good. Bye, Riccardo. I'll see you next time.'

'Bye. But where do you live?'

'In another part of town.'

'In Palermo?'

'Yes, Palermo.'

We say goodbye. As I walk away I can't help but be proud of having made it here without sticking out like a sore thumb. I'm beginning to shake things up and to liberate myself from the softest ideology in existence. It's soft because it wears slippers and not shoes: Platitudinism. When I turn around, Riccardo is still watching me. I say goodbye one more time.

When I get home, it's almost time for dinner. My brother opens the backdoor for me so I don't have to ring the doorbell. I gave him the signal by calling our house phone. I go into my room and Manfredi gives me an update on the negotiations. His diplomatic efforts as my ambassador to the country of Unable-to-Understand-an-Adolescent have resulted in an acceptable outcome. I can go to Brancaccio until everyone leaves for the summer vacation at the beach. I'll go with them, and that's non-negotiable. The cost for my course in England will be reimbursed even though we cancelled at the last minute. The cost of my flight won't be reimbursed. So I'll have to get a job to pay it back.

'Deep down inside, Dad is proud of you. He'll never tell you that. But I was able to convince him that you haven't lost your mind. Mom, on the other hand, is terrified that you're going to end up going down the drain, just like the bourgeois revolutionaries.'

'Who are the bourgeois revolutionaries? Have you ever been able to figure that out?'

'I think they're the ones who have a vacation home.'

'Is there anything wrong with that?'

'Not that I know of.'

I can hear Mom calling us to dinner. I apologize to my parents and life begins anew. At least, I let them believe that.

35

'Weren't you supposed to be leaving?'

'I'm here to pick up some starfish.'

'But what happened?'

'Giuseppe.'

'Malaspina?'

'Yes. What was the point? I would have learned the language and the customs of another city when I don't even know what's happening in my own city.'

'What did your parents say?'

'If they had their way, they would send me to a mental hospital. They lost the money that they spent on the ticket. But the cost of the course was reimbursed. Either way, they think I've lost my mind.'

'People are always sad when it rains. But when someone in love goes to visit his girlfriend, he can't help but start singing. He seems like he's crazy when, in fact, he's the only normal one. So are you going to help me?'

'Would I be here if I wasn't? Don't make me regret it.'

'Should we make a bet that you won't ever leave?'

'Let's make a bet.'

Don Pino smiles and hugs me.

'Thank you.'

I hug him back and I feel at home. It's a home with rooms that still need to be decorated, but with solid walls and lots of light.

'Let's take a walk and I'll explain on our way.'

The shadows seem to have been sent into exile by the sun's ferocity. It's as if they have fled into people's homes, where they are hidden and cared for.

'We need to walk around the streets and let people see that we are here. With our heads held high, afraid of no one.'

'Why?'

'To let people know that there are other things they can harvest besides poison darnel.'

'What's that?'

'Do you remember the landowners that I was telling you about a few days ago? Those who sold their land became very rich. As often happens in Sicily, Mafiosi rose from their ranks. They continue to demand protection money from people who have homes in their territory. They have substituted farming with extortion. The poison darnel of the Mafia continues to grow unabated, thanks to ignorance and poverty. I see Brancaccio as an enormous field, where wheat and darnel grow side by side.'

'I still don't understand what this "darnel" is. Is it something you eat?'

'You're not paying attention. It's a weed that looks like wheat in every way. The difference is that when you thresh it, the wheat becomes grains. Darnel also becomes grains but the grains are unusable and if you mill them, the flour is poisonous. There's plenty of wheat here but it's too often suffocated by weeds.'

'Are the politicians doing anything about it?'

'Politicians? Politicians aren't interested in saving men. Politicians are often part of the problem. The thing that counts is the choices that individuals make. You are politics, my boy, the choices that you make every day as you walk these streets. Do you remember the boy that hit you? What did you want to do to him?'

'I wanted to kill him.'

'I know. But if you don't learn to love, you will continue to be a child just like him. Loving children like him is the only thing that can change Brancaccio. Judging him is too easy. Blaming the political system? Too easy. You have to let the wheat grow together with the darnel. They grow and will always grow together. Darnel grows fast. It has shallow roots and is perfectly camouflaged in the wheat fields. You can't rip it out without harming the wheat. There are no "good" and "bad" people. But there is wheat and darnel in everyone. The difference will emerge at the right moment. You use wheat to make bread, darnel to make bonfires. We need to reduce the influence of darnel little by little.'

'But I don't know how to do that.'

'Does anyone know how to? *Quannu l'amuri voli, trova locu*, the saying goes. *Love will find a way.* But love is something that belongs to the world of men. We can learn anything. We can be taught anything. But love, the most important thing and the most difficult thing, is something that no one teaches us. Yet, if you don't learn to love, you remain an illiterate liver of life.'

Old folks sit in front of their homes. Worn playing cards lie idly on a table. Some of them say hello to Don Pino, who answers with a nod and a smile. Not far away, children hurl rocks at glass bottles lined up on a little wall. When they burst in the sun, they look like hailstones of light. A young man with hair hardened by gel burns through the tires of his moped turning in circles, going nowhere. A woman plows along the street with her shopping bags that seem to nail her to the ground with their weight. A girl in slippers sweeps the sidewalk in front of her house as she shouts her rage and frustration in a dialect known only to those inside. The world before my eyes expands and my muscles melt slowly from the same tension that an explorer feels as he enters deep into a tropical forest.

'It won't be a war on the Mafia that will change Brancaccio, but the patient and constant resistance to ignorance and misery. I need to get the summer games ready for the kids and take them to the beach and to see the stars. Then we will do the sports tournament in honor of Borsellino. It's the first useful Sunday since the anniversary of his martyrdom. I need you to give me a hand.'

'Sounds like a good idea. But how is it that you are never discouraged?'

'Jesus is with me always. And I always try to be like a farmer. I try to treat everyone like wheat. If they are wheat, then they become bread. Charity is not enough. It takes love. You can see the signs of so many defeats on the faces of the kids, the wounds from too much humiliation. My job is to walk these streets and love everyone.'

Don Pino speaks of love as if it were a concrete thing. It's kind of like what Petrarch does when he writes Love with a capital L and he compares it to an invisible presence. Invisible but looming and determined.

'If I had been born and raised on Via Hazon, I wouldn't have had a choice either,' he continues. 'If you are born in hell, you need to see at least a fragment of what hell is not to understand that something else exists. And this is the reason that you need to start with the children. You have to get to them before the street eats them up, before a crust forms around their hearts. That's why we need a preschool and a middle school. It doesn't take strength. It takes the heart and mind. And it takes hard work. You have no idea how much can be done with these three things.'

You can't take anything for granted on the other side of the train tracks that I crossed. What have I seen up until now?

'And then there are the girls. They are still adolescents, in need of safe places. They go out with someone who gets them pregnant. And they "elope." If things go well, they get married. But most of them end up as teenagers with a child to raise, alone like a mother dog with her pups.'

I notice Don Pino grimace and clench his jaw in rage. I've never seen him like this, and have no idea where it's coming from.

'I don't want Lucia to end up like that.'

That's what I said. Or at least, someone inside me with whom I have yet to become acquainted.

'She won't.'

'She seems like she's different.'

'She's not different. She's just like the others. But she has been brought up in a different way. This is what makes the difference between those who become men and those who become just another member of the pack.'

Even the name itself, Brancaccio, seems like a pejorative for something rapacious: *branco*, the pack, the gang. Who would ever believe that at the beginning of the second millennium it was an Arab–Norman Eden full of fruit trees and plenty of water?

You can still see some of the faded signs of this water that nourished everything here: The Castello della Sorgente, 'the castle of the spring', the Favara (from the Arabic *al-fawwāra*, meaning 'spring'), and Queen Constance of Sicily's *camera dello sirocco*, 'the chamber of the sirocco', where legend holds that Frederick II's beautiful mother cured her sunburned skin. Back then, Palermo was a verdant city despite the heat, thanks to a system of underground canals that had been devised by the Arab settlers toward the end of the first millennium. They gushed throughout the city into wells and grottos. The miracle-workers of the era were the water-diviners. They were able to conjure water from the rich water table beneath the city. And everything seemed to flower on that land. Unaware of the divining arts, many visitors believed that Palermo's gardens were sacred in origin.

Don Pino walks across the asphalt desert and, like those masters, he conjures that water from the deepest depths as he digs, digs, and digs. The water hidden in the stone of every human heart, even the most arid one.

The Mafia is pushing the city to abandon its water table, to drain it, and convince the people of Palermo that they have no water. Little by little, people start to believe that they really don't have any water and that it will be given to them only by virtue of charitable donation. Instead, it simply hasn't surfaced. And in the place of the green parks and gardens, weeds grow, like darnel. The city could use water-diviners, but it is the lords of the sirocco who proliferate instead.

'Do you know where I was born?'

'You weren't born in Brancaccio, were you?'

'In the United States.'

'Really, Father?'

'I'm telling the truth.'

'But you don't know how to speak English.'

'That's true. But I'm talking about another United States. It's the poorest part of Brancaccio, the ghetto within the ghetto. It's bordered by not one but two sets of railroad tracks. It was built for the railroad workers who came from other parts of Sicily and Italy. And so it seemed like it was foreign. My grandfather lived there. He was a railroad worker. And that's where Lucia lives.'

'When were you born, Don Pino? In the nineteenth century?'

'You rascal! I was born in 1937. September 15, 1937, with the sound of trains and the clanging of the couplings in my ears from when I was just a baby. I used to watch the trains and dream of traveling far, far away. And yet the train of my life brought me back here as a priest, in October 1990.'

'Do you ever get lonely?'

'I'm not alone. The Mafia is strong. But God is omnipotent.'

'Then why doesn't He do something about it?'

Don Pino doesn't speak. He smiles at me. He gestures for me to come closer to him, as if he wants to confide a secret.

'He did do something.'

'What's that?'

'You and me.'

'With all due respect, it's not much. He could have done a lot more.'

'My friend Hamil knows the desert well and he always says that *those who plant date palms don't eat dates.*'

'What's that supposed to mean?'

'It means that it takes at least two generations for the date palms to bear their fruit. If I plant a tree today, in fifty years someone will eat the dates and cool off in its shade.'

'I see. So what's in it for the person who plants the date palms?'

'You'll understand that when you become a father.'

'But I want to understand now.'

'I'm getting worried about how combative you're becoming. A father takes joy in the joy of his children. His joy multiplies and it becomes much greater than his own personal joy because it is nourished by everyone's joy.'

'Is that what happens to you?'

'Every day.'

36

The sun is stuck behind the sea and the last stars are winding up like ivy in the twilight. How beautiful it would be if the sun were to rise on a new and changed city, full of gardens and men who work and love. Men whose work is a bridge between dreams and reality and not an exile from themselves. In the dark, a man inhabits the city of God.

I found heaven in hell.
It's much smaller and briefer than hell.
It resembles the corner of a garden or a moment. But it's
*   everything.*
It is the fulfillment of everything.
Of the seed in the rose.
Of man in man.
Of woman in woman.
Of God in all things.
And it triumphs in silence even when it shows just an incomplete
*   face of a beauty that seems almost foreign. In exile.*
Heaven becomes wider and nothing and no one can grab and
*   cage it.*
Intrepid like truth, indomitable like beauty.

Have pity on me for all the times that I have slowed the
flowering.
Have pity on me, dear God, have pity on me for having built that
hell through my own sloth. It's not enough to avoid evil. One
must also do good.
There is little in me today that evokes the light. But every seed
hidden in the blindness of the earth is shaking. Perhaps that
seed does not evoke the light but invokes it.
And so I invoke You. Like a seed.
Too small for a land so desolate and dark like my own.
Help me, dear God, to not remain alone.
Help me to find faith in You.

In that city, in Him, it becomes real. It frees you from the most enduring of dreams like the ancient master who knew how to find the water, even in stone. In the meantime, the sea breaks on the solid shore like dogma and it forces that endless port to have faith in that which is constant. You cannot help but hope where there is a never-ending port.

37

'Will you tell me the story of Turiddo?'

'Again?'

Don Pino likes telling stories. It's the best way to teach anything, as he often tells his students: The Italian *parlare*, 'to speak', comes from *parabolare*, which means 'to tell stories'. Don Pino never stops teaching. And for fifteen years now he's been a schoolteacher, even though he's had to reduce his hours recently in order to devote himself to the neighborhood. He's taught thousands of kids over the last fifteen years. Eighteen hours in eighteen different classes at a crowded public high school. Every year, he had somewhere between twenty and thirty students in each class. That makes nearly 10,000 students who were greeted by his smile over fifteen years. And he knows what difference one smile a week can make in the life of a teenager. He'll never leave teaching. Who knows? In the end, that number could reach 100,000 students. You can change a nation with 100,000 teenagers. But even 10,000 are enough for a revolution. Every teacher is the most dangerous military threat of any given nation, a fuse capable of triggering unforeseen atomic reactions.

In another time, it was his mother who told him stories, when they didn't have a television or even a radio. They were traditional stories, the type of story that threads its way through the alleys of

Palermo and then lingers like an echo from the past. A people that holds onto its stories always harbors some hope that it will be saved.

'Well?'

With the fingers of one hand formed like an inverted bird's beak, Francesco makes the Sicilian hand gesture used to ask for something. He closes the beak two or three times with his fingers pointing toward his chest, as if he were going to knock on it like a door.

'There was once a boy named Turiddo . . .'

'No, no! You have to tell me the first part, about your mother and how she was a seamstress and how she had the fastest hands.'

'You're a hard-headed one, aren't you?'

'Just like you.'

'One day, my mother, who was a seamstress and had extremely fast hands when she sewed, told me that God is like a mother in His mercy and like a father in His strength. And I could understand the part about His strength but not the part about His mercy. And so I asked her to explain it to me. She was a simple woman who hadn't had much schooling. But she knew how to tell stories and how to use stories to explain even the most complicated things. And so she told me the story of Turiddo.'

Francesco's eyes open wide as he waits, once again, for the fable to reveal the secrets of the world. Nothing can distract him from a good story. Useless thoughts and even the hidden pain inside of him just vanish. Everything just disappears. And Turiddo enters into the scene.

Once upon a time, there was a mother who had lost her husband and children to the plague. Only one of her sons had been spared. His name was Turiddo and he was his mother's favorite. She was so poor that she had to break her back day and night to raise him. She washed clothes for rich folks, and that allowed her to buy prickly pears for him to eat so that he could grow properly. He loved prickly pears, especially the ones that were red like his hair. And so he was able to grow. And indeed, he became a healthy boy, full of dreams. But he began to hang around with friends whose souls were the color of night. They were always playing cards. Sometimes he would win. But, for the most part, he was the one who would lose. His mother would sit in her kitchen and wait for him every night, sometimes until dawn. And every night she would set out a plate of fresh red prickly pears for him. He would eat them without saying a word. But he had made a silent vow to change his life.

One day, Turiddo had lost all of his money and so he had decided to bet his future earnings. He needed to repay his debt. Otherwise his fellow gamblers would have killed him by beating him with a stick. Or they would have hanged him or drowned him like an old donkey.

So he fled into the night and sat down on a little wall with his head between his hands and pain in his heart. Dogs were barking and the moon was so scared that it practically disappeared. Then something moved. It was the giant cape of a man with an old hat that was darker than night. It was so big that it even covered his face. Turiddo was frightened.

'Who are you?'

'I can help you,' he said. 'Come tomorrow at midnight to Hangman's Crossing with your mother's heart and I will give you the money you need.'

'But who are you?'

There was no answer, and the cape was swallowed up by the night. Turiddo fell even deeper into despair. He couldn't hurt his mother. She had suffered greatly in order to raise him right. But the barking of the dogs reminded him that an awful death awaited if he didn't pay the debt. And so the next night, as she was sleeping, he cut into her chest with a knife and took her heart.

He wrapped it up in a towel and rushed to Hangman's Crossing. The night was blacker than ink. The stars had disappeared. He was so scared and so mad at himself for what he had done, Turiddo ran like a crazy, tortured soul. But it was mostly because his mother's heart, which he held tightly under his arm, wouldn't stop beating. It reminded him of one of the prickly pears that she would set out for him every night.

He wanted to be rid of it as soon as he could and the hour of his appointment was nigh. The road was bad and Turiddo, in his haste, stumbled. The heart was still beating, all covered in blood. It fell out of the towel and rolled along the path. Turiddo could hear a quiet voice coming from it. He thought that he must have gone crazy. But when he bent over to pick it up, he could hear the voice loud and clear. It was a sad, piercing voice in the silence of the night.

'My son. My blood. Did you hurt yourself?'

The heart was asking its son, the blood of its own blood, if he had hurt himself.

Francesco's mouth is hanging wide open. Wonderment and silence are a gauge of the truth of any given story. Once a story is finished, if you return to thinking about what you were thinking about beforehand, or if you immediately start talking, the story is not a good one. Or the narrator is not a good storyteller. But if those listening to the story remain silent, perhaps with their mouths half open, you can rest assured that it was a good story. And it will surely liberate someone from the prison of desperation or boredom, which represent life's great lie. That's why only children know how to listen to a story, even when the story never changes, because they never tire of listening to the truth.

Turiddo paid the debt. And when he returned home, he found a dish with fresh prickly pears on the table and he cried every last tear he had.

'My mother told me that God is like the mother. For God, a son will always be a son.'

'Why do you like this story so much, Don Pino?'

'Because it reminds me of my mother. It was she who taught me how to forgive.'

'What ended up happening to Turiddo?'

'I don't know. My mother never told me. Who knows? Maybe he repented.'

'Either that or he went to hell.'

'With a mother like that?'

'If you have a good mother, does that mean you won't go to hell?'

'Yes.'

'If you are bad?'

'Even if you are bad.'

'Have you ever been to hell?'

'Every once in a while.'

'What's it like?'

'What's the worst thing you've ever done, Francesco?'

'I don't know.'

'Think about it. Think about what you did after you suffered terrible pain and didn't have a way to escape it.'

Francesco hesitates. He can't stop fiddling with his hands. He closes his eyes and puts his hands over his eyelids.

'The time I kicked the dog.'

'What was wrong about it?'

'Because the dog hadn't done anything.'

'That's it. That's hell. The loneliness that you felt after you kicked the dog. Hell is all the times you decide not to love or you cannot love.'

'Does that mean I will go to hell?'

'No. Not if you ask forgiveness.'

'Who do I need to ask?'

'Jesus. And then the dog.'

'And how do I do that?'

'By confessing to Jesus the loneliness that you felt after having visited hell. It's like telling a story. And Jesus loves all of our stories, even the saddest ones.'

'How does he hear me?'

'If you tell me the story, I'll make sure that he hears it.'

'Alright. I'm going to tell you the whole story then.'

Francesco tells him about the dog. And then about the time he spat on his friend Antonio and the time he punched his mother. The time he stole a bike. The time he burned lizards and the tail of a cat. The time he threw rocks at the other team and cracked open a kid's head. The time . . .

Don Pino listens with his eyes closed and nods. When Francesco finishes, he opens his eyes and smiles at him.

'Is that it?'

Francesco lets out a deep breath like someone who has revisited all the evil that he has inside. And then he calms down.

'That's it.'

'I absolve you of your sins in the name of the Father, the Son, and the Holy Ghost.'

He guides Francesco's hand to help him make the sign of the cross. And then he gives him a hug.

'What did you just do?'

'I didn't do anything. God has erased hell. Those things never existed. They have been erased.'

'And so now I can go to heaven?'

'Yes. But you don't *go* to heaven, Francesco.'

'You don't?'

'You are either *in* heaven or hell. You don't go there.'

'I don't understand what that means.'

'Both are inside of us. It depends on the space that we give to the one or the other.'

'Can you say that again?'

'When you kick the dog, you are giving space to hell. If you pet him, you are giving space to heaven. If you kill someone, it's hell. If you save someone, it's heaven. You decide.'

'This makes me happy. Very happy.'

'See? There you are! You are in heaven.'

38

The Hunter knows that what needs to be done must be done. Now more than ever, now that Mother Nature has chosen him. The thing that needs to be done now is to kill a man. That's what they told him. And they told it to him because his greatest assets are speed, determination, and the guarantee of precision.

He was a tireless worker up until the time he was twenty. He had worked all his life like a mule. He did it because he loved his wife and their first child. Then things had gone the way that they do in the world: Wrong. He lost his job and he needed money. He knew the right people and so he began with robbery.

The path toward bigger things was like walking up a staircase. And then there was money. Lots of money. And easy money. Without breaking his back. When he opened a sporting goods store and it didn't take off, they gave him 2 million lire a month in living expenses. Then his devotion and obedience took it to 5 million. To think that when he was working in construction, he practically had to kill himself and he barely made more money than someone who is disabled.

Today, all he has to do is kill someone every once in a while. Nothing pays like determination. And no one is as determined as he. You don't pay state taxes on determination. Maybe on your soul, but that itch passes quickly, especially if you have a family to take care of.

When there's someone who needs to be killed, the Hunter is a sword that's already been drawn from its sheath. Silent and sharp.

That's why Mother Nature chose him. He wanted him in his army, in his firing squad.

He sees the man leave his house. He's around forty years old.

It's the early afternoon and the street is empty and there's a festive, tired silence in the air.

The Hunter detaches himself from the wall like a stone that has come to life. The handle of his gun presses against his abdomen and his belly, full from a Sunday lunch.

The man turns the corner on to an even more deserted street. Words tumble from televisions and evaporate as soon as they hit the street. The man is walking at a relaxed pace and his cigarette smoke accompanies him as the Hunter moves up beside him and shoots him directly in the head. The pistol's silencer shares its whimper with the man. It's a merciful whimper, after all, because the man doesn't even have time to suffer.

The soul departs through the hole that's been opened up in his head and it blends in with the voices from the televisions. And then it evaporates like the voices. A piece of iron and a piece of flesh. Then the Hunter shoots the traitor two more times in the heart and he continues to walk on. The laundry continues to dry, suspended and unsullied between the sky and the earth. The wind caresses it and everything seems simple and pure.

But the blood spreads.

He takes a walk around the block and rids himself of the pistol by hiding it in the usual store. He goes home and caresses one of his children's heads and plays with him. Then, an hour later, he hits the street again and moves toward the crowd of people who have gathered around the dead body.

The police are already there, collecting evidence.

With circumspect piety, the Hunter asks about what happened.

A little girl is kneeling next to the man's body. She has a half-naked doll next to her.

Her mother is trying to move her away from the blood as it stains the little girl's knee.

'Will Dad come back after everyone is gone? Will the blood disappear and will he open his eyes?'

The mother turns away and sobs as the child holds her father's hand. He's already been relegated to the realm of memories, and the last memory of him will remain a border that cannot be crossed. His face has been misshapen by the gunshot. His heart has been splattered inside his ribcage.

The Hunter has no eyes. He observes the scene like someone watching a film for the umpteenth time when there is nothing good on TV.

That which needs to be done must be done.

39

Today is one of those days on which the wind softens the streets, blowing not from the sea but from the land. It covers the din of televisions that stagnates when the heat is deadening and sets everything into cautious motion. I'm on the bus that takes me to Brancaccio and I watch the homes and people go by. My soul is brimming with words that I'd like to write.

I am reminded of Italian class from my freshman year, on the earliest written examples of the Italian language. One was a riddle that compared writing to a black seed that had been planted on a white page. That sheet of paper was as fertile as a field of crops at the time of planting.

'Without words, things almost don't exist,' our teacher told us.

'Especially words that lie underneath a layer that covers them. The page is the soil and once it's been plowed, tilled, and nourished, it generates complete, precise words. These are words that name things and allow them to exist within us because they cannot yet show themselves. These words bring things to light or they shed light on things.'

Then we learned about the second document, the one in which a builder inveighs against the poor workers and flogs them with violent words: 'Pull, you sons of whores!' he says to them. And our teacher told us that this is another thing that words do. They can be hurtful. But words also allow us to feel their exhaustion, their pain, and their frustration beneath the burden they carry. They must bear the weight of their existence.

I love the fact that in early Italian literature, writing is described as a seed and bad words are used. In the end, what are words for if they are not used to speak of good and evil? To bless and to curse. This is what words are for. And once again, it's what you choose to make of them.

I come upon Don Pino as he is arranging fresh flowers in a vase near the altar.

'I have to say a blessing over the dead. Come with me.'

'We're getting the day started off right . . . Who died?'

'I don't know. They shot him.'

Bless the dead. Who knows if it can even be done?

●

40

The Hunter cuts a baby goat into pieces.

'The meat of a milk-fed kid is more tender than lamb. It's very delicate. The flavor and aroma are less intense, and that's why you need to cook it well, with wine and the right spices. It will melt in your mouth.'

'Does "milk-fed" mean that it's little?'

'Yes, that's right, but the important thing is that you give it only milk to eat and no grass. Just look at the color of the meat.'

The knife cuts through the pink fibers with meticulous skill. The skin lies bunched up in a pile in a corner like clothes that someone has taken off. The kid seems more and more naked and shameless. Its eyes stare into the void and its lifeless tongue is stretched between its teeth.

The Hunter pulls out the entrails and they wiggle in his hands as if they were still alive. He sections the animal with the patience of a surgeon. Its compact muscles give way under the sharp blade. The fat is white and solid and the meat shakes as if those cuts continued to hurt.

'I need you to do something for me.'

'Just tell me what,' replies Nuccio as he watches the tip of the knife detach the tendons that bind the meat to the bones.

Then the Hunter sticks his hands into the ribcage of the animal and searches it. When he pulls them out, he is squeezing a little heart that drips with blood.

'When you chop this up and cook it with the liver, lungs, kidneys, sweetbreads, salt, chopped onion, and bay leaves, it tastes like heaven.'

He gathers all the innards in a bowl and they float in the blood. Now all that's left of the kid is its tender meat.

'We need to burn down a few doors.'

'That's it? That's child's play.'

'Take it easy, Nuccio. You're getting ahead of yourself. Don't get cocky and don't fuck this up.'

'You don't need to worry about me.'

'Once upon a time there was a Roman emperor who liked to kill his slaves on the lawn in front of his palace simply because he liked the way the fresh blood looked on the green grass.'

'Who told you this story?'

'I don't remember. I read it somewhere. Or it might have been in my son's history book and he told it to me.'

'Why are you telling me this?'

'Because we don't do that type of thing. That emperor ended up being killed by his own guards. They cut off his head as he tried to hide in a latrine. They dragged his naked body across the city and in the end, they threw him in the river.'

'He deserved it.'

'Yeah, he deserved it.'

With just a single blow, the Hunter cuts through the neck of the goat and its head bounces on the table, alive for just an instant, as if it were aware of this last injustice.

41

The coffin is in the center of the room. It's open and surrounded by black dresses filled with women. The men come in and bow and after a few seconds of silence, they leave. Laments, curses, and prayers are mumbled. The boy is standing, stuck in a corner. Everyone looks at him inquisitively. Then they return to their whispering overflowing with hypotheses. Don Pino sits down next to the little girl with the doll. He recognizes her from the toy. She's been cleaned up and she smells nice now. Her wild eyes are full of tears and she has a runny nose.

Don Pino prays in silence.

'What are you doing?' she asks.

'I'm saying a prayer.'

'What good will that do?'

'I am speaking to him.'

'But he's all full of holes. He's lost his breath. That's what my mom told me. He won't ever come back.'

'That's not true. He's in heaven.'

'But I want him here. Not in heaven. Well, what I really want is for him to be at the beach because we used to go to the beach every Saturday and he would teach me how to swim, a little bit at a time, because I'm really scared of high tide. But he wasn't. Now my dad can't come with me anymore.'

'He's alive and he doesn't want you to feel alone. He hasn't left you.'

'He has left me. Because he can't hold my hand anymore when we cross the street to go to the beach.'

'I'll take you to the beach to learn how to swim.'

'But do you know how to swim at high tide? You seem a bit . . .'

'A bit what? I swim like a fish!' Don Pino lies to her.

He's probably more afraid of high tide and choppy seas than she is.

'If he's alive, I'm going to leave him the doll that he gave me. Can I put it there in the box?' asks the girl, pointing to the coffin and revealing a few missing teeth in her mouth.

'No, no. He gave it to you and it will make him happy if you play with it. He wants you to play with it. So that when you dress it up, when you talk with it, when you caress it, you'll remember him.'

'Are you sure?'

'Of course I'm sure. Just look.'

Don Pino rummages around for something in his pocket and he pulls out some rosary beads.

'What is it? A necklace?'

'Yes, it was my mother's and I always have it with me and I talk with her.'

'And she answers you?'

'Yes, she does, of course.'

'What does she say?'

'She tells me not to be afraid. She is always with me.'

'Well, then, I'll keep my doll. And that way, my dad can talk to me.'

'Yes, I think that would be best.'

'What's your name?'

'Don Pino.'

'Donpino? What kind of name is that? That's a strange name for someone.' The child smiles. 'You know, Donpino, you know that my doll's eyes are always open?' She shows him the doll's wide-open blue eyes.

'That way she can watch over you. What's her name?'

'Doll.'

'That's a fine name.'

A rosary litany fills one's grief with cadenced words, like the waves of an undertow.

> *Tower of David, pray for us.*
> *Gate of Heaven, pray for us.*
> *Morning star, pray for us.*
> *Refuge of sinners, pray for us.*
> *Queen of peace, pray for us.*
> *Amen, Amen. So be it.*

The child falls asleep in Don Pino's arms as he strokes her hair. Seeing death up close is like death itself. It's not the opposite of life but it is life's absence. Life always has life within it, even when it seems to be death, just like a caterpillar's cocoon. But death has nothing within it. It's not the fruit of a painful metamorphosis. And men gave the name of God to the negation of death so that there would be someone greater than death.

42

The lights have been dimmed in the building's stairwells and the neon glows complacently. Three men form the armed shadow of the night, the night of June 29, and they carry with them the fire with which cities were conquered in the epic poems. Then they split up to enter three different buildings in the same complex. The Turk. The Hunter. Nuccio. They are warriors in a war without enemies.

It's a war that has been declared on three fathers whose only weapon is their hard-headedness. Three family men determined to get what Brancaccio is missing: Proper plumbing, a middle school, a park. They are the founders of their complex's homeowners' association. And one by one, they have recruited persons willing to work to lobby politicians and Mafiosi, not to obtain any type of privilege, but simply that which they are owed in the name of naked human dignity, without yielding to the clandestine power of the Mafia. They are the ones who have decided to break apart the logic of the oppressed and their oppressors, a logic that regulates the forces of the neighborhood. They've even reached out to the President of the Italian Republic with their letters. They've managed to get people to pay attention to their call for the construction of a plumbing system. They are evidence of the fact that when someone in Palermo decides to do something, he will die. But they continue to get people to pay attention to them by being the squeaky wheel.

Hard heads are made out of wood, and you burn them with fire. You can hear the gasoline swishing around in the can and it's the only noise that accompanies Nuccio's burning gait. His religion has a single commandment: Mother Nature's approval. There is money. There are women. And there is respect. And this is what needs to be done, just as the Hunter has taught him. He's standing in front of one of the three doors that they need to light up.

Fifth floor. 'Martinez' is written on the doorbell. 'Di Guida,' fifth floor. 'Romano,' eighth floor. The timing will make the fireworks all the more spectacular.

He douses the doormat with gas as the silence permeates the sleep of those who work by day. The fire releases itself from the wood and flares up along the walls that need to be eliminated. Now they'll think twice before they work with that priest. Burning around Don Pino. The local politicians have complained: You can't even manage to keep everyday people under control, let alone priests and workers. It's not as if they are the police!

This is why these doors need to go up in smoke. This is why they torched a van that belonged to a company that was helping to repair the church. The smell of burning wood, the smell of burning car paint, of burning carpets, of car tires: Those smells are always better than the acrid, slightly sweet smell of burning flesh.

This is how one man sucks out the soul of another man in a city where people suck on snails after boiling them in salt-lined pots. They do it that way so that the snails can't escape as they try to save themselves from the heat when not even their homes feel secure anymore.

That's how you buy silence: With fire that subjugates the heart as it squeezes it. It forces people to divert their eyes to the ground and turns their brains into nonsense. That night the children try asking, but no one can offer a proper explanation of what has happened.

And a father needs to care more about his family than about the truth.

But those three – Martinez, Di Guida, and Romano – are different. That is to say, they are normal. And even though people accuse them of making the neighborhood look bad with their home-owners' association, they are reporting a sordid crime with their letters and their requests. Despite the anonymous phone calls on the evenings that follow, in which a woman's voice comes on and cries 'Help, help!' and then the sound of glasses clinking and a terrible raucous voice can be heard, they continue to report and to speak out and to write.

Despite the fire and the barking of the pack, they vindicate a centuries-old code of silence with their words.

They are heroes in an everyday epic.

43

What you are about to hear
Is the tale of heroes and damsels,
A thousand adventures they had to face
Often terrible, often beautiful
And I, the storyteller, want to tell you
The most beautiful one of all.
Lend me your imagination and your ears,
Children, men, women, young and old.

Totò is wearing a stocking-shaped hat and he shakes a wooden sword in time with the words he is saying. His role is that of the *cuntastori*, the storyteller. He's learned the first lines by heart. It's the story that Lucia wants the children to hear.

Lucia's dream is to work in the theater. And together with Don Pino, she has decided to stage a story from the tales of Charlemagne using Sicilian puppets, knights in the form of marionettes. The children will be the puppets. After all, the word *pupo* or 'puppet' in Sicilian dialect originally meant 'child.'

Lucia is a natural director. She is capable of intuiting the best part for each actor. She comes up with plots. She writes dialogue. She fashions costumes. It's like a seed of beauty that she stores up during the winter of the heart for those kids. And with the thawing, it begins to bear its fruit. She has involved mothers, grandmothers, and even a father or two. Everyone will help as much as they are able.

The show is called *Little Orlando Sets Out to Conquer the City*, and it tells a traditional story from the 'Tale of Tales' about the brave young Orlando's childhood.

Orlando was born in the woods with only his mother to care for him and without even knowing his father, who was killed in battle. Even as a child, he displayed cunning and remarkable strength. He had no books to study and so he learned everything by exploring the woods with his faithful friend Virticchiu, who would later become his squire.

Little Orlando has no idea that he is the product of forbidden love. His mother is Charlemagne's sister. After falling in love with a common man, she had to flee to Paris, where she went into hiding.

One day, Little Orlando meets a caravan of travelers in the woods. They are heading toward the city, where they plan to attend a joust for aspiring knights from every walk of life: Nobles and paupers, vagabonds and mercenaries, adventurers and outcasts.

They are all young and eager, just like him. Charlemagne wants to take Little Orlando with him to court. And as he gathers information on Orlando, he discovers the truth: Little Orlando is his nephew. Charlemagne's noble confidant, Ganelon, fearful that he will fall out of favor with his king, decides to eliminate the young heir. But Little Orlando, aided by Pipino the wizard and the friends he's made at the joust, will try to reveal Ganelon's true intentions and his plans to eliminate even Charlemagne himself and take his throne.

Lucia has adapted the story and the text and every week they hold rehearsals at the Holy Father Center. She has to manage fifteen or so boys and girls. Francesco is going to play the part of Little Orlando. The part of Virticchiu will be played by Calogero, Nuccio's little brother. Then there are the ladies-in-waiting, including the girl with the baby doll who only recently joined the troupe. Riccardo is Ganelon and Don Pino himself will wear the good wizard Pipino's beard, even though he doesn't know it yet. Lucia will play the part of Little Orlando's mother.

They are still missing a Charlemagne.

The armor and shields are made out of cardboard. The skirts are emerald green and the bodices are made from blue fabric. The tin helmets have fake plumes. And in the minds of the children from Brancaccio, the plastic tiaras sparkle like tempered steel and hand-made brocade.

'Can you imagine Don Pino's face when he finds out that he needs to wear Merlin's beard and hat?' Francesco says as he hangs on Lucia's arm.

She's trying to sew a decoration onto one of the costumes.

'He's going to have a great time. It will be a birthday he'll never forget.'

They've decided to debut their show on September 15 as a surprise.

'But do you think he'll be able to recite his lines from memory?'

'Don't worry. I've taken care of everything. It will be a surprise.'

Mum's the word, she gestures, drawing her finger to her lips.

'The only problem is whether or not he will arrive on time.'

The children arrange themselves in a circle, each a meter from the other. Totò begins proudly to wave his sword and declares:

> *Ganelon's sword is no match*
> *For the brave Little Orlando's skill.*
> *Strength without smarts is the catch,*

Defeat the brave child it never will.
He and his friends a plan will hatch,
With Pipino's help they're stronger still.
So get yourselves ready for any surprise:
Who will lose and who will take the price?

' "The *prize*," Totò! "The prize." Not "the price"!'

'I don't know why I always get that one wrong. And besides, I'm getting hungry!'

'You'll be fine, Totò. Just try to remember: The "prize" is what the winner takes when he wins. It's the opposite of "defeat." '

'Okay, okay. I'll try to remember.'

The children form a circle around Ganelon. He's dressed completely in black and he's wearing crow feathers. He's trapped and he doesn't know which one to attack because every time he tries to move, the circle closes in around him like an octopus and someone hits him on the shoulders. Then someone trips him and pushes him over before hitting him on the head.

'Give up! I am Charlemagne's nephew. And someday this realm will be my own.'

'You damn kids. Do you think you are a match for a man armed with a sword? I'll slice you up like a cantaloupe!'

'The knight seems nervous. Maybe he needs some chamomile tea,' sings Virticchiu.

'No, he just needs some fresh air. He's suffocating in that armor,' says Little Orlando.

And then he pulls Ganelon's pants down. Everyone laughs as he is forced to take tiny little steps, as if he were a cockroach. And everyone can see his red underpants.

Little Orlando seizes the opportunity to land a blow on Ganelon's head.

'The best things come in small packages,' says one of kids.

'And dripping water hollows out the stone,' declares another.

'Everything big starts little.'

The traitor falls to the ground and they all pounce on him.

'The city is ours!'

'Hurray, hurray, hurray!'

The children celebrate by dancing around the vanquished Ganelon as they sing in unison.

Lucia encourages them by mimicking their movements on the stage.

And to finish the scene, they raise their hands to the sky and shout joyously. This is followed by a moment of silence so that the audience can get its bearings.

Like a river that arrives from far away and empties into the sea, the magic of the story has captured the hearts and minds of the children. And they are emboldened by this fantastic tale. If you don't have a great story to pass down from father to son, then you will always be at the mercy of those in power and their frivolous storylines. Only those who belong to a story can invent their own, just like the flowers of an almond tree that tell the story of spring.

I laugh and applaud from the corner of the room. I always manage to find a corner where I can see but not be seen. I always like being tucked away in a corner.

Lucia turns around.

'What are you doing here?'

'I heard you need a Charlemagne.'

She smiles and the children start clapping.

'That means you're going to be spending a lot of time here. There's a lot of work to be done.'

'Is that so?'

'Yes, it is. I'm the director and if you want to be in the show, you need to follow the rules. Just like everyone else.'

I bow my head as a sign of obedience without uttering a word . . . even though I'm the king.

44

Don Pino is more serious than usual during Sunday Mass. The children sitting in the front pews notice, and it's making them nervous. Francesco is there. And so are Dario, Totò, Salvatore, Riccardo, and Lucia and her siblings. Gemma is sitting behind them with her husband and Signor Mario is sitting in his wheelchair. The fathers whose doors were burned down are there. Mimmo, the policeman, is there. The nuns that help Don Pino are there.

And the wolves from the pack are there as well. They're there to mark their territory. They're there to protect it from unwelcome trespassers.

'Do you know what my favorite passage from the Bible is, children?'

A chorus of 'no' slices through the sweaty air.

'The Beatitudes. It's the one that explains happiness. And this ingredient in particular: "Blessed are they which do hunger and thirst after righteousness, for they shall be filled."

'We're not talking about being satisfied by justice for men. Our justice is often unjust. Nor can someone be happy just because he experiences hunger and thirst for something that cannot be achieved.

'Happiness lies in being filled and not in dying of thirst or hunger. The justice we are talking about is the promise that God has made to man. And that promise is that His strength will always prevail, that love will always have the last word, even when violence appears poised to suffocate it. It's a strange type of justice: It moves through the world in silence, hidden but unstoppable, just like a fugitive who never gets caught. We will be filled because He will do the things that we cannot arrive at ourselves.

'But we are asked to open the door of our lives to allow this justice to enter into the streets where we move. So that we ourselves may become God's promise and that it may be fulfilled. We are His justice. We will relieve the hunger and fill others if we answer God's call.

'There are two questions that God asks man. The first is directed to Adam when he hides after having committed a sin. "Where are you?" God asks us why we are hiding. And we are ashamed of the evil we have done and so we go into hiding.

'We don't allow God's mercy to find us. We think that He wants to punish us. We think that we don't deserve His love. But that's exactly what He wants to give us. For free.'

Don Pino stops speaking and points to the wooden cross. And then begins again.

'The second question is the one He asks Abel: "Where is your brother?" And Abel answers, "Am I my brother's keeper?" Yes, you are. Every one of us is the keeper of those around us, whether a relative, a friend, a coworker, or a neighbor. They need us and we need them, since God does all He can to make us love more and to be loved more. Today, these are the two questions that God asks us: "Where are you?" and "Where is your brother?"

'And how do we answer Him? In a neighborhood where there is no middle school, no public park, and no place for children to play? It's only normal that you will continue to want these things and ask for them. God asks man to fulfill his own will. He doesn't perform miracles where man can make his own miracles by means of his daily toil. But there are those of us who don't want men to live in a dignified manner. And I don't understand why. And I ask such people to come here. Let's talk about it. Face to face. Let's discuss what's going on. You are the sons and daughters of this church. And I await you. Let's meet in the piazza. I was born here and grew up in this neighborhood and I am tired of seeing babies and children in the streets. We can make a new start of it.'

He watches the congregation with a serious look on his face.

Nuccio's nostrils flare and his mouth feels so full of teeth that he can't help but smirk. The children are restless because they can't understand what Don Pino is talking about. He seems angry and it's hard for them to follow his sermon.

Then the priest offers the congregation bread and wine and with the Communion, he also offers every fiber in his body. He watches the children and is reminded of the words of St John in the Apocalypse: 'Behold, I make all things new.' Evil may shout more loudly but a silent spring will nurture those buds and help them along. All it takes is one drop of God's blood to save the entire world, let alone a neighborhood in Palermo.

But God's weak omnipotence without man cannot do anything. Man's freedom is the riverbanks between which God has chosen to confine his omnipotence.

He hands out the pieces of bread to everyone.

And then he begins to smile again. From far away, with a light that doesn't come from the streets of men but from a space that no one can touch. A space that belongs to those who feel at home in the eye of the storm, to those who stand just a meter or two below the stormy surface, where the blue sky is calm and still. His hunger has been relieved and his thirst quenched because he has known hunger and thirst. It's the joy of the journey for those who have arrived at their destination. To him, God is a *never-ending port* and man is a Malaspina in search of a place to dock.

45

'This is for you.'

'What is it?'

'A book.'

'I can see that.'

'Petrarch's *Canzoniere*. My favorite poet. I actually brought it for you a while ago but then a punch got in my way.'

Lucia takes the book. She opens it. She smells it. And then she flips through the pages.

'I've never read a book of poems before. I mean, a book with only poems.'

'It's just like other books, but as if the chapters were shorter.'

'Why did you bring this for me?'

'Because I know that you like books, and I have plenty of books. Or maybe I was hoping you would forgive me.'

'Then why this book? I remember Petrarch being pretty boring at school.'

My hands can't stop fidgeting and I can feel my face turning red.

'How does it end? I can't remember.'

'Not so good.'

'Why's that?'

'Because she dies.'

'And what about him?'

'He keeps on loving her. And he writes about his memory of her.'

'Which poem is your favorite?'

I leaf through the more worn pages and I hand her the book.

'Read it,' says Lucia.

'No, I can't. You read it.'

'You read it. It's your poem.'

I take a moment to clear my throat and then I begin to read slowly. I'm a little bit embarrassed.

> *I cannot find peace and am not at war*
> *I feel fear and hope, I burn and am of ice*
> *I fly over the heavens and lie on Earth*
> *And I grasp nothing and embrace the entire world.*
>
> *One keeps me imprisoned who neither opens nor locks,*
> *Nor keeps me for herself nor frees my bonds.*
> *Love neither kills nor does he unchain me.*
> *He doesn't kill me but nor will he free me.*
>
> *Without eyes or tongue, I see and shout.*
> *I long to perish and I plead for help.*
> *I hate myself and I love someone else.*
>
> *I graze on pain and laugh as I weep.*
> *I dislike death as much as life.*
> *In this state I am my lady because of you.*

'The first lines are beautiful. Also because they're easier to understand. He says that he can't find peace. But then he says he doesn't have anything to battle, and it's full of contradictions. That was about all I understood.'

'I can explain it, if you want.'

'Yes, please. Explain it to me. Who is keeping him locked up in prison?'

'It's Laura. The woman he's in love with. It's like she's keeping him prisoner even though she isn't stopping him from leaving. She neither opens nor closes his jail cell. She doesn't tie him up nor does she set him free. And Love does the same thing to him. See how he writes it with a capital L? Love is a mysterious presence for Petrarch, a kind of shadow that oppresses him, just like when you're in a dark room but you can still feel the presence of someone there. You're sure that he's there but he doesn't say a word and you are afraid to ask.'

I can't muster the courage to look at her while I'm speaking.

'It's strange because he says things that don't go together. Tying up and setting free. Closing and opening up. It doesn't seem possible.'

'They're poems. Things happen in poems that you can't explain. He can explain them. He's someone who's found the right words to say how he feels like he's living a dual life. Because of Love, he's divided into two states at the same time.'

Lucia smiles as she watches me talk with my hands. My words are like juggling-clubs.

'I get it. Then he says he can yell but has no tongue, right? Then he says he can see but doesn't have eyes, right?'

'Yes, exactly. They're called oxymorons. They are words that go together even though they are contradictions.'

'Oxymorons?'

'Yes.'

'I like it. I've never heard that word before. It sounds like the name of some kind of fruit. But what does "I plead for help" mean?'

'I ask for help.'

'What about "I graze on pain"?'

'Pain feeds me. Gives me energy.'

' "I laugh as I weep." Is that an oxymoron?'

'Yes. It's the most beautiful one in this poem.'

'Has it ever happened to you?'

'An oxymoron?'

'Yes. I mean, no. Have you ever laughed while you were weeping?'

'No, I haven't. What about you?'

'Yes.'

'When?'

'That's none of your business. You must like words a lot . . .'

'Words are like anchors for me. They help to keep things steady.' I look into her eyes.

'Petrarch is more interesting than I thought. Our teacher made him seem so boring. By the way, I've been having trouble finishing the script for *Little Orlando*. It's not as easy as I thought.'

'I think it's great.'

'Don't be ridiculous. Some parts could be a lot better. Maybe this book will help me. Thank you,' says Lucia as she takes the book. 'But words aren't enough to make for a great show. It takes time and hard work. It's not easy to get these kids to focus. That's why I told you that you need to come to every rehearsal. I need you to help me.'

'I didn't go to England so that I could be here.'

Lucia doesn't say anything. And then she asks me, 'Why do you want to keep things steady?'

'I get seasick otherwise.'

I've never seen her smile the way she's smiling now. It's one of those smiles that makes you lower your guard. It's as if it were saying to the beholder: *If your intention is to hurt me, this is where you need to strike.*

Oxymorons. Contradictions.

Life itself is a contradiction: To have life, you must lose it first by falling in love.

46

In port cities, there's a moment every evening when the sea forgets about the sky and develops its very own color. It's like the blue in the most beautiful *Triumph of Death* ever painted. There was a fifteenth-century painter in Palermo who painted such a color. No one knows his name. And so he is known only by the painting's title.

The artist must have dipped his brushes directly into the Grim Reaper's palette: When you see the painting you feel like you are meeting death. Death is riding his galloping charger in the center, slicing diagonally through the scene. The horse looks like an x-ray of itself. It's as if you could hear its neighing as Death shoots arrows at rich and powerful men who don't seem to notice its dark presence. A group of poor people implore her to relieve them of their desperation, but she ignores them. The unjust justice of Death.

Look carefully at this scene before the humidity eats it up, like all beautiful things. There's just no way around it: Not even beauty is immortal in Palermo. Death has just shot an arrow into the neck of an elegant young blond man dressed in a blue brocade cloak.

In the opposite corner there are a couple of frightened dogs barking. They will be immortal as long as the painting preserves their pelt. A boy's eyes are wide open and crazed. He clings to life as he offers his hand to a friend. All that the friend can do is grasp it. Otherwise, there's no way to avoid sipping from the bitter chalice of complete solitude.

Removed from its wall, this fresco is now in the same palazzo where Antonello da Messina's *Virgin Annunciate* is displayed. Two of the world's most perfect colors, each preserved under one roof. They represent man's two callings in life. Death and life. The blue of *The Triumph of Death* and the blue of the *Virgin Annunciate*. Colors are the flags that men plant in the realm of light that God has seized from the darkness. The blue serves to take away God's privilege of knowing the secret of life and of death.

At that hour of the evening in which, for just a moment, everything is quiet and it appears that life and death will be overcome, two friends stroll along the banks of that blue.

'Why did you say those things, Don Pino?'

'What would you have done?'

'I would have avoided saying something like that.'

'They set people's doors on fire with gasoline. We will set them on fire with the truth.'

'What truth would that be? Since when is truth spoken in this city? Are you not aware of what happened to Falcone and Borsellino? What good would the truth do?'

'If we keep tucking the truth away in the attic, sooner or later we'll forget that there ever was truth. The problem in this city is that words mean one thing and the opposite of that thing at the same time.'

'It's better to live with double meanings than it is not to live.'

'Don't you understand? I said those things in the name of life, in the name of the neighborhood, the lives of the children, the lives of the women, the lives of the men, life itself! A priest must say these things. The worst thing that could happen is that they kill me. And then what?'

'Please don't say that. Don't even joke about it.'

'Mimmo always says that *you have to die from something*. Hamil, he has a wife and kids. What do I care if they kill me? They'd never kill a priest. No way. They know that all we do is talk, talk, talk. Beyond that, we don't do much.'

PART II

Swooning

Beyond you, oh sea, is my paradise, where
I wore life's pleasures, not its misfortunes.

(Ibn Hamdis, Songbook II, 20–21)

And the children in the apple-tree
Not known, because not looked for
But heard, half-heard, in the stillness
Between two waves of the sea.
Quick now, here, now, always . . .

(T. S. Eliot, *Four Quartets*, 'Little Gidding,' 35–39)

1

The sunlight's aggression begins to melt away as the evening arrives over the sea. This is the hour for resisting and standing tall. But how can you stand tall and resist when you live on the edge of the sea? No matter how abundant, brackish water doesn't quench a burning thirst. And every man is revealed in his bruised mortality.

The boy longs for everything and nothing at all. Don Pino longs for justice. Lucia longs for the beauty in one of her dreams, still intact. Francesco longs to play games with his father. Maria longs for the tenderness of a man's touch. Manfredi longs for a brilliant career. Parents long for their children to achieve their potential. The Hunter longs for a happy life for his children. Nuccio longs for his bosses' approval. Dario longs for a little bit of decency. Totò longs for a conductor's baton. Riccardo longs for easy money.

They are all living creatures. All of them kneaded with love and pain. The God of all swooning stirs within them. Such a heart hurls itself into continuous ecstasy and leaves the body behind. This infinite desire forces the heart to break if necessary. Many call it an empty heart and they heal it with love. But in Palermo it has a special name: Swooning, a throbbing pain caused by too much sea to behold and too many voyages to embark upon.

For those who arrive in Palermo, the city is a never-ending port. But for those who were born here, it's all about leaving, all about desire, all about flight. Never satisfied in the belief that it won't happen to them, they are always waiting for what comes next.

Infinite voyages, real and imagined, originate in the never-ending port. It's the debt that must be paid to the city. But it's also part of the city's delicious charm: The call toward something that always lies beyond the horizon.

A mmari a nnome ri Ddiu. That's what the fishermen say when they start their day and throw their nets into the sea. 'To the sea in the name of God.' The Mediterranean is the most fertile gift given to us by the continental drift. There is no space more sacred or richer in memory than the sea. Today, it collects the fishermen's sweat. In another era it was the repository of heroes' tears.

In Italian, *a mare*, meaning 'to the sea', and *amare*, meaning 'to love', sound the same. And everything here that is ambiguous is true. The heart longs for life but life will never satisfy its desire.

The boy suddenly finds himself without his books. He reads directly from the pages of the sea and the horizon appears to him like the last line of a book. His eyes and heart put out to sea: The infinite resides not only in books and libraries. It's in every neighborhood. It's in every life that seeks its meaning.

Later, he leaves the port behind and slowly re-enters the belly of the city, behind the port. In the Kalsa neighborhood: *al-Khalisa*, Arabic for 'the chosen one.' It's where the sultan lived with his court because the fresh water of the Oreto river runs through it. Once you move beyond what remains of the river, you arrive at what were, once upon a time, the fertile lands of Brancaccio.

Nearby, there is a market, and the most beautiful palazzo and the museum of Palermo, the botanical gardens, and the Basilica La

Magione, the church where his parents were married a long time ago. He heads along Via Romano Giuseppe. Via Santa Teresa. And Via dello Spasimo, 'Swooning Street.' Yes, there's a street near the shore named after the feeling that comes when you turn your back on the sea. There are certain cities where the streets, by their very nature, make the traveler a part of them, whether they like it or not.

There's a church on that street. It's not dedicated to any saint, male or female, but rather to a feeling. Yes, the church is named after the Virgin Mary but no one knows that. Everyone calls it 'the Spasimo,' the swooning. It has no ceiling. It looks up at the sky just like the port looks out over the sea.

And for a moment it seems that God could return anew to the earth through that ceiling that isn't, just like a sailor who returns to she who longs for him.

A never-ending port for those who arrive. Never-ending swooning for those who remain. A city built out of a paradox, a city where you are always arriving or waiting to leave.

The boy sits beneath the patch of sky framed by the walls of the church and he stares into the sunburned blue.

He knows about the sun. But where love arises, love always changes.

Does such swooning save all of these lives? Or does it punish them?

2

'Will you lend me your guitar?'

'No.'

'I'm taking it anyway.'

'I'll set your books on fire.'

'Come on, Manfredi!'

'What do you need it for?'

'There's this kid who wants to become an orchestra conductor. It's his dream.'

'That has nothing to do with me.'

'It does have something to do with you. Once you get involved, it's always going to have something to do with you.'

'Well, what do you need the guitar for?'

'It would be so great if he could learn how to play an instrument. Then he could see if it's something he really wants to do.'

'And he needs to learn on my guitar?'

'Do you have another solution? Look, I only know how to strum a few chords. Why don't you come to Brancaccio and give him a lesson or two?'

'What? Do you think I don't have better things to do?'

'I'm not saying that you have to move to Brancaccio. I'm just asking you to give up an hour or two of your time, in your own city, just a few kilometers from here.'

'I'm not wasting any more time talking about this. I'll lend you my guitar but you are responsible for it. If you break it, I'll break you.'

'Just relax. I'll take good care of it.'

'That's exactly what worries me. Your ability to break and lose things is legendary.'

'The important thing is not to lose your soul.'

'Who told you that?'

'I can't remember.'

'That's all we need: The bad poet. Make sure my guitar doesn't get lost in your soul.'

3

'What's the deal with this bicycle?'

'You need to learn me how to ride it. Damn, I'm the only one who doesn't know how!' answers Francesco in a bossy tone.

A six-year-old boy and a nearly fifty-six-year-old boy stand before one another.

'Right you are. Come on, let's go. Let's see what you can do.'

'I'm not scared at all.'

'If you're not scared, why are you telling me that?'

'Because I'm a little bit scared. But don't tell anyone that.'

'What's wrong with being scared?'

'No one respects you when you're afraid.'

'There's nothing wrong with being scared, Francesco.'

'Are you scared?'

'Yes, I am.'

'Of what?'

'High tide.'

'And what else?'

'Of pain.'

'And what else?'

'Of dying.'

'Who would ever want to kill you?'

'Nobody. Nobody at all. That's not what I meant. What are you scared of?'

'My mom leaving me alone.'

'Your mother will never leave you.'

'How do you know that? Sometimes she says mean things to me.'

'She always says nice things about you to me. When she says mean things like that, she doesn't really think them. It's just that she gets mad sometimes.'

Don Pino grabs the bicycle. It's an old Graziella. He looks it over.

'Where did you get this?'

Francesco doesn't answer.

'Did you steal it?'

'Someone threw it away.'

'Really? I bet they threw the chain away as well.'

'What do I know?'

'Alright. I'll teach you how to ride a bike. But then you need to put it back.'

'What if I don't?'

'Then you better watch out.'

'Okay. Damn! You're sharp, Don Pino.'

'I'm not sharp, Francesco. That's a word you use for someone crafty, someone who takes things that don't belong to him.'

'In life, you have to be slick or else things might not turn out so good for you. The slickest person always wins.'

'And who told you that?'

'I can't remember. But everyone knows that.'

'Come on. Get up on the bike.'

Francesco sits on the seat but it's too high. He can't even touch the ground with his feet.

Don Pino holds him up and, like all fathers do, he has him go around in circles and lets go for a few seconds every so often.

Francesco quickly learns what it feels like to fall off a bike and he scrapes his knees and elbows. Everyone remembers their first fall from a bike and the scrapes that come with it.

After a while, he can finally ride on his own and he rides away.

Don Pino looks out over the deserted street.

'Children. Sooner or later, they need to ride away.'

4

'How do you become an orchestra conductor?' Totò asked me a few days ago.

'First of all, you need to learn how to play music,' I told him.

At least that's what I think you need to do. Honestly, I've never really understood why the man with the baton in his hand is so important. It's not like he's a wizard. We start with the first lesson anyway. Manfredi's guitar has crossed the city with me and here it is, being played in a world I couldn't even imagine before.

We start with some exercises to get his fingers used to playing the guitar.

The strings leave marks on Totò's fingertips from pressing against them.

'I didn't know it was going to hurt.'

'It hurts at first but then it stops.'

Just like everyone who learns to play for the first time, the only sounds he can make are grating. But he doesn't care. He's already fascinated by the notes and how different they sound from one another.

His right hand quickly finds its place over the bridge. It seems that he has a sense of rhythm.

'You've got talent.'

'No, I didn't bring it with me.'

'Don't you know what that means?'

'Talent?'

'Yes.'

'What's that?'

'You're good at it. You have a gift for playing music.'

'Are you telling the truth?'

'I am.'

'What talent do you have?'

'Causing trouble.'

'Like what?'

'Like making my parents mad.'

'I'm pretty good at that myself. What other talent do you have?'

'I like words.'

'What do you do with words?'

'What do you do with notes?'

'Music.'

'You can use words to change things.'

'Like what?'

'For example, you didn't know the word *talent*. But now that you've learned what it means, you know you have it. You didn't before.'

'Wow! You're right! You need to teach me words, too! Then I'll have lots of things!'

'Okay, sure.'

'Like what?'

'What do you mean?'

'Like, teach me something else.'

'Let me think . . .'

'Teach me something that has to do with music.'

'Harmony.'

'Music you make with your arms?'

'No, harmony. With an H. It means that there are different voices or sounds and each one is different. But when they come together they make a harmony that's more complex.'

'I don't understand this at all. Can you tell me something that's easier?'

'Okay, hold on. I'll try. Well. These are the strings: E A D G B E. If I play them by themselves, they each have a different sound. If I play them all together, they make a harmony. Can you hear it?'

'Yes.'

'Harmony is when different instruments and voices play and sing together.'

'Now I understand. Wow! You're good at explaining things. Now let me make a harmony. That's what an orchestra conductor does, right? There are all these instruments and he puts them all together by waving his baton.'

'Do you have a baton?'

'No, not right now.'

'We need to find you one.'

'Wow, that would be great. But you'll have to teach me.'

'Teach you what?'

'Harmony.'

'I can try.'

'You're so good at words. You can teach me a bunch of things. You're better than my teacher at school.'

'Don't get carried away.'

I look around the room full of children busy drawing, playing, reading out loud, dancing . . . they are the harmony of life.

Don Pino comes in.

'Should we have a little snack?'

The children answer him in unison and all follow him to the

main room where the table has been set with Coca-Cola, bread, and Nutella. Other brands are allowed as well but without Coke and Nutella there would be a revolt.

I'm hoping Lucia will see me there, but she's too wrapped up with the children. She's talking to Dario and explaining something by moving her hands like they were the wings of a seagull gliding. I can't stop staring at her. More words that I've committed to memory emerge from somewhere deep within me, somewhere new and unfamiliar:

> *Love found me completely disarmed*
> *And opened the way from my eyes to my heart.*

The room is almost empty and I begin to gather my things before heading back home.

The guitar is missing.

I feel my heart sink. Manfredi's guitar.

I look everywhere for it. But it's nowhere to be found. Prophecies always come true, especially when they are negative ones.

I turn the center inside out but still no guitar. Then I go into the room where they've been rehearsing the play. In the darkness, I can hear the strings being plucked. I go over to Totò, who is sitting in a corner. He's playing and listening to the sounds. He's got his ear practically glued to the guitar.

I'm really angry because I'm going to be late for dinner at the pizzeria where I'm going to say goodbye to Gianni before he leaves for the summer vacation. I can already hear them telling me that I'm crazy: You picked Brancaccio over Oxford?

Totò gets up and looks at me as if he just woke up from a dream. His eyes sparkle with joy. He's smiling. He's disarmed and disarming.

'I've never had anything as beautiful as this.'

I sit down next to him.

'Keep going. I'm lending it to you but you have to take care of it.'

As I listen to myself say this, I can't help but think that I am making the umpteenth big mistake.

I see the better but grab hold of the worse.

Totò smiles with his still-bright eyes.

'It's my talent,' he says as he kisses my brother's guitar.

He hugs me.

I know I'm a dead man. That's what one part of me says.

I know that I'm alive, says the other part.

5

The evening is punctuated by dim lights and the alien glow of electric mosquito-killers outside the sidewalk cafes. You can smell the blend of burning mosquito coils and fried food. The girls' exposed skin and the mousse in their hair reawakens the hunt in streets that are ruled by the survival instincts of the species.

'You're only an hour late. Where were you?' Gianni asks me.

'I had some things I needed to do.'

'In summertime? You've got to be kidding.'

'So tell us what happened to you. Why didn't you leave?'

'There's got to be something you're not telling us. Is she blond with blue eyes? Have you already gotten . . .?'

It's an eloquent gesture.

I order a pizza and a beer. And then I tell my friends everything. As they listen, they find it hard to believe, but they also show compassion.

'Why don't you guys come with me?'

'Where to?'

'To give me a hand in Brancaccio?'

'We're on vacation, Federico. I don't know if you're familiar with the concept.'

'My brain isn't on vacation. Just the opposite. I guess you could say that it just got back from a very long vacation. We are organizing an event to commemorate the first anniversary of Borsellino's death. There will be athletic competitions: Track, cycling, and tug of war. There will be a cake-baking competition for the mothers and there will be plenty of food to eat. It needs to be a day that people remember! And we need help to make sure that it's all done in the most professional manner possible. All we need is for everyone to give a little bit of their time . . .'

They all nod. Of course, of course. We'll begin getting organized. I just need to find a free moment. Definitely, before it gets started. This is definitely going to take a lot of work. Unfortunately, I have to go the beach with my parents. Otherwise, I'd be there in a heartbeat. Maybe when I get back. I volunteered for something once. I'll be there for sure. But I'm already busy that weekend. Don Pino is still the best. The thing is, my grandmother isn't exactly doing so well.

The litany of excuses continues in the form of clichés and platitudes.

'Why don't you just say that you're not coming instead of giving me your lame excuses?'

'Just because you've decided to be a hero doesn't mean that you need to think you're better than us.'

'Hero? What are you talking about? I'm asking you to give up a couple of hours of your time when you don't have anything to do anyway.'

'Has Don Pino brainwashed you? I've always said you should stay away from priests.'

'You have no idea what you're talking about. You guys are nothing but a bunch of lame excuses.'

'Excuse us for not being heroes,' comments Gianni sarcastically. He's always defended me at times like this. But now I realize how distant we've become.

'What do heroes have to do with it? As always, you haven't understood anything. Heroes are just men with balls. You don't even remember where you left your balls.'

'It's too dangerous. Just forget it, Federico. It's better to avoid people like that. I'm telling you as your friend,' Gianni concludes as he cuts me off.

'How would you know?'

'There are certain things you just know. You are talking about Brancaccio, Fede. Let me just say it again: Brancaccio.'

'You know what? Go to hell. Let me say it again: Go to hell.'

'Calm down. What's wrong with you?'

'What's wrong is that you are breaking my balls.'

I get up and leave.

Just let me go for a walk. No destination. I just want to lick the wounds of this city with my eyes. The winding, light-speckled streets form a maze that is too complex for my legs tonight.

A scooter rolls up beside me. It's Gianni.

'Did you think we were going to say goodbye like that? Get on.'

I hop on his souped-up scooter without thinking twice about it. And we head to one of our favorite places. It's where we smoked our first cigarette. It was also my last cigarette, since it was followed by a cough that made me feel like I was being asphyxiated for two days.

It's a spot near Vergine Maria beach where they used to keep the tuna boats. No one has used it for years. It has a tower with a balcony that looks out over the sea. It looks like it came straight out of a fairytale.

All you can see before you is the black darkness of the sea. It rises up like an immense beast that's exhausted from the heat of the day. It pants slowly.

'Tell me what's really going on, because I don't get it.'

'I've fallen in love.'

'With who?'

'A girl from Brancaccio. Her name is Lucia.'

'Why did you have go to Brancaccio to fall in love? With all the girls here in Palermo? What about Agnese? She's been after you for months now.'

'This isn't a game.'

'Are you boyfriend and girlfriend?'

'No. We've only spoken to each other three times. And one of those times was a fight.'

'Come on! That's just what you call your average Platonic love. Snap out of it, Fede!'

'But there's more to it than that.'

'What is it?'

'Everything.'

'What do you mean, everything?'

'Everything else. Life there just seems more real to me than ever before. I couldn't go on living in unreality. If I had gone to England, it would have been like swimming in the kiddie pool after having swum in the sea.'

'So what's so real about Brancaccio?'

'The children. And the things that you can do for them, even though it's hard to make a difference. And then there's Don Pino. He has so much energy. I don't know where he gets it.'

'You're not converting, are you?'

'Converting to what?'

'How should I know? Have you started praying as well?'

'No. I'm talking about living without feeling alive. It's as if up until now I had lived in the magical world of children who have everything going their way, just the way they want it to go. It's different there: Things happen only if you have the courage to make them happen.'

'So what's this Lucia like? Does she know how to speak Italian? Or does she only speak Sicilian?'

'Don't be an idiot.'

A gentle gust of wind caresses the tops of the palm trees and makes the stars shudder slightly.

'She has beautiful green eyes and black hair like the sea tonight. She likes reading. She's not like other girls.'

'The last time I checked there was no shortage of black hair, green eyes, and books where we live.'

'Sure. But she's real.'

'I sure hope so, Federico. This wouldn't be the first time you fell in love with a girl that only exists in your imagination.'

'What I'm trying to say is that she is brave. She doesn't run away, she doesn't back down. She takes life as it is and she doesn't let it crush her.'

'How could you know that? You just met her.'

'Come and see for yourself, Gianni.'

'I'm about to leave, Fede.'

'How are things going between you and Giulia?'

'Good.'

'What do you mean by "good"?'

'It has its ups and downs.'

'You could stay a few extra days in the city. You should come. You could even bring Giulia.'

'To do what?'

'You could give me a hand with the kids' soccer games. Giulia could help Lucia.'

'I don't know. It would be tough to change our plans at the last minute.'

'I know a little about that, actually. When you do it for the first time, it gives you independence.'

'Didn't your parents get crazy mad?'

'They're the ones who wanted a second child. And this is the child they got.'

'Lucky them.'

I give Gianni a gentle pat on the shoulder and we sit there in silence watching the sea. You could do this for hours without getting bored. Now the sea looks like it's been paved with the darkness of the night. Maybe it's harder to stay and endure on land than it is to put out to sea. It's even harder not to embrace the vastness that the sea has stuffed into your heart.

6

I've invited Lucia to come over to my house to work on the script for *Little Orlando*. I couldn't wait to show her my room but now everything seems inadequate, including myself.

Lucia arrives dressed like herself. Total simplicity is one of her best traits. It's thanks to her that I learned the difference between a girl who shows off and a girl who shows herself. The first type of girl interposes a demonstration of who she wants to be between herself and others. And before she'll have anything to do with you, you need to move past her layers of feigned insecurity. The second type of girl doesn't protect herself with any demonstration. She simply wants to be the product of who she already is.

I have nothing to add. Lucia doesn't wear makeup. Her skin is like that described in medieval Arab poetry, the art of spices and the unwitting exoticism of this land. Maybe I'm idealizing her. It's all Petrarch's fault. I'm still afraid to say it, but I believe that *the name that Love wrote in my heart* is hers.

Lucia is made of calm light and fresh shadows. Of clear water on days of thirst. And here you are in my room, in my port. Now that you see my things, I understand how pitiful they are and how little I have to offer you. But you can dock here, in this serene little port.

'Are they all yours?'

'Yes.'

She examines them one by one. My books. Underlined, dog-eared, and worn. I go into battle with my books.

'Why do you underline certain sentences?'

'So I can remember them.'

'You want to keep all of that in your head?'

'Is it wrong to want that?'

'No. But I believe that life is much greater than what we can fit in our heads. Sometimes it seems that you want to break everything down into little pieces so that you can keep it all under control.'

'That doesn't seem like such a bad thing to me.'

'But it's impossible to do. You can't control everything.'

'Maybe it's just because I'm a little scared.'

'Of what?'

'I'm not sure.'

'There you go with your "I'm not sure." It always comes to that. You make me laugh.'

'It beats crying.'

Lucia smiles.

'What are your favorite five words, Lucia?'

She doesn't seem to be surprised by the question. She thinks about it. She takes one of my books and opens it. She writes something with a pencil. Then she turns suddenly and mixes the book in with the others.

'You'll have to find it. Now can we get to work? I have a problem with the finale, and some of the rhymes aren't working. Let me show you.'

I try to commit to memory the area where she hid the book. And then I focus on Lucia's handwritten script. My mother comes in with a pitcher of iced tea.

'Who is this pretty girl?'

'Lucia.'

Lucia gets up and shakes her hand and smiles.

'You have a beautiful home, ma'am. It has so many different rooms, and it's full of things and light.'

'Thank you,' says my mother. She seems uncertain as to whether or not she understands what Lucia is saying.

'Do you go to school with Federico? I don't think I've ever seen you before.'

'No. We're just friends. We met in Brancaccio.'

'Ah, you're from Brancaccio. Federico never tells us what he does there. All we know is that he gave up a trip to England so he could go give a hand there. So what do the two of you do there?'

'You should ask your son,' says Lucia dryly.

'Ah. Okay, I see. I'll leave you two to your work. I hope I didn't interrupt you.'

Neither one of us says anything.

'Why do you think you're better than us?'

'What?'

'Did you hear what she said? "He gave up a trip to England." As if we were sick people who needed help.'

'I don't think that's what she meant to say. She just wanted to . . .'

'She wanted to point out that you came to Brancaccio because we were begging for help. We were doing just fine before you arrived, you know?'

'You're getting carried away. You told me not to judge others but now you're doing just that.'

'I'm not getting carried away. We are too different, Federico. It takes more than having a big house and plenty of money to be better than someone else. If I ever go to England, it will be with my own money. And God only knows how much money it will take.

Life for you has always been a piece of cake. And now you want to teach others how to live? It's not as easy as that.'

'I don't want to teach anyone anything. It's hard enough to know what I should do myself. I came because Don Pino asked me to. He needed someone to help him.'

'I know that. And you did the right thing when you told him you would. But I don't ever again want to hear about how you "gave up" your trip to England.'

The Lucia of my literary dreams is turning into a piece of raw reality. But I can't hate her for what she just said. I'm ready to change, to improve myself, to transform myself.

'I don't need anyone's help, Federico.'

I put my finger on her lips so that she will stop talking. Then I put my finger on her cheek. She stops, surprised. And for a moment she rests her face on my hand. It's the first time in my life that I have experienced a caress. And no caress ever described in a book comes even close to this contact.

As if right on cue, like a jellyfish when you go swimming, Manfredi pokes his head in. I knew he would do this.

'Sorry, Federico, but I need my guitar. Oh, sorry! I interrupted you. I didn't know you were busy.'

'This is . . .'

'Lucia, I imagine.'

Manfredi's dramatic entrance and his contagious grin make Lucia smile.

'All my brother does is talk about you. And I bet when he's not talking about you, he's thinking about you.'

'Cut it out.' I'm trying to get him to leave. I can feel my blood welling up in my cheeks. And I can see it in Lucia's as well.

'So what about my guitar?'

'Yes, your guitar.'

'Yeah, my guitar. You know? The one with the oval thingy and the neck and the strings. Do you remember it? I used to have one and then I lent it to you. I'd like to play it a bit now.'

'Sure. It's not available right now.'

'What's that supposed to mean?'

'I lent it to that kid I was telling you about.'

'You lent it? My guitar? Are you crazy?'

'Yes, he is crazy. I told him so. But your brother has too big of a heart and when he saw how happy that boy was, he just couldn't take it away from him.'

Manfredi seems taken aback by Lucia's easy-going confidence.

'In the end it's just an oval with a neck and some strings, right?' she adds, smiling.

'Yes, that's true. But it happens to be *my* oval.'

'That's just another reason you should be proud! Just think how great it will be when Totò discovers how talented he is, thanks to your guitar. Isn't that great?'

'I guess so.'

I can't understand if what is happening is real or if I am part of one of the best films possible. Lucia has won Manfredi over. You can tell from the little dimple that just appeared on my brother's right cheek. If he likes her, then game over.

'What do you do? Are you a student?'

'I'm studying neurology.'

'What's your specialization?'

'I want to become a neurosurgeon. To study and cure cerebral pathologies. Illnesses of the brain.'

'Does that include Parkinson's disease?'

'Of course.'

'My grandfather has Parkinson's. He has to use a wheelchair. And he drools all over his bib. Lately we can't understand anything he says. I can't tell you what I wouldn't give to see him get a little bit better.'

'What therapy does he do?'

'I don't know. All I know is that he takes a lot of pills.'

'They're experimenting with new cures that will help people to better manage their paralysis.'

'Maybe you could take a look at him. You might have some ideas for how we could help him get better.'

'I'm still doing my training. I'm not a doctor yet.'

'But you will be a doctor one day. I don't see what the big difference is.'

'In some ways . . . What do you do?'

'I'm going to teacher's college to become a schoolteacher. But there are so many other things I'd like to do.'

'Like what?'

'Theater.'

'Do you want to be an actress?'

'No. I want to direct. Which reminds me. You're invited to come see the show that your brother and I are working on in Brancaccio together with the kids.'

In just five lines, Lucia has explained what I haven't been able to explain in weeks.

'Is he in it, too? He didn't say a thing.'

'He's playing the part of Charlemagne. He's great.' She enunciates the last words solemnly and then she looks up at the ceiling.

My brother bursts out laughing.

'Him? He's still afraid of the dark,' says Manfredi, really pushing it.

'Every king has his weakness,' answers Lucia.

They both smile. I watch them, speechless.

'So I'm just going to have to come myself to get my guitar back.'

'Sounds like it,' says Lucia.

'Sounds good. I'll leave you two to your work. And you and I will settle up later.'

As he leaves, he takes advantage of the fact that Lucia has her back to him: With eyes wide open, he gives me a sign of his approval as if I had just scored a goal at the World Cup.

'So where were we?' asks Lucia.

'Here.'

I put my hand on her cheek and then she puts her hand over mine.

7

The girl screams into his hand as he squeezes her neck. He lunges her body toward the darkness and it swallows her up.

In another time, bandits would lay in wait for merchants. They would stop their carts in the dusty streets and demand the *pizzo*, payment for protection. They knew full well that they were robbing working fathers from poor families, and they would only take a small portion of their wares.

The *pizzo* was always the most hidden and most precious part of the wagon. It was a heavy plank of engraved wood that was placed under the strong box to protect its weakest side. It was often decorated with a sacred image so as to ward off bad luck and bandits. Without it, the axle could easily break and the weight could break the wagon and the merchant's back. And without the wagon, there would be no income.

'If you don't give us money, we'll make you pay with the *pizzo*.'

They did not kill. They were men of principle. But they needed to make a living like everyone else. They just had to be paid. Otherwise they would smash your *pizzo* and your wagon would be ruined.

The merchant would pay and continue on his journey. It was a tax and it came with guarantees. It was always the same bandits and so there wasn't any room for others who wanted to take your life.

The owner of the shop hasn't paid. And Nuccio has come to take what he's owed.

The suffocated screams are those of a girl whose spirit is being broken by Nuccio.

He leaves, struts out with justice in his hands. He's proud of having done what needed to be done, even though no one asked him to do it.

He can't feel a thing. Hell is deaf and dumb.

8

The days roll by in a calendar of light and darkness.

The preparations for the July 25 event have reached a feverish pace.

Dario, with his deft and steady hands, is helping Lucia to hang banners. Every once in a while, with his brush in his hand, he stops and stares into the distance. It's as if he has forgotten which letter to add.

'Come on, Dario. We don't have a lot of time,' says Lucia as she wakes him up again.

He watches her with a serious look on his face.

'What are you looking at?'

'Can you give me a hug?'

Lucia goes over to him and wraps her arms around him, and he buries his face into her chest. He sobs uncontrollably and hugs her so tightly that it hurts.

'What's the matter, Dario? What happened?'

He slowly breaks away but can't bear to look up at her. Then, brimming with shame, he runs away.

'Daddy, can you put me on your shoulders?' asks the child.

'Why?'

'So that I can see better. I don't want to miss anything from here. I'm too little.'

'Right you are. When you're not tall enough, your daddy is plenty tall.'

He picks him up and puts him on his shoulders. The child grabs his forehead. Suddenly, the blue expanse reveals itself before him. It had been hidden by the beach cabins that transform the Mondello shore every summer into a colorful and impregnable fort.

'Wow! It's great! You can see the entire sea.'

'Do you like it?'

'Yes, Daddy. It's really great. I wish I could always see everything like this.'

'All you have to do is ask and you got it.'

'Would you buy me an ice cream?'

'Only if you're a good boy.'

'I'm always a good boy.'

'Well, not always. You fuss sometimes, too.'

'But I'm a little kid and little kids fuss sometimes. Didn't you when you were little?'

'Every once in a while. That's true.'

'So will you buy me an ice cream?'

'You're sharp, aren't you? Okay, let's go. Do you want yours made with cream or not?'

'With cream! What kind of ice cream would it be if it wasn't made with cream?'

The boy bounces on his father's back as if he were riding a horse.

The Hunter lets his son keep on bouncing and holds his legs together using his strong 'dad' hands.

Lucia asks another kid to take over and she starts looking for Dario. She finds him sitting by himself and staring into the distance.

'What's going on?'

He doesn't answer. He just shakes his head, almost without realizing he's doing so.

'What's the matter?'

'They do bad things to me, Lucia. They always do bad things to me.'

'Who?'

'Grown-ups.'

Dario looks down at the ground and silence wraps itself around him yet again.

9

July 25 is one of those Sundays when the sun roars. But an unexpected breeze blows from the sea and cools things down a bit. It's the day that Don Pino and his team have organized their event in honor of Borsellino, one year after his murder. Brancaccio for Life. A day of track and cycling competitions, all kinds of games, and a big feast. The Region of Sicily had promised financial support but they didn't even pry a single lira from their coffers. Everything was paid for by donations from people who live in the neighborhood. No help was received from any of the local politicians. They only show up for official occasions to scrounge around for votes. They don't lift a finger for Brancaccio.

In the late afternoon, Don Pino's friend Roberto, a professor, reads the speech that they have written together:

> It's seven in the morning on a July day just like this one, July 19 last year. Even though it's Sunday, Paolo Borsellino wakes up early like always. His daughter Lucia is sitting in the armchair in the room where he is working. The morning light is still cool. He doesn't notice her, though. He's preoccupied with that letter, the last page the magistrate would write.
>
> It's the answer to a teacher who has invited him to speak to a

group of young people. After a series of mishaps, the judge wasn't able to participate nor was he able to write back. And so the teacher sent him another letter in which she complained about his silence. Mortified, Borsellino apologizes for not being able to attend the event, and he answers some of the questions that the teacher had asked him.

His work over the last few months hasn't allowed him to spend time with his children. They are always still sleeping when he leaves the house and he gets back so late that they are already in bed. That Sunday, he is determined to spend the day with his family. That's why he's already at his desk at dawn. Lucia says that her father was interrupted by a telephone call and only then did he notice that she was sitting in the armchair in the corner of his study.

He asks her if she would like to go to the beach. She's been studying for an exam at the university and, until now, she hasn't been able to lie out in the sun.

'Maybe you can sunbathe a little.'

He suggests that they go for a swim and then to her grandmother's house before coming back home. He will work and she will study. Lucia turns him down because it's her friend's birthday and she's been invited to lunch. They will do their last bit of studying together for the exam.

While studying in her friend's room, Lucia will hear the bomb explode outside her grandmother's house. The bomb that kills her father and would have killed her as well. It was the Sunday when he was determined not to work and he had taken his wife to the beach. Then he disappeared with a friend of his to spend some time on the water in his boat. His bodyguards watched apprehensively from the shore. That would be the last time he saw his city and its immense port from the sea. It's the same sea from which this cool, refreshing breeze is blowing today.

Today, it's up to us to remember this man, who used to say to his wife: 'Italy would be so great if everyone made a little dream come true and then shared it with everyone else.' And it's up to us to forget instead the word written in the last line of his last letter to the teacher: 'Consensus.'

'The power of the Mafia lies in consensus,' wrote Borsellino.

Today we are here to remember a man who tried to erase this word. And he paid for it with his life.

That's why our homeowners' association, together with the support of the Holy Father Center, has officially asked that Via Brancaccio be renamed Via Falcone e Borsellino. Because, as 3P always says, every great change starts with small things.

There are a lot of people there. A journalist is taking notes. The article he will publish will cost him his job at the newspaper where he works. And he's not the last person who will commit a similar error: Telling the truth.

When the professor finishes reading, for a few seconds silence fills the piazza and the balconies and the windows and the sky. Then applause washes away the silence. It chases it out together with the fear.

I'm watching the kids' sweaty faces. Francesco has a medal around his neck. He won it in a foot race. Totò has a Donald Duck hat on to protect his skin from the sun. Dario's eyes are lost in the sky. A harmony of faces and smiles. Among them, there's one too familiar to be real.

Manfredi. For a moment, our eyes lock: He's proud of me. Brothers who share battles and defeats, who share laughter and tears: They will always have something to talk about over the course of their lives. No organism is capable of preserving memories like a couple of brothers who love each other. Manfredi nods as he watches me, and now I am sure that I did the right thing.

'My brother is here,' I whisper to Lucia as I wipe away a shiny bead of sweat from her left cheek before the sun and wind can grab it for themselves.

'What did you say?'

'Nothing. Nothing.'

She leans on me imperceptibly and that moment becomes a perfect memory. I don't have that sensation of incompleteness that I usually feel when I experience something beautiful. The contact is light but that's all it takes because she and I know, without saying a word to one another, that it was contact that I had desired.

Then the crowd is a mix of salutations and words. Such joy hasn't been seen in this piazza for a long time. And the crowd can barely contain it. For a second, everyone realizes that normality is a luxury around here. It's a luxury enjoyed by those who let hope complicate their hearts and actions.

Even the TV cameras know this since they usually only come to Brancaccio to report on crime. They interview Don Pino, and his words ring out in the living rooms of those who are sleeping and those who never sleep. No one knows which is more dangerous.

'We have been working for three years without any results. In the waiting rooms of mayors, superintendents, the prefect, and even the police chief and the director of the city services office. We've been asking for at least a middle school, a social and health services district, and a little bit of green where the kids can play and run around.

'All of our requests have been endorsed by the neighborhood council and the homeowners' association. The result? Nothing. There is hope for the district: The special superintendent has promised that he will begin drawing up the necessary documents. The buildings are already there. We will never stop asking because the doors will eventually open for those who keep knocking. Even here.'

It's the beginning of an earthquake, and the TV cameras have documented it by letting those rock-solid words roll out into the ether. Antennae will receive them and transform them into signals that travel across cables. Unabated, they will reach TV sets in people's homes like bombs waiting for their fuses to be lit.

Everyone believes that nothing like this has ever been seen in Brancaccio. A target so clear has never been seen.

Manfredi shakes Signor Mario's hand.

'You can see how he is. I think those are all the medicines he takes,' says Lucia. 'Look how many bottles.'

I watch the scene as if I were watching a movie. My brother is at Lucia's house. Everything feels unbalanced, confused. And yet the two men seem natural together: Two different worlds which complement one another completely. It's hard to understand why evolution has driven us so far apart.

In the end, two horses eat from the same trough even after a race where one won and the other lost. And they don't waste time focusing on their differences. They eat in the same manner. We are beings that run counter to evolution. With the same brain and the same hands, we create both *The Divine Comedy* and *Mein Kampf*.

'The medicines are fine but they need to be combined with other drugs so that Mario can have more mobility and more sensation. I'll get them at the hospital and I'll make sure you have them.'

'There's no need for that. We're covered for our costs. All you need to do is let us know which medicines he should take and our general practitioner will prescribe them.'

'Whatever you think is best. But first let me ask my attending physician and maybe we can try them out for a while.'

'Whatever you say.'

Manfredi already seems like a real doctor. I'm proud of my brother. I can see the joy of someone who can alleviate someone else's pain on Lucia and Gemma's faces. Life is simple when it is made so by love.

10

The little girl is sitting in the shade and her dog is sitting next to her. There are three arches over the terrace of an abandoned building that faces the sea. Her doll doesn't say a thing. She looks straight ahead with her ever-open blue eyes.

The sea unfolds disproportionately and it makes for an optical illusion where it ends and blends in with the sky. Somewhere, land contains the sea. And the child doesn't yet know if the land is in the sea or the sea is in the land. She only knows that she would like to get to the other side. Maybe her father is there waiting for her. But she doesn't know how to swim. And she has no one to teach her.

Pieces of glass, condoms, and syringes are scattered on the salt-encrusted pavement.

The child longs for love and she longs to escape.

The white foam on the water looks like little doves and they make the water seem more inviting.

The doll sitting next to the girl keeps her eyes wide open as she stares out at the horizon. The girl describes the sea to her: 'If something as beautiful as the sea exists, then life must be beautiful too, at least somewhere.'

Then she holds the doll to her chest and her tears, the signs of neglect, fall from her eyes.

At a certain point, the tears stop. The barren sea is still there and so are the hunger and thirst that force her to return to the fire.

11

The light speckles her hair like the light of the moon on the night-time sea. She is reading aloud and explaining the stories to the children.

Every question generates another. Lucia never seems to tire and her talent as a narrator is something I never imagined I would find around here.

She moves her hands as if she were a puppeteer. Her words come to life and her eyes become even deeper and sharper and they light up, now filled with fear, as she adapts her expression to convey the feelings of her imaginary characters.

Her way of laughing and taking little breaks touches me deep inside. It explores my soul and reveals otherwise empty zones that lie inside. Her presence gives me a sense of self-possession. The more I watch her, the more I long for someone to lose, someone to cry for, with all the pain that comes with putting someone into your heart's heart.

12

Mother Nature moves without being seen, like God. The meeting takes place in a basement, safe from indiscreet eyes. The muscle of his operation in this territory is the Turk, a nickname not owed as much to his dark complexion as to the cigarette smoke that follows him wherever he goes. The description is spot on and not open to interpretation.

'I read it. I read it all in the papers. So now they have parties for cops in Brancaccio? Journalists, TV cameras, and cops. And more cops. What do they think this is, New York City? It's crazy!'

'Crazy it is. I told you that you needed to be careful.'

'He's making us look like a bunch of assholes.'

'A communist priest who talks shit to newspapers. That's all we need. Who does he think he is? The Pope?'

'So he wants a party? We'll throw a special party just for him, with plenty of little candles.'

'Want me to take care of the cake?'

'Yes, but not right away. They just had their party. Let's wait a month or two. The right opportunity will present itself.'

The Turk gestures with his forefinger and thumb as if he were grinding something.

'Take your time. There's no rush. First let's give him a taste of how it's going to end. Maybe the lost sheep will see the error of its ways.'

'Okay. It's best that the meat be tender for the party. Otherwise it will be too chewy.'

'Speaking of eating, have someone bring me some good bread and some *panelle*. And take one for yourself as well.'

'It's always a pleasure to carry out your orders,' responds the Turk with a smile.

Mother Nature would never accept losing control of his territory. It would be a sign of weakness, and one cannot afford to be weak in the era of the Corleonesi. The words of Don Luchino are seared in his mind: 'You're allowing yourselves to be humiliated by a priest from your territory. That's ridiculous. You should have done something earlier.'

But who even noticed him? He was just doing things that priests do: Communions, confessions, weddings, and catechism for the children.

Mother Nature and his brothers need to reaffirm their hold on power, once and for all. Others blew up a section of freeway and an entire city street. But they haven't been able to break the will of a priest who's only five feet and seven inches tall. There's a dangerous rival in those five feet and seven inches, capable of obtaining what should only belong to them. He needs to be eliminated because he's like them and could take their place. The moment to show their strength has arrived.

The Turk will show it to Mother Nature.

The Hunter will show it to the Turk.

Nuccio will show it to the Hunter.

For ever and ever.

13

'Don't come around here anymore. You understand me?' says a boy who's bigger than me.

There are two of them and they push me up against a wall. The street is depressingly deserted. Only the televisions, inexhaustible, fill the silence. The sea is far away and it has stopped speaking. I can feel my saliva drying up in my throat.

'What am I doing wrong?'

'What are you doing? You've been spending time with a priest who's breaking our balls. And you also need to stop eyeing the girls around here.'

'What are you talking about?'

'Nuccio, this guy's being a smartass.'

A punch lands on my face before I can duck. For a moment, a flash of light shines in my eyes. And then everything goes black. The adrenaline explodes in my legs. With no help from me, they start running and surprise my aggressors. There's a bitter taste in my mouth and my lungs are burning. But I'm running like there's no tomorrow. The alley that seemed so small now seems endless. I'm faster than them. If I can get out of here, I know I can reach safety. Two more suddenly appear and block my escape. Before I can manage to stop, they've already got their hands on me. There's no time for words. Words are useless.

I try to muster all my strength and resist the vise that's pressing in on me. But one of them kicks me in the knee and I'm knocked to the ground. I don't even know if my leg is still completely attached. I kick with my other leg but strike nothing. I feel the pain of a blade cutting my back.

Someone grabs me by the hair and beats my head against the asphalt. I have blood in my eyes. A kick to the stomach and my saliva is transformed into dense, bitter liquid.

'And just be thankful that I didn't kill you. Don't show yourself around here anymore,' says the voice from before. It's hard to make out with all the blood on my face. I'm still on the ground looking for air in my lungs. They've been emptied out by fear.

When I see their four shadows leaving, I spread my arms open to see if they are still attached to my body. I feel like my whole body's been strewn about. As I stare at the sky, my throat is leathery from the dryness. Now I know what violence is.

I try to get up but my knees can't take it. And one of my eyes is closed. I touch my hair with a hand that hardly belongs to me: It's dripping with blood.

I pull myself up and sit against a wall. I feel like crying but the rage and the pain leave no room for self-pity. The only thing I want to feel on my face is the sea and its wind. I wish I were in England or anywhere else but here, in hell.

Minutes pass. Maybe hours. The street is now dark save for the yellowish light of lamps hanging on a wire between the houses.

When I try to move, the pain knocks the wind out of me.

It's Lucia who finds me and she's the last thing I see. I hear a jumble of words being shouted. Then everything goes dark.

14

I wake up in a hospital room.

My head burns like there's a worm grazing on it from the inside. My eye is throbbing and it's bandaged.

'How are you feeling?' asks Lucia. I don't think I've ever seen her this worried.

'Tip-top shape. Doesn't it show?'

'Nothing's broken, luckily. They gave you some stitches on your eyebrow. You're just going to have to rest for a while before you get better.'

Little by little, I discover my body parts through the pain. My knee is wrapped up as well.

'Who brought me here?'

'The ambulance did. Do you want something to drink?'

'I dunno. The guys who beat me up. One of them was named Nuccio. You need to get away from here, Lucia. You've got to get away. It's hell. You need to sign up for college. We could go to another city. I can't leave you here with these beasts. That's what they are: Beasts.'

Lucia comes over to me with a glass of water.

'You're right. It's too dangerous. But it's not all hell. Like Don Pino says, hell is when you are no longer able to love. When you can no longer give of yourself and receive from others. It's still possible.'

'It's an illusion. It's not worth it.'

'Well, I don't want you to come here anymore. You have to stop coming here.'

'You should come away with me.'

'You just don't get it, do you? This is my neighborhood. It's where my family lives. Running away and making a life somewhere else isn't going to make me happy. You just don't get it. You really don't understand, do you?'

'Then forgive me for not getting it. I just risked being killed and I really don't get it.'

'Exactly. So don't come here anymore. We have to stop seeing each other. This is it. Never again.'

She puts the bottle of water on the stand next to the bed and she leaves without saying another word.

'Wait! Lucia, wait!'

The door remains closed and the bitter taste of being abandoned is added to my pain. I try to get up and run after her but my parents come in just at that moment.

'What happened?' asks my father.

'Are you alright, Federico?' my mother cries.

I close my eyes and lay my head on the pillow as I submit to my parents' interrogation, which is at once emotional and rational. My father takes care of the rational part. My mother, the emotional part. Together, they make a complete being. My father doesn't say it but his conclusion is that I deserve what happened to me. Still, he's proud to have a son with guts.

My mother's conclusion is nothing new: This game of trying to be a hero is over and I will never set foot again in that neighborhood. She will talk to Don Pino, and do a thousand other things that I don't remember, because at some point I fell asleep.

I don't know how long I've slept but my brother wakes me up by tickling my foot. Tickling me has always been his favorite form of torture. His top technique was to block my legs by sitting on my knees. And then he would hold my arms over his head with one hand and tickle me under my arms with the other.

I would laugh so hard that I would practically choke. And I would offer him anything he wanted: Setting and clearing the table every day for a month; loading and unloading the dishwasher; folding his pajamas, and other similar favours. When I would finally manage to break free, I was as tired as a beached whale.

He stares at me and starts to laugh.

'You are looking really good. Now you can really call yourself a "beat" poet.'

I smile and a jolt of pain radiates from my eye all the way down to my toes.

'Cut it out. It's not funny.'

'And if I don't? Then what will you do?'

'I hope you get diarrhea!'

'If you were a woman, I would marry you, Poet. You're my hero. You really got clobbered. I would never have had the courage.'

I smile, but cautiously.

'Let me know if you need anything. As long as you're off your feet, you can count on me. My little Kerouac!'

'Go teach Totò how to play the guitar.'

15

The loneliness of the days that follow is so thick that you could cut it with a knife. I'm a recluse, and the only thing that I have to do is to follow the chromatic evolution of my eye from black to purple to reddish-purple with violet undertones. I read and watch every television show, from *Supercar* to *Happy Days*. Don Pino came to see me. And he went to see Giuseppe in Malaspina too.

He apologized to my parents. It was his fault, he told them, that things went the way they did. He agrees with them that I need to stay away from Brancaccio. It's become too dangerous.

'How's Giuseppe?'

'He's as good as he can be. He told me to tell you hello.'

'I barely even spoke to him.'

'He remembers you. He has a good heart, that kid. That's why I can't give up on him. I've learned to tell the difference between those who are simply ill-mannered and those who are ill-intentioned.'

'I think I've learned how to do that, too,' I say as I point to my eye.

Don Pino smiles.

'I'm going to take them to Mondello in a few days.'

'Who?'

'The kids. You should come with us, if you like. That way you could see them and say goodbye.'

'What will my parents say?'

'It's not like you're going to Brancaccio. You're going to Mondello.' Don Pino smiles and winks.

During the first week of August, the sunlight triumphs unimpeded in fantasies that seem like hallucinations. The July heat makes your knees weak. The August heat cooks your thoughts.

How many hourglasses do you need to empty a beach? How long does it take for a bud to become an apple? Is there an average time, or is each a unique event? At what speed does light travel when it lights up the sea in the morning? Is it a precise or an arbitrary distance that allows for combustion between two people looking at each other? Is the black in Lucia's hair the absence of light or the reverse, the complete absorption of light? How much does a secret weigh? What's the ratio between happiness and the broadness of a smile? How do you calculate the volume of the heart?

My brain peppers me with useless questions that go unanswered as I continue to obsess over them in the white loneliness. I feel like Kafka's Gregor, who wakes up one day to discover that he's been transformed into a cockroach and that all of his fears have become reality.

I grab Kafka's book and I find five words written in pencil on page 34: *Waves, darkness, caress, dream, seed.*

Those are the five words that Lucia wrote. If I had never been beat up, I would never have found them. Those five words are the elements of the formula. I just need to figure out how to put them together so that I can tell her: 'My love, how beautiful you are!'

16

'I'm leaving, Lucia.'

'What are you talking about, Serena? Where are you going?'

'Away from here.'

'What's going on? First you disappear without saying anything, and now you're leaving for good? What's the matter?'

'I'm pregnant.'

Lucia is about to hug her but she stops. The expression on Serena's face speaks loud and clear: Something's wrong. Even the smile that instantly appeared on Lucia's face has vanished, as if she felt guilty for her instinctive reaction.

'Nobody knows.'

Serena bursts out crying. Lucia hugs her friend as she sobs uncontrollably.

Nuccio. Violence. The father. A baby. Abortion. Running away. Leaving everything behind. Heading north. These disconnected phrases emerge as if plucked from the waking moments of a nightmare that never ends.

'Did you tell Don Pino?'

'What good would that do? My life is over.'

Lucia's strength fails her. Hell has taken everything, even her friend's womb. They've shared a thousand tidbits of gossip and have chatted for countless hours on end. She's her partner in crime when it comes to makeup and clothes they've bought together without ever trying them on. She's the big sister who will be going to college. And now the only thing that will remain of her friend is a body dried up by pain and a fatally fertile womb.

17

The van limps along but there's no room for complaints since they are all packed in so tightly. The kids are beside themselves with joy because Don Pino is taking them to the beach. Lucia is giving him a hand. They are all sitting on folding chairs. The van doesn't have seats, and so Don Pino has remedied the situation with these chairs. They sway back and forth between the kids' laughing and Lucia's carsickness.

'I've never been to Mondello,' says Francesco for the second time.

'Never?'

'Never. What's it like?'

'The beach is gorgeous and the water is clear. The sand is white and very fine. It looks like flour. And there are wooden beach cabins where you can change into your bathing suit and there are tons of food stands where you can get ice cream when it's too hot.'

'Are we going to get ice cream?'

'Of course we are!'

'When do we get there?' asks the girl with the doll. She's sings her question like the chorus of a song as she taps on Don Pino's shoulder.

'A little bit farther and we'll be there.'

'Wow! Mondello is far away!'

'You'll enjoy it all the more when we get there.'

'What does the doll have to say? Does she have a bathing suit for swimming?'

'No, she doesn't know how to swim. She's just going to lie out in the sun.'

'And what about you?'

'I don't know how to swim, either.'

'You need to learn!' says Don Pino.

'It's easy. All you have to do is float,' Francesco reassures her.

'My father was teaching me but he's not here anymore.'

'Where is he?'

'He's gone.'

'My dad isn't here either. But my mom learned me how to swim.'

'My mom doesn't have time.'

'Well, Don Pino will teach you then! Right?' asks Francesco, making sure to emphasize the word 'teach.'

Don Pino has a serious look on his face for a moment.

'Of course.'

The girl pulls Doll close to her so that she can give her a loving smack on the cheek.

The sun burns Don Pino's skin and beats down on his dark clothes. He's wearing a cap but it's not enough to protect him from the blazing sun. The children seem to keep popping up out of nowhere like waves. They run around and dive into the water while Lucia and I try to keep them under control. Their bodies can't seem to contain their bubbly energy. I didn't know that she would be here and when I first saw her, I was tempted to hide. She greets me with a nod but doesn't say a word to me.

I can't help but be a little ashamed of these kids. They act like wild savages who have never seen a trinket or a bead. I'm worried that I may run into someone that I know. Then I see Lucia's natural ability in catering to their needs and I try, clumsily, to imitate her. I wish I had her freedom from other people's judgment. I wish I had the freedom you get from knowing that you are doing the right thing, even though you are the only person doing it. And then I remember what Don Pino told me: They may be a little ill-mannered but they aren't ill-intentioned. And we are here to help them come into contact with beauty so that they can clean the crust from their hearts as their happiness gushes out. But Lucia is taciturn and her eyes don't shine like they usually do.

The girl with Doll is sitting at the water's edge, just getting her feet wet. Don Pino does the same. He's rolled his pants up to his knees.

'Will you teach me how to swim, Donpino?'

'Are you sure? You're not afraid anymore?'

'If you're there, I won't be afraid. I want to go behind that.'

'Behind where?'

'There. Where the line is.'

'What line?'

'The line where the sea touches the sky.'

'Why do you want to go there?'

'Because there are tons of things behind that line. Even my dad is there. I think that all the trains go there, too.'

'Who told you that?'

'Doll.'

'How does she know that?'

'She's been there.'

'When?'

'A long time ago. She's a traveling doll. She saw all the beautiful things in the world before my daddy brought her to me. She wants me to see the same things that she saw. She always tells me to keep my eyes wide open like hers. But I can't swim there.'

'I can't swim there either.'

'You can't either?'

'We can sit here together, though.'

'No. I want to go where you can't touch the bottom. Just like I used to do with my daddy. You can do that, can't you, Donpino?'

'Yes, I can,' he answers hesitantly.

Without saying another word, she takes him by the hand. They go into the water and it's not clear who's leading whom.

The boy and Lucia are amused as they watch Don Pino go into the water with his rolled-up pants and his undershirt.

They move slowly as the girl squeezes his hand with one hand while she grips Doll ever more tightly with the other.

'It's so cold!'

'Don't be silly. It's warm.'

'You're right, Donpino. It was just an excuse because I'm afraid.'

'Don't worry. We're close to the shore here.'

'No. I want to learn how to float where you can't touch the bottom.'

'Are you sure?'

'Yes, let's go.'

They keep going out into the water but at a certain point the girl needs to hold on with two hands because she can't touch the bottom anymore. She doesn't know what to do with Doll. And so Don Pino takes Doll and puts her under his arm while he helps the girl float with his hands. He's also scared of not being able to touch the bottom, but luckily he'd have to go out a few meters more before that would happen.

'My daddy told me to move my legs like a bicycle.'

'That's right.'

'Look. I know how to do it!'

'Great job. But slow down a little bit.'

'Is this better?'

'Yes, great. Now you need to do something else. You need to move your arms like you're making a circle in the water.'

'How do I do that if I need to keep holding onto you?'

'Just use one hand.'

'Are you sure?'

'Try.'

'Really? You're sure?'

'Yes.'

She lets go with one hand for a moment. But then she immediately grabs him again.

'Don't be scared.'

The girl starts to muster her courage. She lets go and starts making a circle.

'Not so fast, and now start moving your legs, too.'

'Wow! Look at me float! With just one hand!'

'Now we need to try without you holding onto me.'

'How do I do that?'

'Like you just did.'

'And what else do I have to do? Do I need to make another circle?'

'Yes, just one circle but bigger.'

She tries but immediately starts to sink. When she touches the sand with her feet she pushes up and comes back to the surface like a taut spring. She grabs onto him with both hands as she spits out water with her eyes closed. She buries her face in Don Pino's stomach.

'I almost drowned! Thank goodness you were here, Donpino!'

'I'm not leaving you. Don't worry. Should we try again?'

'But I need to rest a bit first.'

'Okay.'

The girl holds onto him tightly and watches him as he smiles.

'You are such a good girl.'

'And you are good like my daddy.'

When we say goodbye, the kids all hug me and chant my name. You can hear it all across the beach. Now I've been fingered as the one guilty of making all that racket. I start blushing. What else is life if not a game played by carefree children?

'When are you coming back?' asks Totò. 'I learned a bunch of chords and I can't wait to play them for you. Your brother is an even better teacher than you!'

'Did you meet my brother?'

'He told me that you were busy and so he substituted for you for a little while.'

So he did it after all! He didn't even tell me. That would have been too much.

I can see the happiness in Totò's eyes and I imagine my eyes look just as happy in this moment.

'I'm going away with my parents now but when I get back, I'll come see you, okay? Now keep practicing!'

'Every day. My mom can't stand it. Yesterday, she was about to throw the guitar out the window.'

'No!'

'You fell for it, didn't you? That didn't really happen. Manfredi told me that if I keep on learning like this, he's going to give me the guitar.'

I mess up his hair, still wet from swimming in the sea.

When I move toward Lucia to say goodbye, she stops me by gesturing with her hand. But she smiles approvingly.

I can't read anything in her eyes anymore.

We can't leave each other like this. Tomorrow I'll go back to Brancaccio before I am sentenced to eternal exile by my parents.

18

'Why didn't you tell me?'

'I had to go out that way and so I made a detour. I wanted to say hello to Don Pino and I also wanted to make sure that my guitar was still in one piece.'

'But then you went back, and you still didn't say anything about it.'

'I didn't want to give you the satisfaction. Have I ever done anything because you told me to do it? And besides, that kid is too cute. You were stuck at home. So what was I supposed to do? Leave him without a guitar teacher?'

Manfredi's scooter cruises through the sun-washed streets. When I confided in him that I wanted to go back to Brancaccio but that I was afraid to, he told me that he would come with me. At least there would be two of us to take a beating. I can face anything if I have my brother by my side.

We park the scooter a kilometer away. We're here for the guitar but we don't want to lose the scooter.

The train crossing introduces us to the other world of our city.

The children are finishing their rehearsal with Lucia. We wait in the corner.

'Charlemagne has returned!' exclaims Totò as he moves toward me.

The others burst out laughing.

'Did you learn any new chords?' Manfredi asks him. 'So, let me hear them.'

The child smiles and runs to get the guitar.

'What are you doing here?' Lucia asks me.

'If I'm not mistaken, you have one of my books. I came to get it before my parents exile me.'

'Okay. But I don't want you to ever come back. I'll go get it.'

'I'll come with you.'

'If you do, they'll see you with me. Are you stupid or something?'

'What should I care? Either way, this is the last time I'm coming here. That's what you told me, right?'

My brother stays with Totò and the other kids and entertains them with his songs.

We walk to Lucia's house.

'You keep telling me that I can't come here anymore, but you never want to go anywhere outside your neighborhood. The only solution would be that I come escorted by my brother or I buy a bullet-proof jacket.'

'You shouldn't joke about stuff like this, Federico. You don't seem to want to understand. Last time you got away with a few scars. Next time you might not be so lucky.'

I can see from her eyes that there's something else she'd like to say. But something is stopping her from saying it. She pushes her hair back over her shoulder with her hand and it looks like a simple wave on the nighttime sea.

We don't say another word until we get to her house. Lucia gets the book and gives it back to me.

'You keep it. It was just an excuse to see you again.'

'You are so hard-headed. You just had to come to Brancaccio to get your head broken again.'

'I also came to Brancaccio to have my heart broken. By you. I'll be fine with a broken head and a broken heart, as long as I'm still alive.'

'You won't be alive for long if you stick around here.'

'Don't get carried away.'

'Do you know who Rita Atria is?'

'No, I don't.'

'So not even you know who she is. We go to school and they don't teach us anything. They fill our heads with ideas but they forget to teach us about life.'

'So who is it? A friend of yours?'

'I feel like she could have been a friend of mine. She belonged to an important Mafia family from Partanna. They killed her father when she was eleven years old. A few years later, they killed her brother, who had also entered into that world. They were very close, and he had told her about all the business that he knew about. So she decided not keep the secrets to herself. She was a big admirer of Borsellino and she wanted to meet him and tell him everything she knew. And do you know what her mother and her relatives did? They disowned her. And she was forced to leave Palermo. Then they killed Borsellino and Rita threw herself out of a seventh-floor window a week later. She had been in Rome for weeks at that point, by herself. Borsellino had tried to get her in contact with her mother so they could reconcile. But it was no use. She was nineteen years old. Do you get that? None of her relatives even came to the funeral. Not even her mother, who had thrown her out of the house. A few weeks later, her mother visited her grave and took a hammer to the headstone and broke the photo of her daughter.'

'I'd never heard that story.'

'That's my point. The silence. As long as everyday people are silent, nothing will change in this city for the people who do decide to speak up. Our heroes are too far above us for us to imitate them. Falcone. Borsellino. They have been placed so high that they are unreachable. We need to do what Don Pino does: We need to give people the courage to stand up for their dignity. Rita didn't make it because they abandoned her. Even in death. One day I want to write a play dedicated to her because she's been forgotten by everyone. You say I should go away. That I should move to another city to go to college. That I should escape. But what use is it to be born here but be different from everyone else?'

I let those words sink in.

'That's why I can't leave you here alone.'

'No, Federico. You need to stay far away, because I love you. Did you see what they did to Serena?'

'Who's that?'

'It doesn't matter. Just forget it.'

'Waves, darkness, caress, dream, seed. I will keep these five words safe.'

Lucia's eyes light up and she turns away.

'One of my teachers told us a story about a Russian poet who was sent away to a work camp in Siberia because he was against Stalin's regime. The only things that he took with him were the clothes he was wearing and his copy of *The Divine Comedy*, which he had learned to read by himself. His wife never gave up on him even though he had been condemned to death and they would never see each other again. And do you know what she did? She learned all of her husband's poetry by heart so that she could keep him alive. Even after she had lost track of him and his body was buried in a mass grave in the ice and mud. Even after all of his books had been burned.'

Lucia looks at me again and her eyes betray an inner battle. It is resolved for a second with a smile that escapes briefly from the chains of fear and bitterness.

I see her in all of her strength and fragility. I will never forget this moment, one of those instances that happen at least once in a man's lifetime: When, on your path in life, you encounter something that resembles nothing else you know. A brilliant wave of joy invades the fatigue that has impregnated life, like a white swan amid trash in an abandoned pond.

'I won't leave you. I will leave you here, but I will stay here, too.'

19

Riccardo watches the scene from afar, with a knife hidden in his pocket. The wheel is flat. The car gasps for another few meters and then Don Pino is forced to stop. He goes home on foot. The first person that he meets is Riccardo, who says hello with a beaming smile. Don Pino smiles back, masking his exhaustion. It's a hot day. Sweat is dripping down his back and his tongue is stuck to the roof of his mouth.

When he sticks his key into the keyhole, he feels like a man lost at sea but who's now safe after having been washed up on shore. He opens the door and before he can close it again, two hooded men come in and throw him to the floor. One lands a punch on his mouth. The other holds a knife to his eyes. He's shaking with fear and doesn't dare move.

'Now do you see how this ruckus is going to end? Those parties of yours? The interviews? The sermons? If you still don't get it, we'll come back and explain it better!'

Don Pino doesn't say a word. Before they leave, they punch him again and leave him on the floor.

He feels like a worm. It's as if his heart is screaming between his temples as he covers his ears in vain, trying to keep the sound out. His body has been reduced to a primordial tremble.

Before that evening, he didn't really know what loneliness was. Lying prostrate on the ground, face down and with blood dripping from his busted lips, he hopes that everything will be over quickly. But it won't pass. From that moment onward, he won't be able to smile like before. Pain isn't erased so easily.

Riccardo counts the money. He's never seen so much money before. All he had to do to get it was slash a tire and run to give the signal that Don Pino was about to get home.

The light from the television screens in other homes tells of moments of peace and tranquility. But it's dark at Don Pino's house. The wounds of the night mustn't be illuminated too hurriedly. Fear won't allow it. He lies there in the dark, looking for a little company. Little by little, the noises of the night quiet down until they are silent. A few hours later, he fights the lethargy that has set in and slowly he pulls himself up. He turns toward the window that looks out at the dark night in Palermo.

My God, why have you abandoned me? I am so tired, my Father. I can't see you. I am afraid. I want to live. I don't want to die. I don't want to leave like a seagull that flies too far out to sea and then drops into the water exhausted in a last dive.

I know that I need to die. But I'm not ready.

Why did you abandon me?

Why, among infinite possibilities, did you pull this one out?

I know that the world can be no better than what we allow it to be. But I am too small.

You are asking too much of me.

He can hear what he calls 'the pi of life' calling inside of him. Exodus 3:14. When God, in the form of a flame impossible to reach and impossible to extinguish, declares His name in the presence of an unarmed and barefoot man.

I am that I am.

God reveals His identity only to the naked man, an orphan of tenderness who has been reduced to a puff of his trembling existence.

My Father.

He repeats it like a breath.

He lifts himself up and gets closer to the window. It's turned white because of the salt deposits left by the nighttime breeze. Everything is quiet. No one is awake, like him.

A flood of tears wells up in his eyes and soul.

Words are finished. He's been left with nothing of his own. The only riches he can offer are his crying and his tears, which flow over him and all things.

20

In the days that follow he goes about his life with a sense of detachment. The usual things that come in the summer are reassuring. Friends, the sea, chats with his father and mother. Rowing on the water with Manfredi in their dinghy. Cold beers and ice creams. Days separated from their usefulness and donated to the temple of the local divinities: Beauty and Abandon.

It's a night of stars and sea like the Night of the Shooting Stars in 1993. One of those nights in which there should be light, since the universe is full of galaxies that know the time before 'once upon a time.' But all we see is the dark because the light isn't fast enough to reach our weak eyes. But in truth, in reality, everything is light in the night.

There's no wind to deviate the trajectory of the stars that drop from the firmament. These are stars full of ordinary memories that come back to life like unearthed fossils.

The boy remembers his science teacher. She was obsessed with the fact that half of the chemistry course could be learned by looking at the stars, since our solar system was born from a stellar explosion.

The elements were dispersed or aggregated in unique conditions on our planet.

The fires of the sky precipitate and in the fragments of each star that decays, the elements of life are blended into new and unpredictable shapes: Lucia, the children, Don Pino, pain, escape, fear, blood . . .

Riccardo counts the stars the same way he counts money.

Even Nuccio is looking at the stars. He remembers when he was a child and his mother would show them to him. But his mother has been gone for too long.

That night, it seems that nothing can erase everyone's swooning in the city of the stars.

Every day has its waiting and every day has its swooning.

But who, among the infinite destinies and desires, will take care of them? Who keeps track of them these days, so that nothing will be lost?

21

The shoes are always the same ones. There's no limit to how many times he will repair them. That's what his father taught him: If the material is good, there is no shoe that can't be reborn. Don Pino will continue to walk the soft asphalt in Brancaccio with those shoes. The street is his home and his shoes are well aware of that. They've seen their share of dust.

His gait has become more cautious but no less determined. He's just like his shoes: Once he's been repaired, he keeps on going and never stops. His strength rises up again, renewed by the difficulties he's faced. It is reborn from up high and it drops over the streets every day. The street takes him to his destination.

'I found an elderly lady who needs a caretaker. You could do it if you wanted.'

'No. It's not for me.'

'But why, Maria?'

'I have security here. At least I have a roof over our heads and a bed for Francesco. And I have all the money I need.'

'But how long do you think this will last?'

'I don't care. I'm living from day to day.'

'No, you're not. You're dying from day to day.'

Don Pino puts his hand on her cheek and closes his eyes.

When he opens them, they shine.

He leaves without saying another word.

The street is still there waiting for him, certain of itself. It's up to him to decode the maze.

Lucia has asked him to meet with her at Serena's house. They need to speak to him.

'What should I do, Don Pino? What should I do?'

Don Pino doesn't search for a humane answer because he has no humane answer. He stares at Lucia's hand as she grasps her friend's hand in her own. It's as if she's trying to absorb some of her pain by osmosis.

'You could put the child up for adoption. I know a place where the child would be safe. I understand that you don't want to keep it. But you can give birth.'

'How am I supposed to keep this pain in my belly? It's cruel!'

'It's the cruelty of men. But it isn't the child's fault. And you would be inflicting more pain after the violence that you've endured.'

'I just can't go to hell like this. The nausea, every inch of skin that stretches. It all reminds me of the evil that was done to me. It's awful. It's my life, my future. And I am supposed to choose this sentence? I have to give life to a baby that will look like the person who has destroyed me?'

'Take some time to think about it. Whatever you decide to do, I will be here for you. And remember that if you add love where there is none, you will receive love. To repair is much more heroic than to build, Serena.'

Lucia hugs her friend as she buries her head in Lucia's chest.

'I don't have the strength,' she keeps saying as she sobs.

'One step at a time, Serena. If you try to illuminate the

entire valley with the little light that you have, you will only be more afraid. Illuminate the next step and then try to make that next step. One at a time. You have the strength. We have the strength.'

22

August belongs to mythological times. It's not part of the calendar. And the rules of utility do not apply.

The Hunter's son comes out of the water with an octopus in his hand.

'I got it, Dad! I got it!'

The Hunter goes over to him, proud of his son. He grabs it from the boy's hands swiftly so as to keep it from wrapping itself around him. He grabs it by its tentacles and beats its head against a rock with sharp, violent blows.

'You have to do it right away so that the flesh becomes soft and tender.'

The boy watches with a serious look on his face.

Then his father puts his thumbs into the cavity of the octopus's head and turns it inside out. He cleans off the dark material that sticks to the walls as the octopus continues to tremble.

'Turn it over and then beat it some more. Hold it by the tentacles. You'll see how the flesh becomes more and more relaxed.'

The son does as he is told.

'Do you feel how soft it is?'

'Yes.'

The tentacles dangle inert. It's one of the most delicious *antipasti* you can make: Octopus legs with lemon.

'Do you see how you do it? You have to crush its head.'

'Got it.'

'Next time, you'll do it by yourself.'

The boy nods and looks down at the ground.

He wanted to build some sandcastles.

23

Then, suddenly, the time has come for the story. The time for the city. September announces its arrival.

As soon as I get back from the beach, I want to tell Lucia everything. And then I want to hear her stories. And more than anything else, I want to hear her voice. We are going to meet at Spasimo. It's sufficiently close but prudently far enough away from Brancaccio. The wind is blowing a bit harder than usual, as if the scent of the impending night had emboldened it.

When I enter the space, which connects earth and sky by confining them to just a few square meters, everything is made right.

Tell me everything. The beach. Friends. Bonfires. And then? And then? And then books and more beach. And you? Now you tell me everything. The kids. The heat. The beach, me too. Books, me too. Petrarch, read cover to cover. There are a thousand words you need to explain to me, if you don't mind. I underlined every one of them. I don't mind. And my grandfather Mario. He's alright, even though the heat is a bit hard on him. My parents are fine. Mine, too. School will start again soon. What a drag!

That is a drag. But it won't be long before it's time for our show for Don Pino. We need to get ready. I wish you could come back. I miss you. But I'm afraid they will hurt you. Over the last few weeks, it feels like I can only see half of what there is to see. After a while, you get tired of seeing things in halves. It makes you feel like you're missing out on the rest of your life. And we only have one life to live. How's Don Pino? I'm worried about him. He seems tired. It's up to us to take care of him. You're right. Is everything here as beautiful as you are, Federico? Where were we when we weren't together? I've asked myself that. I took you with me everywhere I went. Here we are, under this blue-stone sky, and everything is contained in this single instant, unthreatened by time.

More words. And when we reach the limit, then comes a kiss, like the natural fulfillment of our words and their self-evident inadequacy.

I'd like to learn how to play the piano. It's an instrument that resembles me. Everyone is similar to an instrument. I understood this at a rehearsal for a classical music concert to which our middle-school music teacher had taken us. He had a friend in the Massimo Theater symphony orchestra. They explained each instrument by having us listen to each of them one by one. The teacher clearly enjoyed comparing them to different types of people. And each one of us had to choose our own instrument. The flute person is sweet, sometimes pained and gloomy, but then suddenly happy and carefree. The clarinet person is meticulous and careful. The saxophone person is sensual, fickle, and hard to pin down. The cello person is open, calm, and quiet.

I'm a piano person. So far, I've only known my white keys. Then someone comes along who knows how to play my black keys and I discover a part of myself I didn't know, a part that is capable of playing semitones. I remember that the harp was close to the piano, or maybe vice versa.

I don't want to remain a mystery to myself. I need to accept that other hands can reach inside my heart. I need to arm them myself, against me, to show where they can strike me at my weakest. Is loving not loving the hands of another? Tampering with one's soul is the price that must be paid for love. Then, perhaps, that hand will play a score that we never thought we'd hear inside of us. I thought that I *already* was when, in fact, I *barely* am.

Did Love have to come looking for me here? In the darkness?

24

September is summer's epitaph. It finds its way into everything, even the hardest to reach places. The enormous building next to the cathedral shines like a flayed bone on the beach.

A boy dances jubilantly in the hallway as if he had scored a goal in a World Cup final.

'I did it!'

He's referring to his summer-school exam. He hugs Don Pino, who happens to appear in the hallway at that moment.

'Professor, I swear: I am beginning to believe in God. You've performed a miracle!'

Someone else is heading in for an exam. She envies the jubilation of her schoolmate who's managed to save himself.

'Don Pino, say a prayer for me.'

'With a face like that? You look like you are going to a funeral . .'

'I will be going to a funeral if I don't move up a year. My parents will kill me.'

'You'll be fine.'

The priest sees the teachers sitting at the table waiting for the next oral exam. They regret that they flunked the kids. Not because the kids aren't smart. But because they could be at the beach instead of questioning the students about Cicero and Homer with their clothes sopping wet from their sweat. He says hello to his colleagues with a smile and heads to the principal's office.

'I don't think I'm going to be able to make it this year. My workload at the church just keeps getting bigger, and they also need me at the seminary, where I serve as a spiritual director. It looks like I'm going to have to leave you, Antonio. Five days a week at school are too much. And the other things I'm doing are important.'

Antonio watches Don Pino's face carefully. What he is saying doesn't seem like him. He remembers the long walks they used to take in the evenings in Mondello in the late 1960s, when he was a university student working as a teacher and Don Pino was the spiritual assistant at the Roosevelt Institute, where he worked with orphaned children and kids that came from broken homes. His friend would listen to him for hours. Antonio was just twenty years old.

The evenings were cool back then. And cooling off was the whole point of taking walks. Friends do that as evening comes. They head into the night as if mocking its arrival because there are two and not one of them. Then they would get to the tavern where they would eat a hard-boiled egg with salt and drink a glass of wine. Antonio remembers the time when they thought he was the priest's brother. Don Pino got a hearty laugh out of that.

They saw the world through different eyes. One saw it through the eyes of utopia. The other through the eyes of faith. He had been close to him during difficult moments, for example when he was finishing his university thesis. He had gone to his graduation party. Not even his parents had attended. He had never had a friend like Don Pino. Never. His charisma was owed in great measure to his knowing how to be a good friend, but also knowing how to be a father when needed.

'Pino, you know even better than I do that these kids are as important as the parish and the seminary. That's the reason you've never quit teaching. How many years has it been?'

'Since 1978. My goodness. We're getting old.'

'Speak for yourself.'

The principal of Vittorio Emanuele High School grins, but his lifelong friend seems absent in a way that he's never seen before.

'You've already reduced your hours. Let's try to concentrate them into fewer days so that you have more time for the rest . . . But I'm not letting you off the hook.'

'You've always been hard-headed.'

'I had a good teacher. What's going on with you? Are you tired?'

'Nothing. Just some nonsense. How are things with your wife?'

'Not great. Damn, you still remember about that.'

'You are my friend, Antonio.'

'Is something troubling you? You look a little down. I would have never imagined that you would even hypothetically give up teaching.'

'No, it's nothing. It's probably the sirocco. Or maybe it's because I'm really getting old.'

'Well, that's true. Your birthday is coming up in a few days. How old will you be?'

'One-tenth.'

'So, seventy?'

'Bonehead. Five point six. I count one year for every ten. That way I never grow old,' Don Pino says, laughing like a child.

'Okay, let's see what we can do. I'll talk to the scheduling office.'

'Thanks, Antonio. Say a prayer for me.'

'Don't you know that we're not on the best of terms,' the principal answers, pointing to the ceiling with his eyes and grimacing.

'Well, make the effort for a friend!'

'I'll make an exception for you.'

'Thanks. I'm going to need it.'

25

The beach is the point of friction between the land and the sea. And it's at that border that children and their fathers construct castles that will be threatened by the waves. In the same way, a busted lip is the collision point between submission and truth. The strange war in which violence tries to oppress truth will never end. Violence does everything it can to beat it, sweep it away, and to annihilate it. But in doing so, all it achieves is the strengthening of its resistance. For its part, truth eggs it on as if it were a rabid dog. In nature, when one force battles another, the greater destroys the lesser. But the rules of physics don't seem to apply to violence and truth, nor do the rules of men: Violence and truth cannot do a thing to each other.

There are certain hands that enter into a soul to expand it. Others to crush it. The former are strong but delicate. The latter are hard and ferocious. These are the hands that still threaten Don Pino and that beat his face in during an ambush, in a church building late in the evening. These hands function like words. They bless and they curse, they caress and they strike, they sew and they rip apart. Pain causes flesh to contract and the soul curls up in a corner. But not Don Pino's soul: It expands even in pain because it's pain that a father must suffer to nourish and protect his children. His suffering is the origin of the solution.

'What's this?' asks Don Pino as he takes the envelope.

'The spending money for my English visit. It will do more good here,' I answer.

'Do your parents know?'

'It was a gift. I'm the one who decides what to do with my money.'

'It arrives just in the nick of time, as always. Thank you.'

He gets up from the table where he was attempting unsuccessfully to organize some papers and documents. He comes over to me to hug me and I notice that he has a busted lip, a bruise near the upper part of the wound, and rings under his eyes, more pronounced than usual, the type of rings under your eyes that you get from fear and not just from being tired. I recognize those signs and instinctively touch my own lip. But it's completely healed.

'What happened?' I ask, pointing to his mouth.

'I cut myself shaving.'

Don Pino smiles at me. But it's a smile furrowed by the pain that stops him from fully extending his lips.

'That's not a cut. It's a bruise. What happened?'

'What are you doing here, anyway? What will your parents say?'

'I asked first.'

'You are so hard-headed. I hurt myself while walking in the dark as I was going to the bathroom. It's nothing. And you?'

'I've returned from exile. I was able to talk some sense into my parents. I can come to Brancaccio as long as Manfredi comes with me.'

'And where is he?'

'He couldn't come today. But I really wanted to bring you this envelope. Nobody saw me. Don't worry.'

'No, Federico. You mustn't come by yourself. You mustn't ever do this again. Promise.'

Don Pino is clearly upset. I thought it would be a nice surprise. But he has a stern look on his face.

'Promise me!'

'Okay. I won't come again by myself. But what happened to you?'

'Nothing. Nothing happened. I have too many things to do. Now go. Come on. Forgive me, but I have work to do.'

'Was it them?'

He looks me in the eyes and the mask that he's put on starts to soften.

'The Mafia is powerful. But God is all-powerful.'

I've heard him say that many times.

'This God had better get to work.'

We look at each other in silence.

'How's it going with Lucia?'

I know that this is just a way to change the subject but I also know that there's not much else to add.

'She was right. I don't ever want to go away from here anymore.'

'It's where you found love. That's what always happens when you give it your all or when you don't allow yourself to be imprisoned by fear.'

He smiles. But he seems sad.

'She always says that sadness can kill you much more quickly than a virus. You're making me worried, Don Pino. Here I am and you almost seem unhappy to see me.'

'No, I'm not sad. Just a little tired. Forgive me if I've been rude. I'm nervous because we're in a hurry to collect the money we need to finish paying for the classrooms at the center. We need to get to 300,000. But if everything goes well, we'll make it, with the help of God and people like you.'

The old Don Pino smile suddenly surfaces and his eyes, now calm again, reassure me.

'Don't worry, Federico. Everything will be okay. But I'll feel a lot less worried when you come back with someone else.'

'I promise. But will you promise me you'll get some rest?'

'There will be eternal life for resting. I just need you to do me a favor: When my time comes, don't let me die alone.'

'What?'

The answer doesn't come. Don Pino has already left. For a moment he reminds me of those solitary seagulls who glide across the gray sea on a windy day fruitlessly searching for food.

26

The day's colors remind the boy of the maps of islands he had when he was little. It happens on those last days of summer.

Everything becomes primary and elementary: The colors, the perimeters, the shapes, the happiness. Lucia and the boy stroll through the grounds of Villa Giulia in the quasi-seaside splendor of Kalsa. They arrive at the Genie of Palermo statue and admire its features, unaware of its bittersweet essence. An ancient, pagan god, with his scepter and crown and a serpent that feeds from his chest where his heart is. He ambiguously evokes both renewal and ruin, as he sits with the eagle of the city on his right and the dog, a symbol of loyalty, curled up at his feet. And then there is the Triskelion, the head of Medusa with three legs, which represents Sicily as the Trinacria, and a horn of plenty accompanied by an inscription that summarizes the city: 'Palermo, regal and loyal, has the gifts of Pallas and Ceres.'

It's a flattering definition, especially if you compare it to the awful motto that appears in an inscription that you find in ancient representations of this patron God: *Panormus, conca aurea, suos devorat alienos nutrit* ('Palermo, the golden shell that devours her own but feeds strangers'). The Genie of Palermo, the never-ending port and the swooning, summarized in a single sentence.

'Even the genie of the city says it: The gifts of life are here.'

'You're too much of an optimist.'

'No, I'm a realist like Don Pino. Do you know who the water-diviners were? They were dowsers, ancient noble dowsers.'

'What does dowser mean?'

'They were men who had a talent for feeling the water in the bowels of the earth. They would defy the siroccos and droughts as they would search for water. They were not optimists. They were realists. That's what we need to do for our city.'

They continue to travel through the maze of streets, unafraid of getting lost.

They happen upon a market that has the solemnity of a cathedral. That's the way it is in Kalsa, one of those places where the profane becomes sacred through the excess of feeling and feelings.

The stands are laden with goods and the sellers' hawking drowns out any conversation. You need a trained eye to see the carts in the market. You need to view them without searching for folklore. You need to view them without searching for pain. The goods rear up. Fruit and flowers dance like a flamenco of colors between sky and earth. Watermelons explode, red as if they contained the juice of the entire earth. Wrinkled as the bark of a tree, the lemons shout out their yellowness. The pale green zucchini slither like harmless snakes. The baskets of cod look like they are full of dead moons. The mullets enflame the white of the ice they rest upon. The cuttlefish and octopus are so fresh that they seem like they are about to melt. The carcasses of animals appear crucified as they hang from their hooks. The garlic wreaths dangle as if hanging from gallows as they ward off witches and the evil eye. Bundles of peppers together with hump-shaped broccoli, bunches of aphrodisiacal oregano, tins full of unmentionable entrails. Spiny but sweet artichokes and prickly pears. And baskets that brim with olives of every color and texture. The aromas blend together as they rapidly pass over the nostrils heading straight to the heart.

The history of Palermo is preserved in those crates and those stands. The city of every sweetness, *Ziz*, as the Phoenicians called it, the Flower. *Panormus*, the Never-Ending Port for the Greeks and the Romans, who found its sweet and mercantile essence in the union between sea and land created by its endless pier. The Arabs called it *Balarm*. They didn't stop calling it the port that it was. They just adapted the name to the sounds that came from their own mouths. *Balermus*, Pearl of the Mediterranean for Frederick II. And that's what he made it.

It was too rich and colorful and fragrant not to be plundered. The aroma and the pain of this city are one and the same thing. The scales of oxidized brass continue to weigh all of those goods and all of that history. You can't help but visit those streets like a museum of curiosities. Otherwise it would be just a bright but ephemeral memory. Those who look carefully will discover an Eden of harmony and paradoxes, a continuous swooning that is sometimes self-victimization and sometimes self-sacrifice.

Their hands graze one another as they walk side by side. Her dress is guided by the rare puffs of air that slip through the alleys as they rise up from the sea.

'I'm worried about Don Pino.'

'Why?'

'He's been saying the strangest things lately.'

'He's always said strange things.'

'He's really tired.'

'Did you see the cut on his mouth?'

'Yes. He told me that he cut himself shaving. Then he said he bumped into . . .'

'I don't believe it. I'm afraid.'

'He asked me not to leave him alone.'

'I hope that he doesn't leave us alone.'

27

A row of mandarin oranges on the bookshelf would seem to be out of season. But it's actually what remains from a pastime, or something that has passed with time. Lucia learned it from him.

Using a knife, you slice the peel in half without cutting into the fruit. Then you remove the upper half of the peel. And then you extract the wedges one by one without ruining the stem, which you soak in oil. You make a hole at the top of the peel you previously removed, you light the stem, and then you put the upper half of the peel back on the fruit. It appears to be a whole mandarin orange with a hole on top. But it's actually a little lamp.

She likes watching Don Pino's slow, precise movements. With the smell of mandarin oranges in the air, they seem full of magic. He's making those same movements now as he eats the fruit that she brings him together with the sandwiches. Those sandwiches help to remind him that he does, indeed, have a body. The fragrance of the lamps is just a memory, but such a powerful one that his essence seems to emanate from it.

'Don't forget that you women have 300 grams of extra heart. That's why you suffer more and why you fall victim to the egotistical calculations of men. They have 300 grams of extra brain. But not because they are more intelligent. It's because they are more rational and more calculating.'

'Is that so?' answers Lucia. 'Then I shouldn't trust any of them. But I like Federico, Don Pino. It's your fault for bringing him here!'

'Lucia, falling in love is like looking out of a window. At first, it's too high for you and you can't even reach the windowsill. But then the moment arrives when you look outside and you are attracted by the world. And then, little by little, you feel the need to open the window and then to lean out of the window and then to go out through the window onto the balcony. Until you are ready to run downstairs and walk into that panorama that you saw from up high. It's one of the most beautiful passages in life. But remember: They are moments of great change and therefore great instability. Often, the expectations that you form from up high are excessive. That's what happens with anything you see from far away. And this can cause serious pain. Don't forget it. You shouldn't lean too quickly from the balcony. Otherwise you'll end up falling and hurting yourself. You need to go down to the street and walk together.'

'I'll be cautious when I look out the window. And besides, you'll be there to give me advice.'

'Who knows where I'll be?'

'Why would you say that?'

'No, that's not what I meant. I'm just saying. We priests, one day we're in one place and the next we're on the other side of the world. When you don't know what to do, pray. Prayer helps you to remain faithful to the truth. And only the truth can set you free. It's opening that window every day. Today, people think they are free because they have millions of possible choices. But freedom isn't having a lot of choices. It's choosing the truth. Prayer is the best way to remember to choose the truth, even when you have to pay a price for doing so.'

'But sometimes I get bored when I pray.'

'Even the people who love each other get bored. But their love never stops being true.'

'I don't get bored when I'm with him.'

'He is your prayer. Remember that all love works incognito.'

'What does that mean?'

'It means that they work undercover, on God's behalf. Federico is a good boy. I have a lot of faith in him. You need to protect him a little, you know? He has a big heart and sometimes he risks getting carried away.'

'That's exactly what I like about him. Love is a revolution, Don Pino!'

'Love is a revelation, Lucia.'

He smiles and touches her cheek.

28

Works and Days is an epic title from an ordinary epic that transforms lines of poetry into everyday prose. And this month of days and works is an epic one, without respite. Time is made out of grains of longing. And it's no coincidence that man chose sand for keeping time. Sand is what remains of materials exhausted by the sun, sea, and wind. Don Pino fills his days with works and his works with days. His thoughts aren't easy to inhabit. And yet, his indomitable heart continues to hope. And to tremble.

September 13 is a grain of sand, an unusually gloomy day for the season. The sky is filled with yellowish clouds yearning to pour sand on the city and to sully car bodies and the windows of homes by reducing the summer to a dusty memory.

Don Pino underlines passages in his breviary, something he's never done before. The lines are from St John Chrysostom, who wrote aboard a ship that was carrying him into exile. As the ship pushes off, he watches the port with its trembling fires from the stern. And from the bow, he sees the sun setting as it spots the horizon with blood.

> *The waters have risen and severe storms are upon us, but we do not fear drowning, for we stand firmly upon a rock. What are*

we to fear? Death? Life to me means Christ, and death is gain. If Christ is with me, whom shall I fear? We brought nothing into this world, and we shall surely take nothing from it.

He will meet his death during the voyage and his last words will be: *Glory to God for all things!*

September 14 is another grain of sand, the Feast of the Holy Cross. It commemorates the discovery of Christ's cross by St Helena, the mother of Constantine the Great. She unearthed it in the ruins of the Temple of Venus, which had been built by Emperor Hadrian a few years after Christ's death at Golgotha. By erecting the temple on this hill, Hadrian was attempting to substitute Christians' bitter love with the sweet wine of pagan Eros.

Don Pino celebrates Mass for the community of teen mothers that he works with. In the chapel, there's a copy of Antonello da Messina's *Virgin Annunciate* with her face suspended between a smile and fear. She is framed by that blue veil. To call it 'blue' would be blasphemy: It was painted with the color of the sea stuck directly onto the canvas, with the golden shimmer that the sea has on sunny days.

Don Pino explains to them that Mary was seen by the people, and even by Joseph, as a teen mother. Her conception had no human author and so it certainly wasn't something easy to explain. That's why you can see fear and peace on her face at the moment of the annunciation. It's a paradox that only those who know God can experience. It's the most beautiful paradox of faith.

Don Pino scans the faces he sees before him and he recognizes the girl from the painting: One hand held out before her in a sign of defense, the other clutching her dress closed, because love has already flowed through her and the fruit of her womb needs to be protected. He sees her in one girl's black hair; in the dark skin of another; in the tired and fearful eyes of all of them; in the eyes full of hope belonging to Serena.

Yes, that's her. She arrived late and sat at the back. She smiles at him from afar, with her hands fidgeting in her lap.

Reinvigorated, Don Pino can hear the words flow even more powerfully.

'Look at where Maria is looking when she knows she must face her shame. Look where she is looking in this painting. Look at God. And have faith. He will not leave you alone.'

Then he talks about the celebration that day and how it transforms every defeat into victory, every minus sign into a plus sign, just like the shape of the cross from which Christ forgives his persecutors, who are unable to comprehend what they are doing. He reminds them of the blood that Christ shed in the Garden of Gethsemane.

'Christ felt lonely and he asked three men to stay with him. But they fell asleep and the fear that flowed through him was so great that he began sweating blood. Death and love dueled inside of him. Love won but the fear of death made him bleed. That is why we are never alone in fear and in pain. Because he had to go through fear and pain, and he triumphed. They are a passage toward a greater life and infinite love. We invented the cross and it belongs only to us. It's not what he carries. He invented love: Love for those around us, for the persons whom life has entrusted to us. A sweet burden, just like that of your womb. You, too, are called upon to do this every day. The cross is not pain. It's not suffering. It's just love that cures and heals through its gift.'

The girls stare at him. They haven't understood much. Serena smiles through her tears because she knows that he is speaking to her about her renewed courage. His face smiles now so openly that even the others end up thinking that, no matter what he's said, it must be true.

29

That same day, when the light cautiously moves across the surface of the sea like a cat on a roof and the waves are paws that toy with their prey, turning it over and over, the boy and Lucia walk in silence. The sea stretches along the coast with the peacefulness of someone who doesn't hurry because he knows what he is doing. The boy observes the expanse of water frayed with blood by the tired sun as it sets. The reddish light flares up. No one has ever invoked something small as his witness for big promises. No one has ever declared his love in a garage, unless he was forced to.

Those who love each other hold each other's hands as they walk along the shore. They whisper secrets and say 'I love you' as the horizon, uniter of sky and earth, watches on. And thus the boy turns toward Lucia, who watches him and waits with the mixture of fear and astonishment that every woman feels the first time someone tells her 'I love you.' When it happens, all women would like to grab those words with their hands and put them inside their hearts and keep them there for the rest of their lives.

'I want to love you, Lucia,' says the boy as he fixes a lock of her hair that has been moved behind her ear by the wind. He meant to say 'I love you', but this was the sentence that came out of his mouth.

She turns for a moment toward the sea, toward the sky, toward the sand, toward the mountains. And she calls them as her witnesses. Then she gazes again into the eyes of the boy, marked by his longing. They are clear eyes, the type that belong to those who seek truth. But they are also fragile eyes, the type that belong to those who are fearful and those who would like to experience everything in life without being crushed by it.

Like a rose in bloom, she puts her head on his chest and in the suspended silence of things at dusk, she answers him: 'Never leave, and I will be the summer that never ends.'

An anchor and an encore. A *be still* and a *still be*.

The boy squeezes her in his arms as if he could circumscribe life inside a circle where he could protect her from every attack and failure. And everything around them becomes timeless and frozen in all of her senses, as if they were elements of happiness in the periodic table: Sand, rocks, undertow, wind.

It's September. The month that has within it the end of summer and the budding of fall. The sea isn't capable of containing both of those spirits, and so sings them together.

'Tell me the most important thing about you,' she asks him suddenly with a black gust of her hair.

'My heart is full of desires, dreams, beautiful things. But I don't have any armor,' he answers. He immediately regrets having foolishly offered his essence so immodestly, as if that were his fragrance once his life has been distilled and his peel has been thrown.

Lucia smiles.

She wants to be my armor. And my amore.

I'm that boy.

Federico.

30

Then the day of Don Pino's birthday arrives. September 15. It's the day dedicated to Our Lady of Sorrows. A mother who cries for the death of the fruit of her womb. She longs for him. The grains of time are finished and there are prayers that are like premonitory dreams.

You always wanted me to call you by your first name. Now let me do that.

I gave up a woman for you. I gave up a family and children.

For a family, you gave me this wretched neighborhood of delinquents, misfits, and saints. And children.

You promised me that it would be enough.

Where are you?

Inside of them?

How do you love someone who spits in your face?

How do you love someone who kills you?

Loving your enemies is the craziest thing I've ever believed in.

People call them and me the same thing. Don.

Don Giuseppe Puglisi. Don Giuseppe Graviano. Parrinu, the godfather and the priest. The same word for all of us.

Where do you think these people are heading? To those who have strength, or to me with only my books and words? God of armies? God all-powerful?

Weak and silent God.

Is this how you treat your friends?

That's why you have so few of them.

I'm not abandoning you. You have given me everything.

Now take me. Take me up high into the light and the air and let me unfurl my wings.

Let me be the way I was when my mother would hold me in her arms and cover me with kisses.

Let me be the way I was when my father, surrounded by a mountain of shoes to repair, would put me on his shoulders and let me see everything. You could even see the sea from those shoulders.

Put me on your shoulders and let me see the sea.

From up there, I'm not afraid of that dark sea to cross.

I don't have heaven inside of me but I will go to heaven.

I am not afraid of death.

I am afraid of dying.

I look for your face. Don't hide it from me.

Now and at the hour of my death.

31

Birthdays are for celebrating the fact that we are not immortal. At twenty years of age – so they say – you still have the face that they gave you. But at fifty, you have the face that you deserve. He's turning fifty-six and his face has a clear-cut geography: The dark rings under his eyes carved from exhaustion and the soft, plentiful reliefs of his smile. Just this: Love and giving. Otherwise, he has the face of a child.

The light is perfect on September 15. No dark thing can escape it. There are strong shadows destined to wear out. But they are just illusions. Darkness triumphs when light is taken away. But it's only the appearance of victory and it's only temporary.

The blue shines in the gold 'marvelously' as the first of the poets wrote. He belonged to a land of endless colors that occur naturally here: Amaranth, orange, vermillion, ivory, lilac, almond, mint, coral. But if you look closely enough in the city of men, enamel and debris overlap, like heaven and hell. And while a mother caresses a baby and a newlywed kisses his wife, others break their backs, lives, and faces.

In the afternoon, Lucia and the children are busy with dress rehearsals for the show. Excitement, fear, and concentration come together on the stage. They generate the same feeling of being lost that students feel when they believe they have forgotten everything they have learned right before an exam.

But where there are children, happiness always prevails, free from judgment and regardless of the performance. What counts is being there, everyone together. They all look forward to the pizza to celebrate Don Pino's birthday after the show.

'We're going to surprise him. We're going to sing "Happy Birthday" outside his house,' explains Francesco to the others for the umpteenth time. They know full well that's what they're going to do but he loves to roll surprises around in his mouth, just like candy.

'Seriously, don't tell him anything,' reiterates Lucia.

Besides my role as Charlemagne, there's also Wizard Pipino, aka Don Pino. He doesn't know it yet but he's the surprise guest.

Totò announces my entrance with his pretend sword.

> *Little Orlando wails at this late hour.*
> *The evil Ganelon, back at his lair,*
> *Has locked him up in the castle tower.*
> *That cuckold, stinking betrayer!*
> *Desperate to be saved, he's a sorry sight.*
> *In that cell, he will die of hunger, he fears.*
> *But a light reawakens the knight*
> *And suddenly Wizard Pipino appears.*

I enter the scene with a fake beard that makes even my teeth sweat. And I have a Merlin's wizard-hat that droops over my eyes. And I burst out laughing.

'I can't do it. I just can't stop laughing. "Wizard Pipino!"'

'That's true. It's a strange name!'

'Oh, come on. It's meant to poke a little fun at Don Pino.'

'Exactly.'

Lucia scolds the children and they all stand at attention again.

'Take it from the last two lines, Totò. And you, stop laughing!' she warns me.

But a light reawakens the knight
And suddenly Wizard Pipino appears.

I try to keep from laughing by pinching myself on the thigh.

'Don't be afraid, little boy. Here I am.'

'But who are you? I don't know you. Are you here to kill me?'

'Kill you? What are you talking about? Do you think that someone with a beard like this could hurt you?'

'I don't know if I should trust a beard.'

The wizard leans down and Little Orlando touches his beard.

'I'm here to free you from Ganelon's clutches.'

'But even if I escape and my life is saved, I'll still have to go away.'

'No, you won't. You just need to be brave and let your friends help you. Together you will set a trap for Ganelon and you will become the true and only heir to Charlemagne.'

'Really?'

'Come closer.'

Little Orlando moves toward him and cups his ear to hear him more clearly. Old Pipino tells him something that the audience cannot hear. Little Orlando's face lights up. But just at that moment, Ganelon enters and engages in a terrible duel with the wizard.

'Run away, Little Orlando! Run away! Don't worry about me. I will always be here.'

Little Orlando is hesitant.

'Go on! Now is your chance. Don't waste it. Do what I've told you to do.'

Little Orlando exits.

The duel continues and Ganelon wounds the old man with his sword. The wizard is armed only with a stick and it's no match for the knight's steel blade.

Ganelon chases after Little Orlando and follows him off stage.

The wizard's body lies inert in the center of the stage.

The children stare at him in silence, as if he has really died.

'Excellent! Now the lights come down. Pipino exits the stage. Now it's up to Little Orlando to rally his friends and to share with them the secret that the wizard told him. They all follow him off stage astonished and excited. The audience will be dying to know what their plan is.'

When a pack of wolves can no longer find any prey; when it can no longer find a prize to gnaw and to nourish itself; when a pack of wolves loses its hunting grounds and the burrows where it feeds; when it loses its strength . . . It reacts by slaughtering the weakest animal in the pack. It feeds on its own flesh. Man-wolves do the same thing. They sacrifice those closest to make them feel strong. And they choose the weakest one. In doing so, they regain control and recoup their power. But among men, it happens that the sacrifice of the weakest reawakens those who are standing to the side, those who are indifferent or those who are afraid. The blood of the weakest nourishes them even more than the wolves that devoured it. On September 15, a pack of hungry wolves roams Brancaccio. Its only purpose is to satisfy its hunger.

Don Pino arrives late. The couples in his pre-marriage course have been waiting for a half-hour. It's a day like any other. He's already officiated at two weddings and he also attended the umpteenth meeting at Palazzo Aquile for his request to use the spaces on Via Hazon.

'My apologies.'

'Were you late the day you were born?'

'I know you're joking, but do you know that my birth certificate says September twenty-fourth when, actually, I was born on the fifteenth? I have nine bonus days. That's why I'm always late.'

'If you ask me, you used up your bonus a long time ago . . .'

Don Pino looks at them carefully. He's thankful to be there. He has been working with them for months to guide them toward the sacrament of marriage, which is now around the corner.

Then, clearly absorbed by his purpose, he tells them: 'The most important thing isn't the dress or the reception. The most important thing is that the two of you become Christ. That the life of Christ enters into you and, from that moment onward, love rises again every time it dies. It's not magic. It's what actually happens if you make space for Him in and with your lives.'

The future wives and husbands listen to him with the eyes of those who dream of a love that never tires.

'When you live it like this, human love – with its weaknesses, its imperfections, and its setbacks – can be a true corner of heaven. Many have marriages that are like hell. But this won't happen to you. Hell is when you don't love each other. Will you promise me that you'll love each other?'

'Of course! Why else would we be here?' says one of the future husbands. He moves over to Don Pino and whispers something in his ear as he slips an envelope into his jacket pocket.

'This is our contribution for the Holy Father Center. It's not much but it's what I can swing with my job.'

Don Pino hugs him.

'Thank you, my son. Little by little we are doing something big. We are going to find the 300 million, one piece at a time, just like the mosaics in Monreale.'

'How far along are we?'

'More than halfway there. But the work in the church has been paused. I have a feeling that the construction company gave into some kind of outside pressure. What can we do?'

His words remain suspended in the air, but they are swept away by a chorus of birthday wishes from the couples. Don Pino has given them everything he can, including his smiles and even a scolding now and then. They are joined by some of his closest friends with a tray of *cannoli* and *cassatine*, little candied cakes. One of them has a candle in it.

Don Pino stares at it with a smile as wide as an open port.

He looks at them.

'Thank you.'

And he blows out his fifty-six years.

You can't see even a centimeter of moon in the sky. The next day will be a new moon. There's only room for the stars and the vague glimmer of headlights in that still-incomplete darkness. The night inks the sea as it caresses the immense port. It seems that anything could happen, that some sort of creature could come out of that black liquid in the shape of a mermaid, a triton, or a sea monster. Four of them head out from the night like hungry wolves, knights of a provincial apocalypse. A pack of hump-backed demons in the blinding darkness. They rush to pay their debts with the sirocco god. The sea slows down and almost becomes marble. It prepares to listen to the demons' sabbath between the deserted streets of Brancaccio and the light gait of a small man. The streetlights yellow the dark without managing to wrest away any of its senses.

The demons advance to interrupt, to impede, shatter, trample, crush, and rupture God and to derail his plans. To break his bones. To peel away his muscles. To dig out his eyes. To put iron into his flesh. To close his mouth. To stop his heartbeat. To throw him a birthday party.

One cigarette leads to another and helps to dilute the tension. They just need to sniff out the priest's tracks and follow him. They need to study his movements so they can find the right moment. But the right moment is now because those movements, those footprints, and those tracks are something special: The priest is going home, walking through the streets of the neighborhood. Then he goes into a telephone booth.

'Let's do it now,' says the Turk.

'Without a motorcycle?' asks the Hunter.

'What do you need a bike for? He's all by himself. It needs to seem like a robbery.'

They hurry to the warehouse. The Hunter surveys the weapons. A .32 Automatic would do the trick. They don't need a shotgun or a .38 Special or a .357 Magnum. A birthday party calls only for a tiny little candle.

And he's going to be the one doing the shooting.

He stops for a moment and asks himself why. And the answer is simple: Because he was ordered to.

They don't even bother using stolen cars. They use their regular rides. This is going to be a stroll in the park, too easy, really, for one of the most ruthless Mafia crews in history. What could this weakness be? Aren't they about to hurl themselves against it like an angry mob?

'Maria, listen to me. You simply have to find a job. I'll give you some money for the moment. But you have to promise me that you are going to stop selling your body. No, Maria. You have to promise me. Now, yes, now. Do it for Francesco. No, please don't cry. Listen to me! Go to that center that I told you about. You can stay there and they'll feed you. And they will help you find some sort of work. I received a donation for you. The next time I see you, I'll bring you the money. It should last you until you find work. You can do it. You are a strong girl. You are a splendid mother with a splendid child. I have to go now. Don't cry. I will always be here for you. You'll see that everything is going to be okay.'

He exits the phone booth and heads toward home. The last person he meets is Riccardo, who wishes him a happy birthday and kisses him on both cheeks.

'Don Pino has grown old!'

'What is that supposed to mean? I'm still a kid.'

'Happy birthday, Father.'

He winks and hurries off.

They are waiting for him with two cars. Their arms dangle from the window so as to let the smoke dissipate and the ashes fall to the ground. Two of them are in one car, the other two in another car as backup. The two passengers get out at the same time.

Don Pino is almost at the front door and he searches for his keys in his bag. But he doesn't manage to open the door.

A man he's never seen before blocks his path. He's about to ask him if he can help him with something. But the man beats him to it.

'Father, this is a robbery!'

'I was expecting this.' Don Pino smiles at him.

The Hunter is now at his side and shoots him from a distance of eight inches like he was the last of the traitors, like he doesn't have the courage to look him in the eyes. But even from the side, he can see his smile.

The last words of a man are the ones that count the most.

They are the seal of his life.

He says: 'I was expecting this.'

He says he was ready, at 8:40 p.m. on September 15, 1993.

And he smiles.

These are his last words.

He was waiting for death.

He was waiting for it like someone who goes to an appointment or receives a visit after a long wait.

He dies with a smile.

He doesn't see his two assassins. He sees two sons. He was expecting them, with a smile, like a father who rushes to embrace a child who's been away for a long time.

He sees through them. He sees beyond them. And in his gaze, they see themselves as they were when they were children.

The Hunter had a different nickname them: Ricciolino, 'curly,' because of his hair. It was the nickname his mother gave him. That smile takes him back to that time. That smile says to him: You don't know what you are doing; you are not this. That smile is the worst punishment that can be inflicted on an assassin. And the Hunter will no longer be able to sleep at night. There are certain crimes that seek out their punishment. And they end up finding only forgiveness.

Don Pino now sees who was waiting for him.

He sees who he's always seen in all things.

He feels the weight that crushed him be lifted, as if on the immense wings of a king from on high.

He sees God. Face to face. And he smiles at him.

The semi-automatic Beretta M1935 with silencer fires from a distance of eight inches from the back of his neck. It's a pistol for common criminals and amateurs. But from this distance, it's plenty and then some.

The bullet explodes on the back of his neck and shows his soul the way out.

Don Pino falls and kisses the street with his lips. The bitter taste of blood is blended with that of the dust.

They take his bag. It's supposed to seem like the result of a robbery by a desperate man.

The body is still on the ground. It's almost 9 p.m.

The pack heads back to its den. It's a warehouse for a shipping and transport company, the ideal place for those who ship souls to the afterlife.

The Hunter's hand is shaking. He puts the pistol away and opens the priest's bag.

'This time we were the ones to say the blessing.'

He finds the envelope. It has 50,000 lire in it and a greetings card.

'To Don Pino, who treated us like a father when others only judged us. Happy birthday.'

'We sure gave him a good birthday present. Look at this!'

There's another envelope with a lot of money in it. It's says 'For Maria' on it.

The Hunter slips it into his pocket without letting anyone else see. The money from Federico's English visit.

They don't find anything else in the bag. No secret messages. No trace of working with the cops or contact with the police. Nothing. Just a few banknotes, a driver's license, and the greetings card.

The other guy rips the stamps off the license.

'These are always useful.'

They divvy them up, one for each of them.

They laugh, clearly proud of themselves. They drink an ice-cold beer. It relaxes their foreheads, which have been made shiny by sweat from the tension.

'Now it's time to hit the tobacco store,' says the Hunter with a feverish tremble.

'A great night! What are we doing?'

'Burning it down.'

The pack is still hungry. The prey they just finished sacrificing was too weak. And they always want more. That pack of wolves is preparing an attack that has never been attempted in the history of the Mafia: A car filled with TNT in front of the Stadio Olimpico in Rome, to be detonated when the game is over and people are leaving. It's a huge leap forward. A checkmate for that papier-mâché idol otherwise known as the government. Like the Italian word for *has-been*, the *stato* – the state – is the past. They are the present and the future.

32

In the silence of Piazza Anita Garibaldi, the air is still. Minutes pass slowly as the blood exits the wound in the back of Don Pino's neck. It has exactly the same rhythm and possesses the same dripping awareness that his life does.

These seconds are filled with absolute and tremendous lucidity.

There are five things that a person regrets when they are about to die. And they are never the things they consider important during their life. We won't regret the trips that never went further than the window display at the travel agency. We won't regret the new car, a better salary, or a woman or man that we dreamed of. No, at the moment of death, everything finally becomes real. And there are five things that we will regret, the only real things in a life.

The first is not having followed our inclinations in life instead of being prisoners to others' expectations. The mask of skin that made us lovable, or made us believe we were lovable, will fall by the wayside. And it was the mask created by fashion, by our false anticipation, to heal the resentment of wounds we never faced. It's the mask worn by those who are content merely by being lovable. But not loved.

The second regret is having worked too hard, having allowed ourselves to be overwrought by competition, by results, by running after something that never arrived because it existed only in our minds. We regret having neglected people and relationships. We wish we could apologize to everyone. But there's no time left for that.

Our third regret is that of never having found the courage to speak the truth. We will regret not having said 'I love you' enough to those close to us, not having said 'I'm proud of you' to our children, not having said 'I'm sorry' when we were wrong or even when we were right. We preferred festering resentment and long silences over the truth.

Then we will regret not having spent time with those whom we love. We didn't bother to worry about those we always had around, for the very reason that they were always around. And yet the pain reminded us every so often that nothing lasts forever. But we underestimated this as if we were immortal. We continued to put it off, giving the right of way to what was urgent and not to what was important. How did we manage to endure so much loneliness in life?

We tolerated this because it was ingested in small doses, as you do with a poison so as to become immune. And we suffocated the pain with tiny, sweet little surrogates. We couldn't even manage to make a call and ask how things were going.

Lastly, we will regret not having been happier. And yet, all we would have needed to do was to let bloom that which we had inside and around us. But we allowed ourselves to be crushed by habit, by apathy, by egotism. Instead, we should have loved like poets and we should have sought knowledge like scientists. We should have searched the world for what the child saw in his maps: Treasures. We should have searched for what the adolescent discovers as his body thickens: Promises. We should have searched for what young people hope for in the affirmation of their lives: Love.

* * *

Don Pino doesn't regret any of these things. He knew all of them through love. To him, everything was already real. That's why he smiles as he crosses over the threshold. He has only one regret: Leaving his city, his neighborhood, his friends, and his kids. He misses their faces and thinks about the pain that his leaving so abruptly will cause. Maria, Lucia, Francesco, Totò, Federico, Dario, Serena, all of his old students and the ones that he would have had that year and others. Their names start to become jumbled because his brain is burning like a fire and the bitterness is grabbing at his heart. But he senses a light that slowly guides his way in the grip of death.

The love that he has given will remain intact and it will continue forever, indestructible, because that love didn't originate with him. It passed through him like an open channel. He remembers the phrase written at the top of the first page in his notebook of maxims from his years at school: 'The Priest: Ring that connects God and man.' A connection that has twisted his limbs, which are now growing slack as he tries, in vain, to call them back to his body.

The last thing that he hears is the voice of the sea and the last thing he smells is the aroma that permeates the city he loves. He now needs to leave those streets like – when he was six years old – bombs fell over Palermo. Never-ending port and longing. He has arrived at his destination and he is leaving again. It's the same thing. His heart slows and his longing fades.

He now enters into a place where every paradox melts away.

He enters into God and his embrace, where every desire is a possession and every possession a desire. Devoid of pain. Every departure is an arrival and every arrival a departure. Devoid of pain.

The grains of sand are finished. Fear is finished.

He cannot regret anything: He has given and received everything.

He sought to bring water to life in the path of burning thirst. He sought to plant trees in the cement of the city. He sought to open the sky to the streets. He sought to bring heaven to hell.

He sees his mother and father's faces again. They smile at him and take him by the hand and they swing him just as they did when he was a child.

Every time, they swing him higher and higher.

The world's show comes to an end and so does hell's laughing.

The cycle of dreams and blood subsides.

History and every one of its moments are fulfilled.

Dying abruptly is the only way to get on with goodbyes. He will trust that those who remain will *go with God*.

The last thing he sees is the sky riddled with stars. The galaxies flow swiftly through the hands of the Creator, so rapidly that their light is late in reaching our eyes. He opens his arms, utterly exhausted. Now all that he has longed for is finally his.

33

A little girl moves toward Don Pino's lifeless body. She arrives before the others who were finishing up at the rehearsal. She wanted to be the first. She and her doll. She dressed up for the occasion and she is afraid of the moonless evening sky because everything has to be just right: It's Donpino's birthday.

She smells nice. And in her eyes, you can see a little girl dancing in the sunshine. She knows the way by heart. When she arrives, she finds him there, on the ground, covered in blood. And she understands that he is not sleeping, just like her father. He will not wake up again. He has gone beyond the sea. He has gone to where all the train tracks end. She sits beside him. She puts her hand on his head and caresses it, without saying a word. Her little hand gets covered in blood. He is smiling. And she smiles back with her eyes as black as night and tears like the sea. They have taken another father from her.

Nothing seems capable of breaking that silence.

But then suddenly, a scream slices it cleanly in half.

The undertow grinds in the background like a pack of strays and the clouds look like scratches against the metallic sky.

Mimmo, the policeman from the second floor, comes out with his cigarette in his mouth. He leans over the motionless body with its inert arms and the keys in one of its hands. Those keys were for opening a door other than the door to death.

A doll is lying next to him and it stares at him with its glassy eyes. It has no answers and no questions. There is a little girl standing not too far away.

'What's your name?'

She disappears into the night.

When the other kids arrive with Lucia and the boy, Don Pino is no longer there.

'He wasn't feeling well and they took him to the hospital.'

'What's all this blood on the ground?' asks Francesco.

'He hit his head when he fell down.'

'You should always keep your head held high.'

'What are you saying?'

'You should always keep your head held high.'

'What does that have to do with anything?'

'That's what the wizard Pipino whispers into Little Orlando's ear,' says Francesco. Then he starts running. He doesn't even know exactly where the hospital is. But it's nearby.

The others follow him. Everyone looks out at the swarm of children as they cross the street heading to God knows where.

34

They put him on the gurney for a post-mortem examination.

The night is just halfway over and the demons are all still on the street.

Some say that to know a city, you have to see how its people work and love. But especially how they die. And nobody knows that better than she does. She knows every detail about death. The doctor who carries out the examination looks over that body and she sees the entire city.

It's still not rigid and the skin temperature is gradually going down. Blood oozes out of his right ear. There is a wound on the left occipital lobe with ecchymosis around it.

The bullet is lodged in his head and it has transfigured his face. The parietal-temporal-occipital area is swollen. The cranioencephalic trauma stopped the bullet, which was deformed by the silencer. A face made unrecognizable by iron.

And yet, you can still discern the last thing he did, a testament to the man: Smile.

The doctor has never seen anything like this in someone turned into a cadaver through violence. She can certify that violence has been defeated. Violence unmasked by the victim himself. Weak violence against the weakest.

That smile leaves her serene.

In the meantime, the fire carries out its conquest. A ferocious, fast fire. It turns a tobacco shop into dust together with all the dreams of someone who didn't bend to the bitter demands of the gods of the neighborhood.

And the sabbath continues, more furious than ever, and the flurry rises again. It stinks up the streets that have been lost to the night, twisted by other fires and other murders. The light has been trampled upon in a macabre dance. But between the sobbing, it doesn't stop revealing the faces of all the victims in history.

The Hunter laughs bitterly. He has killed a man who smiles.

35

The visitors' room is crammed with children.

I lean over Don Pino's body. He's still smiling even though life has left it. I have so many questions yet to ask. I almost hate him for having left us so early.

You, who opened the space between my heart and my mind.

You, you showed me that courage belongs to those who know they are weak.

You, who helped me shed the scales of boredom from my eyes. You, who were my teacher and my friend.

I put my head over his heart so I can calculate how big it is, and it's as wide as the whole city. I cry like a baby who has lost his father. I look up at the other children, the real children. No father can have this many in just one life. And they are all there, as only they could be in the face of death. In silence and in anticipation that the deceased will get up and walk once again.

Only the older kids allow themselves to cry. The younger ones ask where he has gone but they are skeptical when told he's gone to heaven. They want to know where he is so that they can go visit him or at least call him. Riccardo stares at him without shedding a tear because now Don Pino has shown him the way to get to heaven. He leaves without saying a word.

Francesco holds Father Pino's hand and won't let go.

'You promised me that you would show me a miracle. You are supposed to keep your promises. You are supposed to keep them!' he repeats to himself.

Totò has his arms crossed and his head bowed. He cries into his glasses.

Then he comes over to me and asks: 'Why doesn't God keep the people he has instead of letting them die and making new ones?'

I try, in vain, to offer an answer as I watch those kids. They are pieces of a broken vase. There is more love in putting back together the fragments than in taking for granted that the vase is in one piece. Once it's repaired, the vase takes on an inexplicable new beauty, more similar to life. It takes someone who can see the beauty in the broken pieces. I watch each of them one by one. We are all orphans of a man whose fatherhood was stronger than blood but it took blood to show that. The memories I dig out of my pain grab on to my heart like octopuses in stormy seas. Every movement rips through my flesh.

When Don Pino used to come into the classroom, we were always hungry for surprises. Other teachers just went with the program. But to him, we were the program, with our lives and our questions. And there was never a question that he ignored. He began every lesson by reading a passage from the Bible. Then he would ask us if we had experienced what he had just read about.

I remember when he talked about the Penitent Thief who died on the cross next to Christ and who asked Him to remember him when he entered into his kingdom. He received a guarantee that he would go to heaven.

'He is the only man that we know for certain is in heaven.'

'A thief and a murderer?' I asked rebelliously.

'Yes, but the difference is that he recognizes Christ's innocence and his own guilt. And he asks at least for the privilege of a remembrance on behalf of the man that dies next to him. He suffers the same pain but he is serene.'

'This God of yours is too good. He's giving the place of honor to a thief,' I joked at the time.

'He must have been a pretty good thief: He managed to steal heaven . . .' answered Don Pino without skipping a beat.

Many of us laughed when he said this. But he wasn't simply making a joke: 'The thief was a murderer who ended up there because of his crimes. Someone who found himself next to God as a consequence of his actions. It was his being lost in evil that brought him to the right place, where he found peace and forgiveness.'

He didn't give us the answers, but he allowed those words to dig deep into our hearts and stay there. He knew they would come in handy at some point in the future.

I remember the time we spoke about sex. Yes, at school and with a priest.

'It's not the body that contains the soul but the opposite. Think of a caress and a smile. Could a hand caress someone and the eyes smile without a soul inside?'

After a break when we were all supposed to think about our own expressions of affection, he added: 'And if we send our souls into exile, our bodies become orphans and our expressions of affection become mere masks.'

He read all kinds of newspapers, liberal, conservative, and everything in between. He always started off with the local news. He never shied away from reality. And he never avoided stories that could make others uncomfortable. He brought the world into the classroom and he never excluded anything the way other teachers did.

He had a courage that I have rarely seen in other adults.

I can see everything again with the same extreme clarity that you get from keeping your finger pressed on the contrast button on the remote control. Who loved this neighborhood and this city more than Don Pino? His heart had no bounds. He hugged and transformed every person he met.

I won't leave you alone. This is what you asked me. No, I won't leave you alone.

Take away love and you will have hell, you used to say to me, Don Pino.

Give love and you will have what hell is not.

Love is protecting life from death. Every type of death. A litany of your sayings comes to mind now that you are gone.

Don't leave me alone. Don't leave me.

Then something happens that no one could have foreseen.

The children all squeeze in around Don Pino's body.

Totò begins suddenly in the silence. He starts reciting lines from the play, one after another.

Without any masks, without any costumes. Because there is no longer any need for them.

All they want is for Don Pino to be the only audience member, on the day that the show debuts.

Ganelon's sword is no match
For the brave Little Orlando's skill.
Strength without smarts is the catch,
Defeat the brave child it never will.
He and his friends a plan will hatch,
With Pipino's help they're stronger still.
So get yourselves ready for any surprise:
Who will lose and who will take the prize?

Don Pino's smiling face seems to approve. And it shows that happiness doesn't lie in lengthening your life but in expanding it.

36

Maria finds him there. Francesco won't let go of Don Pino's body. He's standing with his hands wrapped around the edge of the coffin, as if, from one moment to the next, his friend would wake up.

'I think this is some kind of joke.'

Maria doesn't say anything.

'Can't you see that he's smiling?'

Maria shakes her head. Only then does the child throw himself into her arms as he starts to sob uncontrollably.

'He's coming back. I know he will. He has to come back.'

Maria caresses him and holds him close to her chest. She looks at Don Pino's face and can hear his voice over the telephone. His last telephone call and the last request of a man condemned to death were both for her. His last wish.

Francesco suddenly breaks away from his mother. He takes an envelope out of his pocket and offers it to her. It says 'For Maria' on it.

'Who gave this to you?'

'I don't know him. A grownup with curly hair. He told me to give it to you.'

That envelope resembles an unexpected will and testament.

She can't contain the pain. She cries and laughs at the same time. She squeezes her son even more tightly, as if she were giving birth again.

She shows him the other mother that she can feel growing inside.

The only tile of the mosaic that's missing is Dario. He didn't rush here with the others. He ran away and hid at the abandoned construction site. That's where he stores his wings. Don Pino is now gone and he needs to try to reach him. Nothing will hold him any longer in the maze.

He won't be hitting the streets tonight. He's never going back to the maze again. He leans over the roof. People like to toss dogs off that roof. He's put on his wings, which he patiently built with kite paper, just like Don Pino and Lucia taught him. The sheets are colored and well-assembled, with just the right amount of glue. He closes his eyes and he feels so light in the wind of the night that he could go anywhere.

He just needs to learn how to master the movements and he needs to stay far enough away from the sun at dawn. The sea stretches out before him, even though he can only see a few white-caps. The weight of his body disappears into the darkness. No one hears him fly away.

It's still nighttime and Riccardo is throwing rocks at dogs when he comes upon Dario's broken body. He starts crying because he knows that he helped show him the way to heaven. The dogs bark at his rocks. He had no idea that evil could multiply itself so fast.

The silence of the earth seems to meld with the silence of the sky. The mystery of the city and the sea combine with the mystery of the stars. I'm standing before a barren sea. But suddenly, as if someone had mowed me down, I kneel on the salty beach. My land. I can feel something sink inside of me. It's a clear and almost tangible sensation. The sea wets my knees and feet. It would like to wash me away like a sandcastle that you build during the daytime. The pain is so strong that I am tempted not to offer any resistance. But I promised I wouldn't leave him alone. My mouth and face are covered in sand: This is my land, no matter what the taste. Petrarch was wrong. In life, there are certain dreams that last forever.

The little girl sits silently looking out over the sea. It seems compact and motionless. She watches it from the empty arches of her refuge. Now that she knows how to swim, she is less afraid of it. The sea is still there, as if nothing had happened, and the stars shine furiously. Who knows where Doll has gone? Then, suddenly, she gets up and starts walking. Nothing and no one can stop her. There is nothing and there is no one who awaits her in this port.

37

The newspapers talk about the priest. Fifty-six years old. Thirty-three years in the clergy, three in Brancaccio. Those are the figures released by the local press.

'These are the type of murders that give you satisfaction,' says the one who is driving.

'If you ask me, we should have kept this quiet,' answers the other one.

'He had it coming,' the first one reassures him.

'Stop for a second. I need to take a leak,' says Nuccio, interrupting them.

The car stops in the middle of the countryside.

Nuccio walks through the burned stubble as the evening forces the sun to slow its fix on people and on things.

'Let's do some grilling tonight.'

'That sounds great,' says Nuccio without turning around.

'We need to get the meat.'

'What meat should we get?'

'Mutton.'

'Where should we get it?' asks Nuccio.

'Here.'

'What do you mean, here?' He zips up his pants and turns around. He doesn't understand.

The other one points a gun at him.

'What are you doing?'

'I'm going to kill you.'

And he fires. The countryside swallows up the sound.

Nuccio keels over, landing on the ground. He tries to crawl through his own urine.

He has a helpless look on his face, like a child who doesn't know why he's being punished by his father.

'This will teach you not to take advantage of the orders you are given. Maria's money. Skimming your protection money. The daughter of the furniture store guy. You haven't learned what it means to follow orders. We are not punks who do things like this.'

He grabs Nuccio by the hair and lifts up his head.

'What's that you're saying? I can't hear you! Speak up!'

The boy tries to say something but he's unable to comply with this order after his head is blown into a thousand pieces by another shot fired just an inch or so from his face.

'Die!' growls the one who's doing the shooting.

They burn the body sufficiently, put it in a bag, and leave it in the trunk. This time, Nuccio will follow his orders to a tee.

Totò has a straw in his hand and he's waving it in the silent air of the kitchen.

His mother starts laughing when she walks in.

'Sweetheart, have you lost your mind?'

'I'm conducting, Mom,' answers the boy.

'Conducting what?'

'A concert.'

'A concert with no instruments?'

'Can't you see them?'

'No, I can't.'

'What are you saying? They're all there. Strings, percussion . . .'

'I can't hear them.'

'What do you mean, you can't hear them? Now the woodwinds come in.'

He cues them with a wave of his hand.

'You're making all of this up.'

'No. It's a concert in honor of Don Pino.'

'I know it's very sad, Totò. But Don Pino isn't with us anymore.'

'But he's right here listening. And he's smiling.'

'They killed Don Pino. Who's going to be the referee at our soccer games now?'

'What referee?'

'He used to let us play soccer and he would be the referee.'

'Referees are losers and cops.'

'Not him. He was good at it.'

'Someone else will take his place. How hard can it be to be a referee?'

'But where will we find someone who doesn't cheat?'

'You can still play even if you don't have a referee.'

'Why did they kill him, Dad? Was he bad?'

'There are no good people in this city.'

'But he seemed like he was a good person.'

The Hunter doesn't answer. He has seen plenty of dead people in his lifetime. But the deadest of all is the boy that he used to be.

Giuseppe comes into the room with his head held low. He sees me and Manfredi. I wouldn't have been able to make it here without my brother today. After everything that has happened, I need to stay away from Brancaccio for a while, even though I did go to the funeral with my family. My father said that I should tell this story someday. And I promised him that I would.

Giuseppe's eyes are filled with tears. He sits down, crumpled over himself and sobbing. He has the copy of *Pinocchio* that Don Pino gave him and he hugs it like it was his friend's arm.

Manfredi is standing in the corner and doesn't say anything.

'What am I supposed to do now?'

'I'll come and see you if you want. I promised Don Pino that I wouldn't leave him alone.'

'What does that have to do with me?'

'Aren't you kind of his son?'

Giuseppe dries his face and eyes by rubbing them on his arm. He nods.

I'm really all that's left of him, even though I am the Federico who likes to say the word *though*.

Hamil walks along the Cala, the seaside promenade. The sea frightens him.

As the poet from his land says: *I do not ride the sea because it frightens me / with its perils / I am mud and it is water / and mud dissolves in water.*

On this day, life seems like the sea and he feels made of mud. He no longer has his friend at his side and he no longer has anyone to whom he can tell the stories of his land.

A carriage with a couple of tourists heads down the street. A gray horse is pulling it along with a lazy coachman at the reins. It reminds him how stories can save the listener from desperation and how those who know how to tell stories mustn't ever lose the fire that drives them to tell those stories.

*   *   *

Lucia rings Serena's intercom fruitlessly. The blinds at her father's store are lowered. Sometimes it happens that things disappear into the sea without leaving a trace. With the same desperate abandon, Serena turned back around for the last time from the stairs to the airplane and she looked out over the blue expanse. She no longer has an anchor to keep her in that city, nor does she have the strength to face it. Never again. Never again.

The school principal looks at the schedule that has been formulated expressly for Don Pino. The boxes with the name 'Puglisi' written in them hurt more than a cemetery headstone.

Once he happened to see a flock of wild birds fly over a cage filled with birds of the same species. The birds had been raised in captivity and had never learned to fly. Fearful but seduced by the sight of the other birds, the caged birds tried to flap their wings like the birds they saw. They were restless and full of hope. But they were also uncertain of their surroundings and their possibilities. It was with the same grace that that man, with wings unfurled, passed over lives that were sometimes in cages. And when he would do so, it would generate restlessness and hope.

They were counting on his teaching load. And the principal knows that he won't be able to find a substitute: The kids in those classes will become orphans.

Lucia and I walk the streets in silence, as if the funeral procession had never ended after the funeral. It's a sort of ritual of reconciliation with what has happened. We sit under the protection of the Genie of Palermo in the middle of the pathways and geometric spaces on the grounds of Villa Giulia.

'I miss him.'

'I miss him, too. But we can't allow the pain to ruin everything. We'll do what people do in the country. We'll build a wall around the citrus trees so that the hot wind can't burn them.'

'I'm scared that I won't be strong enough.'

'We'll try, together. I promised him I would.'

'No.'

'He asked me to take care of you.'

'Will you?'

'I promised him I would.'

We sit there in silence and stare at this sky streaked with clouds and wounded by the flight of a seagull or two. The shell shape of the port opens up like a hug. The light seems to be coming out of things instead of being poised upon them. And the shadows are all part of the masterpiece, which would not be there otherwise. There is no such thing as a painting made only from light.

'I wrote a poem for you.'

'Read it to me.'

I open a sheet of paper with my best handwriting and I begin to read. You can hear a little bit of shyness in my voice.

Where are you when I need my soul sewn
Silently?
Girl full of light,
Can you mend a boy
Made of wind?
I search for your name,
Though you don't have one.
I found you where darkness
Seemed endless,
Between the waves of stormy seas
You emerged, like a seed

That arrives from afar.
Small like a caress
It settles on virgin land
To bear its fruit.
I am that land,
Your name is not a dream.

'You're worse than an octopus.'

'Why?'

'You squirt ink when you need to defend yourself. You'd be lost without words.'

'It's true. But those are my five words, plus yours. That makes ten words to make us.'

I look at her and I realize that I must have a comical expression on my face because she lets out a little laugh, like a wave splashing.

She touches my face with her fingers.

'Well, I like you as an octopus.'

Lucia puts her ear on my chest in silence.

Everybody thinks that life is what's supposed to make you happy. But I have realized something: All you need is courage to be happy. To embrace the sky and the earth in your heart, you need quite a bit of it. But I also know that that courage is somehow inside of me, like a seed that is small at first and then becomes a tree with big, strong branches, limbs that can provide shade and safety. It's capable of being wounded and taking in the seasons. Of dying every winter and budding every spring, summing up its life and death in rings that grow wider and wider as they unite sky and earth.

I gently touch her lips and our shared longing subsides for a moment as it unites our breath.

38

From his balcony, Mimmo the policeman watches the crowd that has gathered in Piazza Anita Garibaldi. It's a faint image of the funeral winding its way through the astonished streets of Brancaccio. It is a fearful sight for those who know something but say nothing and for those who don't know anything and still say nothing.

He's a cop with a pot belly but his head is as sharp as Detective Columbo's. And like Columbo, he smokes incessantly. His mind spins around and around like a top.

Two contradictory things happened.

The body of a boy, burned and nearly unidentifiable, was found that morning at dawn a block from the piazza where the execution occurred. In Mafia code, this means that he was the person who committed the murder. Priests aren't murdered. The Mafia doesn't murder them.

Actually, the Mafia likes to keep things clean. The dots begin to connect: The stolen bag, the robbery, and the .32 Automatic point to someone with little experience.

They haven't been able to identify the boy. His face and body were too burned. It was probably a stereo and car thief who didn't live in Brancaccio. Or it could have been a drug addict. And so it was this low-level criminal who killed Don Pino.

But Mimmo isn't buying it. Around here, dissimulation is a fine art. The message is clear: Where there is no government, the Mafia will run things. Once again, people can feel safe. The Mafia feeds on the neighborhood and it provides the neighborhood with food. Just like God. Actually, better than God, because God makes you work too hard for your daily bread.

Then something else happened that definitively convinced him that the boy's execution was a decoy. The funeral procession went down Via San Ciro. On the door of a framing shop on that street, someone posted a photo of a fat, smiling man sitting at a table during a family gathering. In the confusion of the funeral, no one bothered to look at it carefully. But it was a photo of Totò Riina together with a noted family from Brancaccio. Order has been restored. And its patron saint, from the sanctuary of his prison cell, is being shown in the streets of the neighborhood.

The messages are contradictory.

The photo on Via San Ciro is a secret confession. It will be seen by those who are meant to see it.

The burned body of the boy is a false confession. It will be seen by those who are meant to see it.

Actually, there is no contradiction.

During Don Pino's commemoration, some politician – good with words but not so good with facts – quoted the very Sicilian answer given by Gaspare Uzeda to Massimo D'Azeglio. In the novel *The Viceroys*, Uzeda is one of those gentlemen landowners who were the progenitors of the Mafia. He was told that 'We have made Italy and now we need to make Italians.' And he answered: 'We have made Italy and now we need to make our own fortune.' And he was right. In fact, we still have to bring unity to Italy and to the Italians, but as far as shared values are concerned, they are already united in their own self-interest, especially in Sicily.

Mimmo smokes his cigarette calmly while his thoughts race like bats: Blind and yet confident in their nocturnal movements.

He wishes he could hear what Don Pino thinks of all of this, but that's no longer possible.

He's not the type to cry. But this time his eyes are red. The air is stale and gloomy. He can hear the voices of the kids who preside over the place where Don Pino was killed. They cross through the piazza like a cool wind. Mimmo watches them. They have gathered around the spots of violet-red blood. Someone tried to wash it off but he was rudely chased away by the kids themselves. Mimmo talks to his friend as if he were there to hear him: 'You have to die of something, Father. But there's one thing I'm sure of: You found out what kind of death no one wants to die.'

The time remaining is monopolized by the children. The world of adults runs out sooner or later. It becomes exhausted. The children, on the other hand, resemble budding grain that leaves room for the possibility that they will someday become someone else's bread. They wander the streets, swarms of kids looking for games to play.

One of those games entails climbing up the little wall that runs along the train tracks and attracting dogs using rotted meat, stolen from some butcher shop, as bait. They throw rocks at the dogs: If you smash the dog's head open, you win, but you can also score points by striking their bodies or legs.

Francesco is standing on the wall and he has a rock in his hands. He's about to throw it at a dog's muzzle. The other kids have thrown their rocks without hesitation and now it's his turn. The dog barks and tries to chomp down on the meat. He growls at the devil-children. Francesco gets down from the wall and moves slowly toward the dog. The others egg him on to strike from close range.

The dog is a mutt and one of its forelegs is bent backward, just like Nino the cripple, who begs outside the supermarket. It's black with snow-white spots, as if someone had sprayed it with bleach. There's a piece of meat between Francesco and the dog. The child moves toward it with his arm raised. He's holding the rock snugly in his fist. The dog can't decide between danger and hunger. He chooses hunger and jumps on the meat but the child is faster. Francesco grabs the morsel and throws it as far as he can. The dog stops, uncertain of what to do. Then he runs, limping, in the direction of the food. Curious as to why he did this, the pack shouts furiously. Francesco follows the dog with the rock loaded in his hand. Whimpering, the dog is about to disappear behind a car.

'Get out of here! Go away!'

The dog stares back at him and barks.

Francesco pretends that he's throwing the rock and the dog flees. The other kids can't see him anymore and they call for him to return. He yells back that the dog has run off. And then he leaves.

He finds the dog around the corner. He's licking his paw as he waits for a better moment to look for the meat. Francesco moves toward him slowly and crouches down near him.

'Are you hungry?'

The dog looks at him. It's calm only because it's desperate.

'Come with me.'

The dog knows that this is his only hope.

'What's your name?'

It smells him without answering.

'Would it be okay if I called you Pipino?'

The dog continues to smell him.

'Come with me, Pipino. I'll be taking care of you from now on.'

He offers the dog a candy he has in his pocket and to his

surprise, the dog takes it right from his hand, delicately. It then follows him.

> *We should fear alone those things*
> *That have the power to harm.*
> *Nothing else can frighten us.*
>
> *It is God's grace that makes me so*
> *That your affliction does not touch,*
> *And neither can these fires assail me.*

I remember the time that Don Pino quoted these lines from Dante's *Inferno*. He was talking about fear. Only now do I fully understand them. Don Pino's sacrifice wasn't his death. That was the consequence. His sacrifice is what the word *sacrifice* tells us: Making things sacred. Don Pino made everything he touched sacred. He protected it like you would any precious thing. I read these lines and take them as a testament: I no longer need my anchor-words from Petrarch. Now I need bow-words that contain all the courage necessary to face the open sea. It doesn't matter how complicated the maze is. All that matters is the thread that binds us to love.

The little girl. What happened to the little girl? Mimmo only has one clue: The doll. This time, he has decided to give up on his inert thoughts, however perfect they may be. He's hit the streets like he used to when he was young and didn't weigh as much. The mother is looking for her but she's vanished. Mimmo talks to people from the neighborhood and gathers some clues and some ideas as to her whereabouts. It takes him twenty-four hours to find her sleeping near the train tracks.

He recognizes her. Her clothes are filthy. Her arms and legs are all scratched up.

'What's your name?'

She doesn't answer, and tries to run away. But he holds her by the arm and shows her the doll. Little by little she gives in to his tender strength.

'Your doll has been looking for you. You left her alone . . .'

She followed the train tracks until she was so tired that she couldn't walk anymore. Those endless tracks were too much for the legs of a little girl. She surrenders to the fearful crying typical of children who are looking for something to hang on to.

'I got lost.'

'Where were you going?'

'To see my father.'

'Where does he live?'

'At the end.'

'The end of what?'

'Of the tracks.'

'What's his name?'

'Donpino.'

Author's Afterword

As the years pass, adolescence begins to resemble a dog. It's like a canine that barks as his master attempts to abandon him but then doesn't have the heart to leave. And so he always turns back.

And then comes the time that it seems like it's really going to happen. But then the hound follows the master's scent until he reaches his home and waits outside for him curled up on his doorstep. And this is so that he, the dog, can return home quietly and take his place where he belongs, guarding the memories of the age that marks the end of innocence.

It's an exciting and dramatic age, full of memories both bitter and sweet. And it's marked by the credentials of truth, the 'first times,' the details of days and nights in which love and pain shake one's flesh and cut to the bone. This is why, years later, I love to walk once again through the streets of this story. And with every stroll I take, something emerges more clearly from the port and the memories under which it is buried. It's the port that the dog watches over.

Years ago, someone once told me the story of a man. When he had something difficult to resolve, he used to go to the same spot in the woods. He would light a fire and recite ritual prayers to God and then his wishes would come true. As time went by, his secret was lost. A generation later, another man visited the place in the woods. He didn't know how to start a fire but he remembered the prayers. And all of his wishes came true. A generation later, another man forgot the words of the prayers but all he needed was to reach the place in the woods. And just like the others before him, his wishes came true. And then no one could remember where the place in the woods was.

The Spasimo is my place that the faithful canine watches over: An abandoned and roofless church in the Cala neighborhood of the city. It was built over the border between the sea and the earth, where children and their parents erect sandcastles as they defend their dreams. The walls of the Spasimo still stand there, as if the tide had ripped them up out of the city. Between these walls, light alternates with shadows underneath a sky framed by stone so yellow that it seems like gold as the arches and vaults give way to the purest blue. When I no longer remember how to light a fire and when the words of the prayers escape me, I need just the right place to coax them from memory.

It was here that I found an answer that many are searching for: This is where the Mafia was born.

And it's all Raphael's fault.

He created a painting where the colors look like enamel made of light and the bodies are Greek statues in the moment before they take flight into absolute beauty. And at the same time, it's a dark painting. Christ and Mary have Apollonian faces that contract in Dionysian pain. Just as every man and every woman ask, they ask: Why?

They don't seem to know anything that other men and women do. They don't have any magic tricks to perform. Christ is heading toward Calvary, nearly crushed by the cross. He carries the weight of hell on his shoulders. It's been refined to an art form by men wholly capable of sophisticated thought when their goal is war or torture. The wooden hell of the crucifixion awaits him. A soldier threatens him with a spear and another drags him along using a rope.

He is immersed in the hell of men and he cries over their hell. There is just one man who helps him, someone who just happens to be passing through, Simon the Cyrene. Otherwise, Christ is aided only by the scarce pity of the unknowing onlookers who aren't accomplices in the spectacle.

Christ moves along but needs the help of the Cyrenaicans with every meter of road he covers. The mother cries for her son. He cries because, like every man, he cannot bear the pain of his mother. If she could, she would scoop him with her open arms and hold him close to her bosom. It's hard to say whether or not that maternal gesture is inspired by an arrival or a departure, by receiving or by giving, by the port or by the swooning.

That painting, *Christ Falling on the Way to Calvary*, also known as the *Spasimo di Sicilia* ('The Swooning [Virgin] of Sicily'), arrived in Palermo in that roofless church in 1517. It's a painting that has a story of its own. During the seventeenth century, in circumstances that remain unclear, it seems that a local citizen secretly gave it to the viceroy of Spain and then it was given to the Spanish king in exchange for favors, income, and titles: A 'Don' to precede one's name and the clang of money in the bank.

The Mafia was born that day.

Ever since that day, when the solution to the maze was taken away and the ineffable beauty of Raphael's 'Spasimo' was exchanged for a title, a job, a recommendation, and a favor, the city has been unable to decode itself: The solution has been lost. Even though the absence of the solution could help the city to understand. It's like an armless and headless Greek statue: The bust alone can evoke the beauty of the missing pieces. If the painting were still here, Palermo would understand. But the painting is in a faraway museum in another land.

The inhabitants of the city need to be told that the thing they are missing in order to save themselves is the *Spasimo*. Rome has Michelangelo's *Pietà*. Florence has Simone Martini's *Annunciation*. Naples has Caravaggio's *Seven Works of Mercy*. Milan has Leonardo da Vinci's *Last Supper*. Venice has Titian's *Assumption*. Palermo? It had Raphael's *Spasimo* a very long time ago. Just one of the many 'long times ago's that we use in my city: Raphael bartered for a little taste of power. Would Palermo once again reclaim its title as Pearl of the Mediterranean if we had that painting and that place back?

I'm not sure. The one thing I do know is that the place is no longer there.

Or maybe it is. Because when the man in the woods forgot where the place was, he discovered that all he needed was his wishes. And those wishes were in his heart.

A place where you can escape to. That's what Don Pino and the boys and girls were looking for. He helped them to find that space within themselves. It was the only way to block the violence.

Money, respect, strength? You had to get there before this sacrilegious trinity did. This was one of the reasons that I decided to become a teacher and a writer: To unearth that place, first in me and then in the children. And it needs to be done every day. Otherwise it would mean giving up on the search for the words that you need to cull life from life. You have to find that courage not to barter Beauty with Compromise. And you need to remain faithful to your own desires over time.

My first thanks go to my parents, who shared the light with me in this city. Thanks to my brothers, Marco and Fabrizio, and my sisters, Elisabetta, Paola, and Marta. They are this city's walls of flesh and blood.

Thanks to my professors and classmates at Vittorio Emanuele II High School.

And thanks also to the passionate and highly talented editors who helped me revise this book page by page: Valentina Pozzoli, Antonio Franchini, Marilena Rossi, and Giulia Ichino.

Thanks to the whole team at Oneworld, who believed in this book with passion, especially Juliet Mabey, Alyson Coombes and Paul Nash.

Many thanks to Jeremy Parzen for his accurate translation.

Thanks to my students, their parents, and my fellow teachers. We all sail in the same boat as we face the stormy seas of these uncertain times.

Thanks to my closest friends. It would take up too much space to name them all here. As Don Pino used to say, hope is the result of friendship. And I get all of my strength from my friends.

Thanks to the organizers of the Pino Puglisi International Prize. They shared yet another sign of Don Pino's presence in my life: The award came while I was writing this book.

Thanks to Francesco Deliziosi for his wonderful book about Father Puglisi, and thanks to Roberto Faenza for his film.

They were an inspiration to me.

Thanks to the people who read my previous books, especially the teachers and students that I have met across Italy over the years. I need to apologize to many of them because I don't always manage to answer every letter, email, enquiry, and comment on the blog, even though I read every one.

Last but not least, I'd like to thank you for taking the time to read this book. I hope that the hours you've spent reading this story have been as rewarding as those I spent writing it. I hope that it gave you, like me, greater courage in facing life, even when it hurts to the point of death. And I hope it has been a place you can escape to when the flame goes out and your words fail you. In order to make sure that they stayed intact, they had to be tended like coals under the ash. They burn there together along with our greatest desires.

*   *   *

The basements on Via Hazon were sealed up just a few days after Don Pino was killed. But they were reopened, by a clandestine sledgehammer crew, not long after. Their restoration began only in 2005.

The Giuseppe Puglisi Middle School was officially opened on January 13, 2000.

Oneworld, Many Voices

Bringing you exceptional writing
from around the world

The Woman at 1,000 Degrees by Hallgrímur Helgason
(Icelandic) Translated by Brian FitzGibbon

Frankenstein in Baghdad by Ahmed Saadawi (Arabic)
Translated by Jonathan Wright

Back Up by Paul Colize (French)
Translated by Louise Rogers Lalaurie

Damnation by Peter Beck (German)
Translated by Jamie Bulloch

Oneiron by Laura Lindstedt (Finnish)
Translated by Owen Witesman

The Boy Who Belonged to the Sea by Denis Thériault
(French) Translated by Liedewy Hawke

The Baghdad Clock by Shahad Al Rawi (Arabic)
Translated by Luke Leafgren

The Aviator by Eugene Vodolazkin (Russian)
Translated by Lisa C. Hayden

Lala by Jacek Dehnel (Polish)
Translated by Antonia Lloyd-Jones

Bogotá 39: New Voices from Latin America
(Spanish and Portuguese) Short story anthology

Last Instructions by Nir Hezroni (Hebrew)
Translated by Steven Cohen

The Day I Found You by Pedro Chagas Freitas (Portuguese)
Translated by Daniel Hahn

Solovyov and Larionov by Eugene Vodolazkin (Russian)
Translated by Lisa C. Hayden

In/Half by Jasmin B. Frelih (Slovenian)
Translated by Jason Blake

ONEWORLD TRANSLATED FICTION PROGRAMME

Co-funded by the
Creative Europe Programme
of the European Union

IN/HALF by Jasmin B. Frelih
Translated from the Slovenian by Jason Blake
Publication date: November 2018 (UK & US)

WHAT HELL IS NOT by Alessandro D'Avenia
Translated from the Italian by Jeremy Parzen
Publication date: January 2019 (UK & US)

CITY OF JASMINE by Olga Grjasnowa
Translated from the German by Katy Derbyshire
Publication date: March 2019 (UK) / April 2019 (US)

THINGS THAT FALL FROM THE SKY by Selja Ahava
Translated from the Finnish by Emily and Fleur Jeremiah
Publication date: April 2019 (UK) / May 2019 (US)

MRS MOHR GOES MISSING by Maryla Szymiczkowa
Translated from the Polish by Antonia Lloyd-Jones
Publication date: March 2019 (UK)

Oneworld's award-winning translated fiction list is dedicated to publishing the best contemporary writing from around the world, introducing readers to acclaimed international writers and brilliant, diverse stories. With these five titles from across Europe, generously supported by the Creative Europe programme as well as various in-country literary and cultural organizations, we are continuing to break boundaries and to bring new and exciting voices into English for the first time.

For the latest updates, visit oneworld-publications.com/creative-europe